The Toy Store

A Holiday Romance

Seth Sjostrom

wolfprint, LLC
Camas,
WA, 98607

Trade Paperback
ISBN-13: 978-1-7361026-6-4

1. Blair Cooper (Fictitious character)-Fiction. 2. Romance- Fiction. 3. The Toy Store-Fiction I. Title.

First wolfprintMedia Digital edition 2020. wolfprintMedia is a trademark of wolfprintMedia, LLC.

For information regarding bulk purchases, please contact wolfprintMedia, LLC, at wolfprint@hotmail.com.

United States of America

To Kathi, my muse for The Toy Store and so many wonderful adventures of my life.
To Hayden, the angel on my tree every year.
To Kiara for exuberance beyond compare.
To Logan for striving every day to make life better.
To Ethan for spreading joy and God's word in his wake.

To the Downtown Camas Association for supporting independent small businesses.
To Caffe Piccolo for fuel, a place to launch books and visit with readers, and kindness that embodies the season.
To Jen for your effervescent encouragement and willingness to dive into the words with a courageous red pen in hand.

The Toy Store

A Holiday Romance

One

Blair Cooper used the reflection in her Manhattan office window to smooth her outfit as she scooped up the materials for her meeting. Glancing at the clock on her desk, she wheeled around and stepped briskly into the hallway.

Nearly colliding with her assistant, who was streaking by at her own hastened pace, Blair offered a weak smile to inspire confidence. The expression that was returned denoted her failure.

Halting abruptly, Blair asked, "Am I that transparent, Ann Marie?"

"You seem a bit nervous," the assistant admitted. "Look, you've got this. This is the most amazing campaign I have seen and you getting it put together in such a rush for the holiday season is…well, you will definitely wow them with this." Pausing, Ann Marie faced her boss directly. Straightening Blair's collar, she gave a reassuring smile.

"I don't know what I would do without you," Blair said as she tapped her disheveled pile of documents into the appearance of order. With a deep breath, she nodded, "Let's do this!"

With a boost in her step, Blair led Ann Marie into the boardroom where the entire executive team of Lorent Cosmetics was waiting for them. Flashing a bold smile that disarmed the room, she lined her storyboards along the display wall.

"Thank you for being patient, these are quite literally hot off the presses," Blair shared.

"Not at all, Ms. Cooper," Thomas Lorent waved her off. "We appreciate you even taking on this project with such short notice. Our new distribution deal means a lot for our company's future, and we couldn't make it happen without a solid marketing plan."

Blair couldn't help but slip a smile at the faith her client had put in her and the firm. "Well, let's dig in. I think you will like what you see."

With a nod to Ann Marie, the cover to the first storyboard was removed revealing a gleaming ad copy. "A New Year to a New You. A series of inspirational messages and images staggered throughout the winter season while people are cooped up," Blair explained.

As Ann Marie uncovered a series of messaging slides, she paused at a final storyboard.

"And this," Blair continued, "will make Lorent a consistent presence with your clients around the world, all year long."

Ann Marie revealed the last of the storyboards.

The Lorent team leaned forward as they absorbed the final element of the campaign. Blair described the concept in relation to the images on the boards.

"The first ever Lorent social media campaign encouraging Lorent users to share their own inspirational stories across the web. We can seed the flow with known Lorent clients and even provide Lorent outlets and distributors' links to encourage traffic with their own clients," Blair beamed.

Her eyes danced around the room, trying desperately to decipher the thoughts of the Lorent team. To her dismay, none of the executives gave away their disposition. Blair's heart thumped wildly in her chest as she waited for some sort of reaction.

Mr. Lorent shot a questioning glance to his left, a smartly attired woman that Blair knew to be Lorent's head of corporate communications, Candace Barrows. She also knew that she was shrewd and was resistant to using Blair's firm and sending the campaign to an outside source at all.

Candace split her lips into a smile and nodded, "I think it is brilliant, I really do. I love it."

"I do too," Mr. Lorent beamed, rising from his seat to inspect the story boards. Turning to Blair, he added, "Excellent work, Ms. Cooper. Perhaps after the holidays you could spend a week in Paris at our corporate offices, as our guest."

"That would be wonderful, thank you, Mr. Lorent," Blair smiled, shaking the corporate executive's hand.

Candace stood and approached Blair, "I will admit, I was wary of outside influence. The inspirational message is not one that I had thought of, though inspiring confidence in women is what we are all about at Lorent. Well done."

"It is my pleasure. I look forward to getting to know you and your company even better as we prepare to launch in January," Blair responded.

"Then we will see you in a few weeks."

"In a few weeks. Merry Christmas," Blairs smiled.

As the Lorent team exited, Blair leaned against a wall and let out an enormous breath. "Wow!"

"You did great!" Ann Marie cooed.

Blair looked at her friend, "They seemed to genuinely like it, didn't they?"

"They did," Ann Marie grinned.

"Break for holiday coffees, my treat?" Blair suggested.

"I would say we deserve it," Ann Marie agreed.

Blair sat at her desk, flipping through the Lorent Cosmetic game plan notes. She wanted a jump on the initial phase so that it was ready to launch as early into the new year as possible.

Glancing at her calendar, she circled the dates they wanted her to work in Paris. Lost in her work, Blair was startled when she heard a knock at her office door.

Looking up, she saw Ann Marie leaning into her office. "Sorry to interrupt, there is a courier at the front desk…says he needs to hand some documents directly to you," Ann Marie shrugged, a frown formed on her face.

"Courier?" Blair stood up. "Maybe the contract from Lorent?"

"Maybe. That would be the fastest contract we ever received from a client," Ann Marie replied. With a mischievous hop, she prodded, "Only one way to find out. Let's go!"

"Ms. Cooper?" an anxious man with a sealed envelope asked as they rounded the corner.

"I am," Blair nodded.

"For you," the courier handed her the packet and a pen. "Sign here, please."

Blair snatched the pen and scrawled her name across the tear away card.

"Have a good day," the courier nodded.

"Thank you," Blair nodded, scanning the envelope for clues to its content or sender.

"Well?" Ann Marie leaned in.

"It is from a law firm…," Blair said as she began to pry a corner open.

Ann Marie's cellphone began playing Jingle Bells, "Uh, I should grab this. I'll catch up."

"That sounds good," Blair nodded. Patting the envelope, she retreated to her office.

Slipping behind her desk, she retrieved her nail file from the top drawer and used it to slip into the envelope seal. With a quick slide of her hand, the packet was opened. Pulling a thin set of papers out of the envelope, Blair leaned back in her chair.

Rifling through the papers, she frowned. It was not the contract she was expecting. Her head spun slightly as she absorbed the words on the pages.

Still reeling from the impact of the documents, Blair didn't notice Ann Marie stepping into her office.

"Is everything okay?" Ann Marie asked. "Not the Lorent contract I take it?"

Blair looked up from the papers, "No, I mean yes."

Shaking her head, Blair reframed her response, "It is not the Lorent contract, and yes, everything is okay. According to this, I inherited my grandparents' toy shop in Washington."

"Washington…as in the state?" Ann Marie's jaw dropped.

"That's the place," Blair nodded.

"Wow. A toy store," Ann Marie cocked her head, imagining such a thing.

"I spent a lot of time there growing up. We would spend a few weeks over Christmas visiting my grandparents. It was so much fun," Blair reminisced before snapping her head. "What am I going to do with a toy store three thousand miles away?"

Ann Marie paused and stared at her friend, "What *are* you going to do?"

"Whatever I am to do, according to this, I have until the end of the year to claim it," Blair said, scanning the rest of the document. "I have to go to Washington."

Ann Marie bounced in front of Blair, "It sounds like you have an adventure ahead of you!"

"I don't know," Blair said slowly. "I've got the Lorent deal to prepare for..."

"You've got it locked and it doesn't kick off until the New Year. This is the perfect time for you to go."

"I suppose so. I can get out there, deal with what I need to, and be back in plenty of time before the holidays," Blair shrugged. "Want to come with?"

Ann Marie frowned, "I would love to, but I have used all of *my* vacation. I don't think you touched yours."

Blair tossed the packet onto her desk. Staring at it for a moment, she shook her head at Ann Marie, "I still can't believe it."

Shaking off the December chill, Blair glanced around the restaurant. Finding what she was looking for, she nodded her way past the hostess and made her way across the restaurant.

"Hello, handsome, is this seat taken?" she grinned.

The well attired, clean cut man she targeted looked startled as he pulled away from his phone. Setting it face down on the table, he stood and smiled. Giving Blair a quick kiss on the cheek, he pulled out her seat and helped her out of her jacket.

"How did your meeting go?"

Blair let out a big grin, "The Lorent team loved the presentation, we're in."

"Nice job! If we didn't both have to return to work, I'd say we should celebrate."

"Let's live a little, Todd. We should celebrate anyway!" Blair urged, a mischievous twinkle in her eye.

Todd shifted in his seat, "I…I have clients and a board meeting."

"I know, the hectic life of an accountant," Blair said, a little disappointed. "Couldn't hurt to ask."

"What's that?" Todd nodded towards the packet Blair had brought with her.

A nervous smile creased the corner of Blair's lips, "You remember me telling me about my grandfather passing?"

"I remember you were sad because you were on a business trip during the funeral," Todd nodded.

"That's right," Blair nodded solemnly. "They left me something."

"Your grandparents?"

"They owned a toy store in Evergreen. We used to go there a couple times of year growing up. Usually in the summer and again for Christmas. They left me the store," Blair announced.

"Blair, that's incredible!" Todd exclaimed.

"I know!" Blair nodded. "Catch is, I need to go to Washington to claim it."

"I have some time off coming to me, maybe after the New Year I can go with you," Todd suggested.

"That'd be nice, but I have to go before the end of the year. I'm going to fly out there on Monday."

"Well, not much to do but sign whatever papers you need and then meet with a realtor. Not sure what a toy store in Washington state goes for, but it might be enough to get that apartment on Park you've been eyeing," Todd mused.

"Yeah," Blair shrugged.

"What?"

"I was just thinking, it's going to be a little sad not to have the toy store in the family," Blair said softly.

Todd studied Blair for a moment, "Times change. Things change. Do something with part of the money that celebrates your grandparents."

"That's a good idea," Blair agreed.

"Besides, it's not like you could run a toy store from across the country," Todd added.

"No, I suppose not," Blair replied. "Well, let's order. I have a lot to get done for the Lorent account before I take off."

Two

"Ms. Cooper?"

Blair looked through the crowd of travelers squeezing their way through Seattle-Tacoma Airport to see a dapper man holding a digital placard with her name on it.

"I'm Blair Cooper," Blair nodded.

"Very good. I'm Mason. I'll be your driver into Evergreen," the man declared. "I'll take your bags. Do you have checked luggage?"

"No, this will be a short trip," Blair informed the driver.

Mason grabbed Blair's carry-on luggage and led her through the airport to the waiting black SUV.

Pulling away from the curb, Mason asked as he glanced at his passenger through the mirror, "First time in Evergreen?"

"No, I used to come here ever year with my family," Blair responded.

"Charming town. Especially this time of year," Mason said.

"It is. The way Main Street is decorated, the holiday events. It's been so long, I'm kind of excited to see it all again," Blair said.

"Even have a bit of snow on the ground, though I don't think there is too much more in the immediate forecast," Mason added.

"Has it changed much?" Blair asked.

"The forecast?"

"The town."

"When is the last time you visited?" the driver asked.

"Uhm…," Blair stared at the ceiling of the luxury SUV as she pondered the question. "Since I took my marketing position in Manhattan. Seven years ago."

"Some shops have closed over the years. Evergreen is one of those small towns that seems to be getting smaller. Main Street has maintained its holiday flair, despite a few empty buildings along the way," Mason informed her.

Blair looked out the window as the scenery transformed from dense buildings and bumper to bumper traffic, an endless sea of trees covering rolling hills giving way to tall, snow-covered mountains. "It's so beautiful out here."

"It is. Not too far from the city, but far enough out to be charmingly peaceful," Mason declared.

"Makes you wonder why towns like Evergreen would be shrinking," Blair mused.

Mason pulled the SUV off the highway. "You saw the traffic coming out of Seattle. Pretty tough for most folks to navigate on a daily basis. That is where all the jobs are, I suppose."

Carving their way into the foothills, the wet, green landscape became lightly dusted in a soft covering of snow. "It's as breath- taking as I remembered," Blair breathed as she drank in the scene.

Driving into the town of Evergreen was somehow even more striking than the amazing natural landscape that surrounded it. Blair's heart did an excited dance in her chest that reminded her of how she felt traveling into town with her parents when she was a child.

The very entrance to Evergreen embraced Christmas spirit. A giant archway of green garland and red bows welcomed visitors. Framed in the arch was festive Main Street lined with streetlamps adorned with wreaths. At the end of Main Street was a roundabout encasing a small-town park with a gazebo and tall tree decorated for the holiday.

To Blair, the town seemed like a wonderful Christmas scape snow globe. A nostalgic image of Christmas, if there ever was one.

"Here we are, Ms. Cooper," Mason called as he pulled to the curb alongside a darkened building on Main Street. "I believe Stuart Myers Esquire should be waiting for you."

"Thank you, Mason. It was a lovely drive," Blair replied.

"Indeed a pleasure, Ms. Cooper," Mason said. "I will have your bags for you at the Holly Bough Bed and Breakfast, one block north of Main Street."

"That sounds wonderful, Mason."

The driver put the SUV in park and ran around the car to Blair's door. "Madam."

Blair grinned at Mason, "I could rather get used to charming drivers."

"Yes, Ma'am," Mason nodded and helped her onto the sidewalk.

Striding briskly from the neighboring coffee shop, a man in a well-tailored suit cloaked in a wool overcoat approached, a handful of documents in hand. "Ms. Cooper?"

Blair nodded and accepted the man's handshake.

"Stuart Myers. Welcome to Evergreen," the man declared. "Thank you, Mason. My office will take care of the tab."

The SUV roared away, leaving Blair and the attorney standing on the sidewalk outside of the toy store. While darkened and looking lonely between the open coffee shop and open café opposite, Blair was surprised to see the toy store exterior decorated for Christmas.

"Kind of a sad sight not being open, huh?" Stuart said.

"It is," Blair admitted. "Nice that the facade is decorated, nonetheless."

"It is. Hard to not appreciate this town," Stuart said. "Why don't we step out of the cold. I'll buy you a cup of coffee while we work through the paperwork."

"That would be wonderful."

Blair followed the estate attorney into the coffee shop. Having placed their orders, they sat a booth with their drinks. The attorney handed Blair a series of documents and a pen. One by one, they made their way through the thick packet.

As she had signed the final line, Blair's hand hovered thoughtfully over the page before finally placing her mark.

Stuart cocked his head slightly, "You hesitated, it is a big deal, isn't it?"

Blair looked up at the attorney and nodded. "It is. Since I was born, this was my grandparents' store. It was part of our family identity. I don't feel like I deserve it."

"They had you in mind as part of their estate plan, they certainly felt like you did," Stuart pressed.

"I suppose. I just…I just don't know what I'm going to do with it," Blair confessed.

"It's yours now," Stuart declared as he produced a key from the bottom of the envelope.

Blair stared at the key in the attorney's hand. Reaching across the table, she accepted it. Holding it in front of her, she thought deeply of her grandparents and how much the store meant to them. Now it was hers to decide its fate.

"Well, if you'll excuse me, I need to get back to Seattle," Stuart said. With a nod of his head, "Ms. Cooper."

Blair sat with her papers and her key as she finished her peppermint mocha and thought pensively about her situation. As she finished her cup, a twinge of excitement overcame her. It had tugged at her since she arrived, but she had been suppressing the feeling. Not that she couldn't wait to see the store once again, she knew she was only there to collect it and sell it.

With a sigh, she slipped out of her chair. With a wave to the barista, she made her way back out on to the sidewalk. With key in hand, Blair turned the lock and pushed her way into the store. A little bell announced her arrival. It was a sound that rang a memory filled melody for her.

Blair closed the door behind her. Leaning against it, she slipped the key into her pocket. Looking around the store, it was not a lot different than she had recalled. It was every bit as wonderful as when her grandparents were there to greet her.

The store flowed in sections with a mix of old-fashioned and newest generation toys. There was a section for children's books and, curiously, a section for local artists and craftsmen.

Blair danced through the store, the sights and smells triggering memories from throughout her many childhood visits. She played with a wooden train that sat atop a tall stack of wooden tracks. Straightening a doll's dress as she moved to the modern sets of holiday princesses. Pausing at the local's section, she studied the sundry of wares lining the shelves. Rows of carved children's toys and homemade dolls' clothes filled the bulk of it. An intricate wooden toy chest was opened to reveal a hand carved chess set. Blair picked up a piece, sliding a finger along the design.

Setting it down, she walked behind the register. Running her hands over the keys, she remembered sitting high on a stool behind that counter, pretending to take care of customers who came into the store.

Her grandparents even let her run the register during their annual foster kids' Christmas party. They gave each child an allotment to purchase presents for their peers and siblings.

Settling against the back counter, she drank in the nostalgia, the memories, the reality that at least for the moment, the store was hers. Knowing the task she came to do made her a little sad, though it was the only logical solution.

"If I am going to sell this store, I need to make it look like an operational turn-key business," Blair muttered to herself.

Three

Blair pulled her coat tight and her collar high as she locked up the store. Walking along the streets of Evergreen, she could not help but feel the Christmas spirit flow through her. The town and everyone in it exuded joy. She chuckled with the number of people that said hello and wished her a Merry Christmas. People rarely looked up from their phones in New York, never mind gave a friendly gesture.

The bed and breakfast was only a few blocks from the store and a mere few houses down from her grandparents' house. Walking up the steps, Blair admired the bed and breakfast's charm, especially wrapped up in elegant Christmas décor.

Pushing through the wreath-clad front door, she was bathed in warmth, both literal and in holiday allure.

Within an instant, a cheerful woman burst into the foyer to greet her, "Well my, you must be Ms. Cooper."

Blair smiled, "I am."

"We have been expecting you. I am Loretta Marsden, your hotelier," the woman sang as though her words were a carol. "Come on, come on. I had just set for dinner unless you need to freshen up first."

"You know, I wouldn't mind a moment in my room," Blair admitted.

"Of course, of course," Loretta nodded as the front door burst open and a man strode between them. Giving Loretta a quick kiss on the cheek, he made a beeline for the hallway. "Ah, hem! Luke Marsden, hold it right there!"

The man froze. Slowly turning his head to face Loretta, he flashed a sheepish grin.

Loretta's cheery face fell into a frown, "Don't pull that charming smile on me. It worked for your father nearly forty years ago, I'm immune...well, mostly."

"Yes, ma'am?" Luke responded.

"I need to finish serving supper. Would you be so kind as to show Ms. Cooper her room? She'll be staying in the Frost Suite." Turning her head to Blair, she promised, "It is way cozier than it sounds. I'll save you a place at the table whenever you're ready."

"Thank you. Please don't go to any trouble," Blair pleaded.

"Nonsense, caring for our guests *is* no trouble," Loretta replied and whirled away down the hall.

Luke and Blair looked at each other for a moment.

"Welcome to the Holly Bough Bed and Breakfast. As you most certainly might have guessed, Loretta is my mother and she is the boss around here," Luke said.

"It's a beautiful place," Blair said, giving the bed and breakfast a sweeping glance.

"Mom's right about the Frost Suite, it is my favorite," Luke offered. "Come on, I'll show you to your room."

Selecting a key from a wooden box sitting on a hall table in the foyer, he led Blair up the garland and string light adorned stairs towards the second floor.

"In Evergreen for the holidays?" Luke asked.

"No, as wonderful as the holidays are here, I am due back in New York," Blair responded.

"New York, huh?" Luke cast a glance at Blair who offered a slight nod. "Here's your room."

Luke stuck the key into the lock and gave it a turn. Pushing the door open, he held it as Blair walked through. The room was a blend of blues and shimmering silvers. The décor reminded Blair of a winter princess movie.

"I see why you call it the Frost Suite," Blair said. "It's beautiful."

"I like blue," Luke nodded. Glancing at the modest luggage placed at the foot of the bed, he commented, "You really aren't planning on staying here long, are you?"

Blair followed his eyes, "Are you always so inquisitive with your guests' plans?"

"Just the small-town mindset, I suppose. No harm intended," Luke said. "I'll leave you to your…whatever. Oh, here's your key."

Blair took the key giving Luke a wry smile.

Closing the door, she took in a deep breath. She was enjoying the nostalgia of being in Evergreen, but she could not shake the feeling of guilt in that she was only there to sign off on and sell her grandparents' store. She resigned to do what she had to and get back to New York as quickly as she could.

When Blair arrived at the dinner table, the room fell to a hush. The heads of its occupants turned to face her as she entered.

"I'm sorry, I hope you weren't waiting for me. I had to get out of those airport clothes," Blair wrinkled her nose.

"Not at all. I served the guests so that you could take your time. I have a setting for you right next to me," Loretta offered.

As Blair circled the table to the seat next to the Bed and Breakfast proprietor, a thump under the table was met with a groan from Luke. He grimaced as he rubbed his shin. Rolling his eyes, he hopped out of his seat and pulled the chair out for Blair.

"You didn't have to do that," Blair gushed.

"No. No, I really did," Luke confessed as he shot his mother a look.

Much of the table let out a snicker.

"Ms. Cooper, you have met my son Luke. This charming couple to your left is the Lawson's. They make the short drive from Seattle each year. Next to them is the Cavanaughs from Vancouver…Canada's not our Washington version to the south. Most of our other guests for Christmas will be coming in over the next few days. And this man to my right is Sam Marsden. Be mindful of him, he is a charmer, but a bit mischievous," Loretta raised an eyebrow towards her husband.

"It's nice to meet everyone," Blair smiled awkwardly at the table. She preferred to not be in the spotlight if she could help it.

"Loretta tells me you are only here for a couple of days," Sam Marsden inquired.

Blair shot Luke a glance and nodded, "Yes, that's right."

Sam looked confused, "You are going to be missing one of the most amazing holiday events in the country."

"I know. I used to come to Evergreen for Christmas when I was kid. It is amazing," Blair affirmed.

"Well, if there is anything we can do for you while you are here, you just let us know," Sam smiled.

"Thank you," Blair smiled, looking at the food on her plate. "Ms. Marsden…"

"Loretta," the hotelier corrected.

"Loretta, this all looks wonderful. Do you cook like this every night?"

The woman beamed, "We eat pretty well around here, but I'll admit, we amp things up a bit for the holidays."

"You should see her Christmas Eve and Christmas Day spreads, they are straight out of a magazine," Mrs. Cavanaugh offered.

"Susan, you're too kind," Loretta gushed.

"If you are here Friday, it is the annual tree lighting," Sam said. "It is the official kick off to the holidays here in Evergreen."

"Cocoa, carols and of course, candy canes," Mr. Lawson added.

"The three c's of Christmas…fourth with Christ the inherent one," Sam said.

Blair looked around the table, "It all sounds lovely, just as I remembered."

"You never know what Evergreen during the holidays has in store for you. We were just driving through ten…no eleven years ago. We ended up staying and have been coming back ever since," Mrs. Lawson squeezed her husband's arm.

"It's true. Sam and I used to stay here at the inn as guests. Ended up buying the place and making it our home," Loretta admitted. "Well, however long you are here, I hope you make yourself at home."

Four

Blair woke, startled at not being in her own bed. She traveled frequently for work and the first morning of disorientation was always the same.

Stretching out in what she decided was a very comfortable bed, she lay still for a moment, enjoying the weight of the blankets. Reaching for her phone, feeling guilty for sleeping in, she was comforted that by Pacific Coast standards, it was still quite early.

Wanting to get an early start on the day to assess the store and meet with the realtor, she quickly dressed in comfortable clothes and headed downstairs. She was greeted with the smell of coffee and bacon wafting from the kitchen. Hesitating at the base of the stairs, she was quickly met by Loretta.

"Sneaking out already, love?" the proprietor asked.

Blair wrinkled her nose, "I was trying to get an early start on the day."

"No sense running out without a bit of food in your belly," Loretta conferred. "You drink coffee?"

"I do," Blair nodded.

"Well come on in, we'll get you fixed up before you head out," Loretta urged.

Sensing it to be more of a command than a request, Blair relented.

"You're up earlier than my west coast guests, I figured as much that you might be," Loretta mused. Handing Blair a cup of coffee, the matriarch pointed towards cream and sugar.

"Crispy or wriggly?"

Blair looked up from her coffee, confused, "Hmm?"

"How do you like your bacon?" Loretta asked.

"Oh, a little crispy please."

"Girl after my own heart," Loretta said. "I know you are on a mission, so I won't subject you to a full meal, though you are missing out on pumpkin pancakes unless you'll reconsider."

"No, ma'am. I should get a start on the day," Blair lamented. "Pumpkin pancakes sound delicious, though."

"Very well. Here you are, bacon and egg croissant. It's what I fix up for the boys when they are in a rush. It usually tides them until lunch," Loretta said sliding a plate across the counter. "Sit. I can't imagine a few minutes will change much for you."

Blair obliged and sat at the counter with her coffee and sandwich.

As Loretta worked, she tossed a question towards Blair, "So, what *does* bring you to Evergreen on such a whirlwind venture?"

Blair wasn't sure why she hesitated, but she did. "I had family that lived here. I need to take care of somethings on their behalf."

"Ma and Pa Noelle. You're Susan's daughter," Loretta said across the counter. "It took me a bit because, of course, Cooper is your father's last name."

"Yes, that's right. I am Susan's daughter."

"You came to look after your grandparents' estate?"

"Sort of. There is still a lot to sort out," Blair admitted.

"Well, if there is anything we can do, we'd be happy to. We loved your grandparents. This whole town did," Loretta offered. "We were thrilled to learn there was family that the store would go to."

"Thank you," Blair acknowledged. "And thank you for breakfast. It was just what I needed."

"If you get hungry around lunch time, you just pop by. Anytime."

Blair got up and started to carry her dishes to the kitchen sink.

"You put that down. I'll take care of it. Go on, get on with your day. You have our number, I mean it. If you need anything…" Loretta pressed.

"I will," Blair promised.

Grabbing her coat, she headed out of the bed and breakfast. Off the steps of the porch and onto the sidewalk, she steadied herself as the morning chill was enough to keep frozen spots speckling the cement, leaving her trek to the store a bit on the slippery side.

Walking gingerly towards the store, she was able to appreciate the town of Evergreen in its quiet state. A few early risers ambled about, the bustle that was to come and build towards Christmas had yet to arrive.

Reaching the toy store, she slid the key in the lock and pushed her way in. Walking past all of the richly decorated buildings on her way, she realized the store seemed out of place without Christmas décor. She wasn't sure how useful it would be to help the sale, yet she somehow felt compelled to decorate the interior to match the trimming the town laced on the outside.

Digging into the back storeroom, she began sorting the containers of ornaments and carried them to the back of the store. She was startled to see a woman with a binder standing by the register.

Nearly dropping the box, she was holding, Blair collected herself.

"I'm sorry. I thought you heard the bell," the woman said. "I'm Meredith, the commercial real estate broker?"

"Yes, of course. Thank you for coming," Blair said. Setting the box down, she strode forward.

"So, you want to sell this place?"

Blair hesitated, "Yes…I think so."

"With all the stock?"

"If they want to keep it a toy store. I guess I hadn't considered any other option," Blair admitted.

"You never know. I did some research on Evergreen. In certain economic cycles, you could fetch a solid premium for a space like this. I could have sold this without a second thought to a national coffee chain or drug store," Meredith said, wandering around the store.

"This is not one of those cycles," the broker continued to Blair. "Evergreen draws its Christmas crowd and there are a few tourist locations like the local winery, but with the factory shutting down, there is very little consistency of flow and revenue. I don't know…."

"The factory?" Blair asked.

"Yes. They make textbooks and other such things. Most of that stuff has been centralizing for years. The local plant is shutting down at the end of the year, I'm afraid. My firm has that account too, looks like it will be a long sales cycle if ever to find a new suitor for that space. Too far from Seattle," Meredith said. "Still, this place has some charm, if you can be patient."

"Patient? You think it will take a while to sell?" Blair asked.

Meredith let out a chuckle, "You could get lucky. Seriously, with all of the tourists coming over the holiday, you might find someone romanticizing about living here and owning a toy store akin to Santa's village."

"Hmm," Blair was stumped. The image in her head was a simple process, though she admitted to herself, not grounded in any sort of reality.

"I see you were about to decorate, that is very smart. With this place up and running, your odds are much greater. If you left it shuttered amidst all of the holiday grandeur, I would give you almost no shot," Meredith admitted.

"Open? You mean *run* it?" Blair gasped.

"Well, yeah. A buyer would want to see this place functional, in full swing during its absolute busiest time of the year," the broker said.

"Oh," Blair leaned back against the counter.

"I tell you what, the moment you have the store tidied up and decorated, give me a call. I'll have a photographer drive out and we'll get right to work posting it and reaching out to our colleagues for prospective buyers," Meredith said.

"Ok...," Blair's head was spinning.

The broker left Blair to work on the store.

"I am going to need more coffee...," Blair mumbled to herself, bracing her palms against the counter.

Five

Fresh holiday flavored latte in hand, Blair decided to approach the store a bit more methodically. Instead of allowing the volume of work to be done to overwhelm her, she pulled out a note pad and began making a checklist of what needed to be done. Despite the lengthy list, seeing everything on paper and having the ability to knock one thing off at a time gave her some sense of control.

Moving through the store, Blair took careful inventory of things she needed to do to convey the store was operational and in top form. Dancing through the displays, she reveled in the memories that were triggered while she catalogued her list.

When she had reached midway through her second sheet of paper, she flopped the pad onto the cashier stand. With hands on her hips, she spun around the room, determining whether to tackle items in order or to prioritize them. As she scanned the store, she spied her grandfather's record player.

Walking behind the stand, she opened the top of the player. Biting her lip, she began opening cupboards until she found the stack of records. Flipping through the stack, she quickly found several Christmas albums. The smell of the records themselves welcomed a powerful memory, Blair placed the record on the turntable and set the needle. In moments, after a brief crackle or two over the speakers, Burl Ives began crooning about splendorous, glistening Christmas colors throughout the store

Blair smiled as she listened, it was her grandfather's favorite as well as a hit with the children who shopped in the store. Inspired by the music, she glanced at the first item on the list. Nodding to herself, she found the duster, rags and broom. Before she could decorate and begin to give the illusion that the store was operational, the couple months' worth of dust had to be whisked away.

Singing Christmas carols as she worked, she was startled to hear the bell at the door ring. Holding the broom steady, Blair craned her neck to see down the aisle. A woman near her age was looking around the store. As she came closer, Blair widened her eyes in recognition.

"Nella? Nella Jones?" Blair called out, setting the broom down and striding to meet the woman.

Smiling, the woman responded, "Nella Swanson, now."

"Wow, congratulations," Blair offered.

"It's been a while since we've seen each other, hasn't it?" Nella said.

"It has," Blair nodded. "It's good to see you."

"I was walking by. I heard the music and thought I'd pop in to see what was up," Nella said.

"A little clean up work," Blair nodded towards the cleaning supplies.

"No better soundtrack to do a little Christmas time work. Reminds me of your grandparents," Nella declared. "I could help."

Blair shook her head, "You don't have to do that. I'm just doing a little tidying and thought I'd put some decorations up. This placed looked so sad between the coffee shop and café being so festive."

"That's why I'm here. I hope I'm not being too forward, I helped your grandparents run the store, before…before…"

"Not at all, I'm glad you're here," Blair smiled.

"So, I guess you're my boss now?" Nella raised a brow.

"I hadn't really thought about that," Blair looked confused and bit forlorn. She wasn't planning on opening the store for real, merely get the store to the appearance of being fully functional. She was also struck with the idea that Nella didn't know about her intention to sell the store.

"So where do we begin?" Nella clapped her hands together.

Appreciating her friend's enthusiasm, Blair let out a light chuckle. "Well, I dusted and am just about done sweeping. That means we're on to decorating."

Nella's eyes grew wide, "I was hoping you would say that. Can I do the window display up front?"

"Sure," Blair affirmed.

In a flash, Nella was at the front window, clearing the toys to make room for the Christmas décor. "Your grandparents loved doing the window. They usually started with different ideas but always ended in agreement. Every year was something different, fun and beautiful."

Blair looked off, her mind cataloguing the memories of the window displays when she visited. "Yes, yes they were," she nodded absently. Snapping out of it, she winked, "No pressure!"

Nella opened her mouth wide, "You're right! I better think this through carefully."

With a giggle, Blair went to finish sweeping. "My grandparents loved this store," she said aloud, almost as much to herself as to Nella.

"They meant a lot to this town. It's going to be so nice to see it open again and right before the holidays!" Nella called, removing the last item from the window.

Blair froze in tracks. Squeezing her eyes shut for a moment, "Yeah...right. Open before Christmas. That's, uh, that's the plan."

With a sigh, she swept the last pile into the dustpan. She wasn't sure what to do other than keep moving forward with her plan. Regardless of opening the store for business, it still needs to be decorated. Setting her cleaning supplies aside, she retuned her attention to the rows of boxes.

"Hey, have you seen the tree decorations in all those boxes? I was thinking a classic living room vignette with select toys from the store around the tree. Maybe find some toys from each decade the store was open," Nella called from the front of the room.

"I did," Blair confirmed. "That's a great idea. I'll get it down for you."

Heading into the storeroom, she waded through the boxes she had already pulled down. High up on the top shelf were two boxes marked 'Tree'. Reaching up, her fingers grazed the very bottom of the first box. Extending on her tiptoes, Blair could just tap each side of the box. Scooting the box closer and closer to the edge, she smiled at her resourcefulness until the box reached its tipping point.

Suddenly, stretched to her max, she was trapped supporting the box overhead with the last edge on the lip of the shelf. If she tried to complete the process of removing the box, Blair knew it would topple, perhaps taking her with it.

Hoping Nella was within earshot, Blair called out, "Uh…could you give me a hand? I think I may have bitten off more than I can chew."

Hands reached up behind her and helped to support the box. Blair froze as the hands did not appear to be Nella's and the body she backed into as she snuck out and under the box was more masculine than she expected.

"I got this," a male voice responded.

Blair whirled around, spying the man from the bed and breakfast. "You?"

"Me," Luke Marsden grinned. Setting the box down on the floor, he nodded towards the shelf. "That one too?"

"Yes, please," Blair nodded sheepishly.

As Luke retrieved the second box full of tree decorations, "Sorry if I startled you, it looked like maybe you needed a hand."

"I did," Blair admitted. "I was expecting Nella back here in the storeroom, not you. Not that I'm not appreciative, just unexpected."

"Yeah, I waved at Nella on the way in," Luke nodded.

"What are you doing here?" Blair asked, exasperated. "Again, grateful, just surprised."

"I heard around the grapevine that you were reopening the store at long last," Luke said.

"Well, I…about that," Blair started.

"It's a wonderful thing," Luke interjected. "The town needs this store. This Christmas season is tough on everyone and this is a symbol of Christmas the way it always was."

Looking up at Luke, Blair asked, "How come?"

"The publishing house has been the life blood of this town for nearly a century. It employs half the town. They are shutting down as of December thirty-first. Evergreen has not exactly been growing and its future, the entire town, is in jeopardy," Luke said.

Blair screwed her face in a bit of pain, "That's not a resounding selling point for the store."

"I suppose not, but you being here and getting this place open for the holidays is just that little bit of spark that can set off some Christmas magic for the people of Evergreen," Luke said.

"Right," Blair looked away, biting her lip.

"So, my specific reason for coming here, outside of rescuing this box of very fragile Christmas ornaments, was…," Luke began. Beckoning Blair to the local craftsman section, continued, "Was these."

Pointing to a row of wooden toy boxes.

"You want to buy a toy box?" Blair asked, even more confused.

"No. I make these. And a few other things, that is what I wanted to talk to you about," Luke laughed.

Blair dropped her jaw in surprise, "You *make* these?"

Luke ginned, "I do."

"Wow." Blair knelt down, smoothing her hands over the top of the chest as she admired it. "These are beautiful, I was wondering where they came from."

"Straight from my winery. I use old wine barrels. Even most of the metal bits are fashioned from the metal bands that tie them together," Luke nodded.

"You own a winery too? So let me get this straight, you help out at the local bed and breakfast, cobble genuinely amazing toy boxes and you make wine?" Blair pressed.

Luke let out a knowing grin, "And own the vineyard in which I get my grapes, well most of them, at least."

"You're not the town mayor or sheriff as well?" Blair teased.

"No, I don't have any other job titles that I can think of," Luke chuckled. "I did want to add one other thing to my portfolio, however. Could you stay here for a moment?" With a twinkle in his eye, he dashed out of the store to return a few moments later with a box. Setting it next to one of the chests, he opened the box. Gently, he pulled out a series of wooden items he had wrapped in tissue. Placing them on a shelf, he finally produced a larger wooden piece that he set behind them.

"You made a nativity set?"

"I did," Luke beamed.

Grabbing one of the pieces, a carving of an angel, Blair studied it. "This is beautiful. This whole set is."

"There's a little hook at the peak of the barn," Luke added excitedly.

"You mean the manger?" Blair asked.

"The manger is actually the little feeding trough the baby Jesus is in," Luke corrected.

"Right," Blair offered a little nod as she contemplated the set.

"I would like to sell these here along with the toy chests," Luke offered.

Blair stepped back. "You want to sell these...here."

"Well, yeah. Your grandparents let locals sell their crafts here, I just figured that it would be okay. Unless you don't...," Luke started.

Waving him off, Blair smiled, "Of course. Of course, they're wonderful. It's just, these are treasures. Are you sure you want to sell them here, at a toy store?"

"Are you kidding? This place is an Evergreen institution. This store is *the* place, especially at Christmas time. There's no better place to display and sell, what did you call them...treasures?" Luke assured.

Blair's mind raced with the thought that Luke was hinging his sales of the nativity sets on a store she had no intention of re-opening.

"Great," Luke bounced a bit. "I have to get back to the winery, I'll bring a few more by tomorrow. When do you plan on opening?"

Blair looked down at Nella who was singing along to herself as she worked on the front window. "You know, as long as Nella is available, we should be able to open tomorrow."

"Wow, you work fast. That will be great. Having the toy store open will be like a gift to the entire town," Luke said. "See you tomorrow."

"See you tomorrow." Blair watched Luke walk out of the store with a little wave to Nella.

Chewing her lip, she studied the nativity scene. Each piece was simple in its carving design, with soft, undefined features yet strangely emotive. She took her time to set them up with the stable, until it was all just right.

Taking a step back, she admired the little wooden scene.

"He does nice work," Nella said as she walked up to Blair.

"Yeah," Blair nodded. "These are really good."

"Come look at the window!" Nella squealed, tugging on Blair's arm.

Blair allowed herself to be dragged along by her excitable associate. Slowing by the inside of the display, her arm was yanked. "You have to see it from the *outside*," Nella urged.

Pushing through the door, the pair stood on the sidewalk. Blair's eyes widened, "Nella, this is beautiful!" The tree sat on a little round rug, flanked by an armchair. The tree was decorated with lights and garland, small toys were hung on the branches in place of traditional balls. A toy had been selected from each of the past fifty years adding a touch of nostalgia. "It reminds me of one of my grandparents' best displays."

"I will take that as a *huge* compliment," Nella beamed. "Come on, let's get the rest of the store put together."

As they walked back into the toy store, Blair turned to Nella, "Are you sure you're up for this? I don't know the first thing about running a toy store. I'm afraid this might put a pretty big weight on your shoulders."

"Don't worry, I've got this. By the…well, over the last year or so, your grandparents had me learning about every part of the store," Nella assured. "Really, this season is all about *you* being the face of The Toy Chest, bringing that family connection into Evergreen."

"I'm not sure I can live up to that. Grandpa and Grandma were like the Claus' of Evergreen," Blair shrugged.

"You'll do fine. Just be yourself and make sure you fill up on plenty of Christmas spirit!" Nella grinned. "Come on, let's get going on these decorations!"

"I will put on another Christmas album," Blair suggested. "Any requests?"

Nella's eyes glistened, "Got any Brenda Lee over there?"

"Are you kidding me? One of Grandma's favorites!" Blair beamed.

Rifling through the albums, she slid out the Brenda Lee record and the pair literally began rocking around the Christmas tree as they continued to prep the store for opening.

Nella focused on the register and operations while Blair, hands on her hips, studied the store. Feeling inspired, she began moving fixtures, organizing toys and lavishing each display with a touch of Christmas.

Smiling quietly, Nella admired Blair's attention to the arrangements. At first, she was confused with Blair's intent, yet the more she watched she began to understand. The flow of the fixtures began to tell a story. Families from youngest to oldest had items that would resonate. Blair mixed classic toys with modern toys where before they were segregated in their own sections.

"Impressive," Nella said, peering over the check stand.

Blair swung her head back at her friend.

"Mixing the nostalgic toys with the modern ones suggests that both have their place under the tree," Nella said.

"That's what I was thinking. It's like this store. I was always excited to see what the latest toys were, but was always drawn back to the classics," Blair said, picking a Holly Hobby doll off a shelf and giving it a fond inspection.

"You're good at this," Nella shared.

Blair started to nod in acknowledgment and then quickly put the toy back, almost feeling like a fraud. She was enjoying putting the store together, but she knew it was temporary. Worse, she was working under a false veil.

Turning to Nella, Blair sighed. She had to confess. "There's something…there's something…," Blair swallowed.

Nella's eyes widened, "Missing! You're right! The carousel!"

"The carousel," Blair repeated softly. Her eyes brightened as Nella's had, "The Christmas carousel Grandpa and Grandma always had on the counter! I'll check in back, we must have missed it!"

Blair dashed into the storeroom. Glancing around the shelves with the Christmas ornaments, most of them bare, she stood on her tiptoes to try and peek on the top shelf. Reaching up, she scaled the shelves, placing her feet carefully on the lower section until she could peer over the edge of the tallest shelf.

Tucked in the back corner, she found a dusty gift box. Sliding it forward enough to where she could grasp it, she stepped backward, landing hard on the storeroom floor.

Blowing off the dust, Blair pried up the edge of the box and looked inside. What she found, sent her melting against a rack. The gift box in her lap, she stirred through the contents. As Blair shuffled around the items, her heart fluttered. A wave of warm memories enveloped her.

"Everything okay?" Nella's voice interrupted Blair's slip into nostalgia.

Blair looked up and smiled, "Yeah. I found this. It's a game I made with my brother and my grandparents."

"Wow," Nella circled closer and gazed in on the contents of the box.

Blair looked thoughtful, "There was one year, it snowed so hard for so long, we couldn't get back to Seattle. We were snowed in. So, we sat around a table Grandpa set up by the fireplace and we made this up. The board, the rules, the pieces… it was actually a lot of fun."

"That is so cool, tell me about it."

"It's an advent calendar. We created a minigame you could play each day leading up to Christmas. Each day also revealed a piece to a larger game that we could all play together on Christmas day," Blair's voice rattled excitedly as she recalled the game.

"What a great idea!" Nella exclaimed. Her eyes widened, "We should play it!"

Blair appreciated her enthusiasm, but she glanced at the clock on the storeroom wall. "Maybe tomorrow. You have a family to get to and it is getting late," Blair said.

Nella looked up at the clock and saw the time herself, "Oh my gosh! You're right. I've had so much fun with you, time has really gotten away. Let me help you put the decoration boxes away."

"You go home. I'll finish up here. We were almost done anyway. Maybe I can solve the mystery of the missing carousel," Blair said. Seeing the hesitant look in Nella's eyes, Blair stressed, "I *insist*."

"Alright, but I'll be in early tomorrow morning to finish setting up. We'll be ready to open!" Nella squealed.

"I'm excited," Blair said. Wrinkling her nose, she admitted, "And a bit nervous."

"You'll be fine. We'll be fine. It will be fun," Nella assured.

"Goodnight, Nella."

"Goodnight, Blair. See you in the morning," Nella said, scampering out of the storeroom.

Blair took one more glance around the gift box contents. Closing the lid, she set it aside where it would be accessible.

One by one, she set the Christmas decoration boxes back onto the shelves. One box seemed to have a bit more heft to it. Setting it down, she pried open the top. Moving packing materials aside, she found the prize she was looking for. Gently pulling it free, she carried it to the check stand counter.

Her eyes followed her fingers as she smoothed them along the ornate, snow dusted rotunda and admired the trademark Christmas carousel. The handcrafted decoration eschewed Christmas with its candy cane striped poles and evergreen garland harnesses. Eight reindeer preceded a magnificent sleigh. Each animal looked joyful in their task as a jolly Santa himself waved at all who watched him circle the carousel, his green pack bulging with presents behind him.

Blair found the mechanism to turn it on. Turning off the record player, she leaned against the counter and toggled the switch, letting the music box triggered by the carousel's motor to take over the ambience for the store.

As the reindeer and sleigh made their trip by, Blair's journey down Christmas memory lane was fully engaged. Since she was a little girl, she propped her chin against the counter and marveled at the carousel. She would watch it for hours, studying each detail of the elegant decoration.

There was a charm to the carols delivered by the crude brass machinations buried within its construct.

On top of the rotunda, amidst the gold frames of depicted Christmas scenes, was the logo for The Toy Chest. The artist that made the carousels loved visiting Blair's grandparents' store. Despite their worldwide exclusivity, he even sold a few units from the store. One year, he sent them the carousel as a surprise, one which they coveted ever since.

The realization that the carousel was now hers, made Blair sadden. In particular, knowing that The Toy Chest would likely no longer be in the new year. With a sigh, she turned off the carousel.

Strolling through the store one more time, she drank in the experience of being in Evergreen, in The Toy Chest.

Turning off the lights, she pushed outside and spun to lock the front door. She admired Nella's store window display. It told a story of nostalgia and current days melding together. It looked like a nice, warm, friendly place to spend Christmas with family.

Pulling up her collar to ward off the chilling breeze, she watched the toy store sign wave slightly in the breeze. Its crackled wood belying the years of wet and cold Washington state abuse it had endured over the decades as layer after layer of fresh paint had been applied, making it as welcoming a beacon to the store as ever. Despite the heavy patina on the hardware that held it in place, the joyful sign was an enticement for visitors that fun and love were just inside.

Blair chuckled. The sign was right. With a last longing look, she turned away and began the walk to the Holly Bough Bed and Breakfast.

It wasn't just the store that Blair appreciated. The town itself had a calming, romantic charm to it. The tree lined streets with the magnificent fir trees and foothills of the permanently snowcapped Cascade mountains as a backdrop was an image ripe for the cover of a Christmas card.

The town was decorated for Christmas as complete as any house, a mecca of cheer for the people that lived there as well as its guests. Blair liked this place. It felt like home, even though she was only a visitor herself.

Six

A light flurry danced its way down from the skies delivering a soft wintry shimmer for Blair to walk through. As she reached the bed and breakfast, the classic white house with the large porch sone as a well-lit beacon in the night.

Blair studied the charming residence. In each window, a lit wreath with a tidy red bow adorned the façade. The length of the porch rails were wrapped in evergreen boughs and dressed with strings of white lights. In the center of the front door, another wreath with holly sprigs and berries greeted guests.

Stepping up on the porch, Blair hesitated as she reached for the door. As welcoming as the bed and breakfast and its proprietors were, she felt self-conscious. Barging into the bed and breakfast so late and the expectations of her opening and retaining the toy store made her feel like she was lying to everyone.

Pushing through the front door, the home only proved even more inviting. The stairs were deocrated with evergreen garland and sparkling lights winding their way up the banister. Sam Marsten tended to a roaring fire as he regaled guests gathered around the fireplace. The Christmas tree, with its twinkling lights and elegant decorations, was radiant.

For a moment, she considered sneaking upstairs to her room and avoiding everyone. The thought was fleeting as Sam Marsten shot up from tending to the fire and raced to the foyer to greet Blair.

"Welcome back, my dear. Let me get that coat for you," Sam said, his arms extended to help her slip out of her winter jacket.

Blair hesitated, but relented. Spinning, she allowed Sam to tug the coat off of her and add it next to the others hung in a neat row just inside the front door.

"Why thank you, good sir," Blair curtsied.

"My pleasure," Sam gushed.

A figure appeared in the hall, a towel cast over her shoulder, "Hello, dear. We were wondering when you might turn up. I have a dinner plate set aside for you."

"Thank you, Mrs. Marsten," Blair said. "You're both exceptional hosts." Blair cast a glance at Sam who hovered between her and the coat rack.

"Loretta, if you please," the bed and breakfast proprietor insisted. "Well, come along. I'll get your dinner reheated for you."

Sensing no good would come from anything other than compliance, Blair headed down the hall.

"Long day at the shop?" Loretta asked as Blair joined her in the kitchen.

"Yes," Blair nodded. "Lots to do to get ready to show...open the toy store. It was fun, though. So nice to be back."

"It's good to have a Noelle family member back to run the store, inject some new life into the old place," Loretta said, putting Blair's plate together. "Would you like some wine with dinner?"

Blair thought for a moment and then realized how nice a glass of wine sounded after her day at the shop. "Only if you'll join me for a glass."

"Very well, I wasn't going to let you eat alone any way. Would you be a dear and grab two glasses from that cabinet?" Loretta nudged her head towards a cupboard door.

Reaching for a pair of glasses, Blair followed Loretta to the table. A lone place setting was held over from dinner. Loretta set the plate down and pulled out an adjacent chair. In the center of the table, an open bottle of wine was quickly poured into a pair of glasses.

"To The Toy Chest and Ma and Pa Noelle," Loretta held her glass high.

Blair touched her glass to Loretta's.

"This looks fantastic," Blair said, eyeing her plate of salmon and asparagus. Taking a bite, she smiled, "It tastes even better than it looks. Oh my gosh, what is on this?"

"It's a pomegranate glaze. Sam cooked them on cedar planks out on the barbecue," Loretta said. "Even cooked the asparagus out there. The fish is from right here in Evergreen, or a little ways out of town, at least."

"Well kudos to you and Sam, this is really delicious. Thank you," Blair gushed.

Loretta waved her off, "Nonsense. It is our pleasure. It's just too bad you weren't able to join us for dinner. As well as Sam can grill salmon, he is an even more talented storyteller."

Blair smiled, "I bet."

"How is the store? It hasn't been touched in months," Loretta asked.

"Not bad. It took a little tidying, but mostly it was trying to make it half as festive as Grandpa and Grandma used to," Blair admitted.

"They did have quite the Christmas touch," Loretta said.

Blair nodded, "They did. Nella Johnson...I mean Swanson now... helped a lot. She did a great job on our front window display."

"Well, I look forward to seeing it. I'll make Sam take me to coffee tomorrow and we'll stroll by," Loretta suggested.

"If you do, don't stroll by without stopping to say hello," Blair smiled.

"Wouldn't dream of it," Loretta said. "I'll take care of those."

Blair started to get out of her seat and take her plate. The tone in Loretta's voice encouraged her to quickly abandon the thought.

"I was just about to make wassail and bring it to the living room. I have something I need you to do for me in there anyway," Loretta said.

Blair eyed her suspiciously but averted a denial of the request as stern eyes fell on her. "Can I help you with the wassail?"

Loretta studied the girl and agreed, "That would be lovely."

Leaning against the counter as Loretta filled the mugs and placed them on a tray. "I let this simmer in a slower cooker, great for as many guests that we have. My little secret," Loretta explained.

"It smells wonderful. Like Christmas," Blair said.

"My own exclusive blend of holiday spices. Hibiscus tea and juniper berries really sets it apart," Loretta beamed.

When the last mug was filled, Blair lifted the tray and followed Loretta into the living room.

The hostess was as gallant as ever, flitting from guest to guest. She would introduce Blair as they made their way around the room. When the tray was empty, Loretta pulled Blair aside.

"As I said, there is something I need you to do. It is a Holly Bough tradition to have our guests help in decorating the tree," Loretta declared.

Blair scanned the gorgeously decorated tree, "But it already looks beautiful to me."

Loretta grinned, "It isn't just about the aesthetic, but the experience. Here." She held out a tray of exquisite glass ornaments.

Blair selected a colorful nutcracker, "In honor of the toy store."

"Great choice," Loretta said.

Walking to the tree, Blair found a spot that wasn't overcrowded and slid the ornament on to a branch. She stood and admired the tree, reviewing all of the ornaments that were hung.

"It's beautiful, isn't it?" Loretta said, handing Blair her mug of wassail.

"It is," Blair nodded.

"Have you started looking for places to live? I know a great realtor I connect you with," Loretta asked.

Blair frowned and shook her head, "Oh, I, uh…"

The door burst open and Luke Marsten strode in, his arms laden with firewood. Blair used the interruption to eject herself from the conversation.

"Let me help you with that," she offered, scurrying to unload logs from Luke's arms and place them in a neat stack in a copper bucket near the fireplace.

When she got to the last one, they both held onto it for a brief moment, their eyes flitting on the other's.

"Sorry," Blair scoffed letting go of the log. "I suppose you can manage that one."

"Thank you for your help. It saved me from getting and earful from Mom about hurling the logs into the bin and making a mess," Luke said.

"Luke, are you going to stay for some wassail?" Loretta asked.

"I was just stopping by to deliver some wood. I filled the rack outside and covered it up with the tarp," Luke admitted.

Loretta put her arm around her son. "What could possibly be so important that you can't stay for one drink? Besides, it will chase the chill out of you," Loretta insisted.

Luke knew the futility of fighting his mother, "One. I really do have things to get back to."

"She's a tough one to say no to," Blair smiled, watching Loretta scamper away.

"You're a quick learner," Luke laughed.

"She's sweet, though," Blair said.

Luke looked at their guest, "Yes, she is. Don't let her fool you too much, though. She's not afraid to chase you out of the kitchen with a wooden spoon, believe me."

"I'll keep that in mind and be on my best behavior," Blair assured.

Loretta swooped close and handed her son a mug. She started to join the conversation when a bell ringing in the kitchen pulled her away, "My cookies!"

"Cookies, too?" Blair gushed. "You do spoil your guests."

Loretta whisked away to pull her treats out of the oven.

Luke took the opportunity to gulp down his beverage. "Excuse me, I really do have a lot of work to do tonight. It was nice to see you again."

"You as well," Blair nodded.

Clapping his hand on his father's shoulder, Luke said, "Good night, Pops!"

"Leaving?" Sam asked.

"Lots of work to do," Luke said.

"Winery or workshop?"

"Workshop tonight," Luke said.

"Well, don't cut your fingers off," Sam warned.

"I won't, Pop," Luke assured. As Loretta wheeled in through the living room with a platter of cookies, Luke swiped one and grinned. Giving his mother a squeeze around her shoulders, he said, "Goodnight, Mom!"

Loretta scowled at the cookie theft followed by the abrupt exit.

As Loretta made her way around the room, she paused at Blair.

"They look delicious, but the season is young, and I am sure the temptation for treats will only get worse," Blair said.

Loretta cocked her head, "Snickerdoodles, fresh from the oven."

Blair rolled her eyes, "Fine. I'll have one."

Selecting a soft in the center cookie, Blair took a bite. "Oh my, these are delicious!"

"Award winning recipe from the Evergreen Christmas Festival a few years back," Loretta boasted.

"I can see why," Blair said.

"You can see why I walk around with this," Sam Marsten tapped his on his belly. "Got the store all squared away?"

Blair nodded, "I think we'll be in good shape. Especially with Nella's help."

"Nice girl," Sam said. "She was such a huge help for your grandparents."

"Not sure I'd want to open without her," Blair admitted.

"What did you do before you, uh, before taking over the store?" Sam asked.

Blair swallowed, "I'm in marketing. I put together ad programs for Fortune 500 companies."

"I'm sure that experience will serve you well here in Evergreen," Sam said.

"I hope so," Blair said. "I did run a marketing campaign for an online toy store, 'The Heart of Play' campaign aimed at pulling kids together with friends, siblings and parents."

"Was that the one with the teddy bear watching the kids play?" Mr. Hubbard asked.

Blair nodded triumphantly, "That's the one."

"I loved that ad. The one with the cousins always choked me up," Mrs. Hubbard added.

"That came organically after our first few runs. Customers started to post their clips of holidays and family reunions that brought kids together after long stretches of not seeing each other. They used toys and games to bring them together quickly," Blair said. "Interactivity with the customer is always the golden goal."

Loretta gushed, "I can only imagine what you'll do with The Toy Chest. I'm sure your grandparents would be so proud of you."

Blair's smile faded a bit as she struggled to keep it pasted on her face, instead, she fell melancholy, "Yeah. Well, I should get up to bed, I have a long and exciting day ahead of me tomorrow."

"Goodnight dear," Loretta said, echoed by Sam and the guests.

Blair stepped out of the living room and shuffled up the steps. Closing herself in her room, she leaned against the door. She was enjoying her time in Evergreen, the people and being in her grandparents' store so much. She knew it was fleeting. She was only there for a few days, yet the entire town was under the impression she was there to stay.

She closed her eyes. Blair wasn't even sure how it started. She never *said* she was staying. She never said she wasn't either. She couldn't bear to think of the reaction the town would have when a big "For Sale" sign was posted in the front window.

Her phone buzzing stole her from her thoughts. Looking at the screen, she saw Todd's name flash. "Hi, Todd."

"It's late. I thought you would have called by now," his voice carried over her phone.

"I know, I'm sorry. I just got absorbed in pulling the store together and really haven't stopped until just now," Blair said.

"Did you meet with the realtor?"

"I did. There is lots to do here. I'll probably be a few days," Blair said.

"A few days?" Todd asked.

Blair looked at the phone as she prepared her response, "She wants me to have the store open and functional. She thinks an operational store will inspire a buyer to act."

"That makes sense. It is a good opportunity to maximize profit. You can probably liquidate the stock and whatever junk is left if the buyer is going to turn it into something other than a toy store," Todd agreed.

The idea of the space being anything other than a toy store made Blair's heart sick. "It's not junk. There are some really nice things in stock and some of it is personal stuff of my grandparents."

"You know what I mean. It's stuff you certainly don't need to fly back to Manhattan with," Todd said.

"Yeah, I suppose," Blair admitted.

After a brief pause in the conversation, Todd tried to make his voice more upbeat, "Look, get the store up and running, do it as a last hurrah on behalf of your grandparents. Put their store in its best light. That's all that can be asked of you. But remember, time is money in sales."

"When you've given the realtor what she needs, you can come home, and we can have *our* Christmas. I'll take you skating at Rockefeller and we can order something special for Christmas dinner," Todd said.

"Yeah, you're right," Blair said. "Look, it's late. I'm tired. I'll talk to you tomorrow, okay?"

"Okay. Love you, Blair!" Todd sang through the phone.

"You too," Blair said softly. Her mind was mush. The thought of Christmas in New York was magical and exciting only twenty hours ago. Now it seemed foreign.

Thinking she was just exhausted; she readied her things for a shower so she could slip into bed.

Nodding to herself, she was numb. Yawning, she muttered, "Yeah, I'll get the place going, the realtor can get some action shots and I'll be back by the weekend."

Seven

Blair descended the stairs of the bed and breakfast and already the invigorating aroma of coffee and fresh pastry met her nose. Thinking she would slip out unnoticed, she was almost jolted with the welcoming.

At the bottom of the steps, Loretta grinned with a thermos and a brown bag. "I thought you'd be rushing out of here. It's your big opening. Good luck."

"Thank you, Loretta. You truly are wonderful," Blair said as she welcomed the breakfast and especially the full vessel of coffee.

"Be sure to bundle up, there's a little snow in the forecast," Loretta said.

Blair nodded as she wrapped her scarf around her neck. "Will I see you at the store later?"

Loretta nodded, "Have a good day, dear!"

The door shut behind her, Blair took in a deep breath. The crisp air gave her the slightest chill, but she found it rejuvenating. With a bounce in her step, she glided happily through the still quiet streets of Evergreen.

In a rush of excitement that she did not anticipate, she turned the key in the lock to The Toy Chest and burst into the store. Heading to the back, she peeled her coat and gloves off, laying them over the desk chair. Flipping a series of switches, the store slowly came to life. The store lights and then the Christmas lights bathed the store in a warm glow.

With a skip in her step, Blair made her way to the record player and spun a Christmas record adding to the ambiance. Eagerly tapping into the thermos of coffee Loretta provided her, she stood behind the check stand, her hands proudly placed on either side as she imagined shoppers strolling in, just as they had when her grandparents were alive.

Blair thought of her grandfather and grandmother. The store wasn't just about transactions and toys, it wasn't just business, it was an experience. Chewing her lip, she realized what she was missing. She reflected on her grandparents, especially during the holidays, always had the store especially welcoming. Like Loretta and her guests at the bed and breakfast, shopping at The Toy Chest was like attending a Christmas party with friends.

Moving a row of large, boxed items to the floor, Blair set up a space in the center of the store. Laying down Christmas table runners and finding a few more decorations to spruce up the area, she stepped back and planned what she needed.

Thinking of where she could go, she realized she didn't want to compete with the coffee shop next door. Hands on her hips, she pondered until she had an idea. With a smile and a snap of her fingers, she headed next door.

The coffee shop was busy with employees of the print house stopping in before heading into work. As she waited for the line to clear, Blair studied the offerings. The coffee shop wasn't there when Blair was younger, but it embodied a hometown shop that made it feel as though it had been a part of Evergreen forever.

It wasn't just the ambiance that Blair found the shop to embrace the spirit of the town, but the staff was sincerely friendly, recognizing everyone who walked in and presenting them a warm smile. It felt welcoming. The employees reminded her of how her grandparents ran the toy store. There weren't customers, there were guests, friends.

As she reached the counter, the barista smiled, "It's opening day for you. You must be excited."

Blair paused for a moment; the level of insight wouldn't happen in Manhattan. "Yes, and yes, I'm very excited. A little nervous."

"You'll do great. Just…have fun," the barista said.

"I'm Blair. Blair Cooper," Blair extended her hand.

The barista giggled, "I know. I'm Jessica. My friend here is Patty. And that… is Kris. She owns the shop."

"It's a pleasure," Blair.

"Your grandparents were like, well, grandparents to all of us. They were a treasure and are dearly missed," Jessica said.

"Thank you," Blair said. "That is really sweet."

"So, what can I make for you? Should be something special for your big opening," Jessica suggested.

"Surprise me, and make something for Nella, she should be in soon," Blair said.

Jessica brightened, "I know Nella's seasonal favorite. I'll make two."

"Sounds wonderful," Blair said. Looking towards Kris, she asked, "Could I speak to Kris for a moment?"

"Sure," Jessica shrugged as she began assembling the cups for Blair and Nella's drinks. "Kris!"

The woman strode around the counter. Blair studied her for a moment, she was elegant despite casually attired, exuding as welcoming an affect as her barista.

"You must be Blair. We have been so excited to hear that you were coming to take over the store," Kris extended.

Blair's head dipped slightly as the words met her ears, "Yeah."

"Oh, don't worry. You'll be fine," Kris assured. "So, what can I do for you?"

"Well, my grandparents always had treats for the shoppers that came into the store during the holidays. I thought it would be nice to do the same, but then I thought it might erode some of your business if I was giving away warm drinks," Blair explained. With a little bounce, she said, "So, I wanted to see if I could purchase the drinks and treats from you. Even put a little card up letting folks know where it all came from."

"I see," Kris considered. "That is really quite thoughtful."

"The toy store would just be an extension of your shop," Blair added.

Kris nodded, "It sounds like a wonderful idea, what would you like?"

Blair shared what she had hoped and accepted a few of Kris' own thoughts. The café owner herself, helped carry thermal urns of coffee, cider and cocoa to help set up.

A selection of Christmas cookies and pastries were set on Santa Claus plates that Kris pulled from her back room.

Together, they admired the setup. "This is so wonderful," Blair declared.

"I think your guests are going to like it," Kris approved.

"Thank you, so much. Just let me know what I owe you, we'll take care of it each night," Blair promised.

"Good luck, Blair. I'll be sure to tell everyone who comes in that The Toy Chest is once again open for business and just in time for Christmas," Kris said.

Nella walked in just as Kris walked out. "Good morning, boss!"

Blair grimaced at the title. "Good morning, Nella."

"It smells great in here, like Christmas," Nella exclaimed. "Wow, this looks great! Is this what Kris was doing here?"

"It was. I remembered my grandparents having treats out, I wanted to do something similar, but not take away from their business next door," Blair explained.

Nella nodded approvingly, "I like it."

"There's just one thing missing. We need candy canes," Blair frowned.

"I can take care of that," Nella said. Pulling out her phone, she dialed a number. In seconds, she hung up triumphantly. "The grocery will send some in just a little bit."

"I love this place," Blair smiled.

"It's a community. That's how it works around here," Nella shrugged. "You ready for this?"

"I think we are," Blair nodded. Her phone buzzed, "Ooh, I should grab this."

Taking a step away, she hit the green button on her phone and announced herself.

"Blair, it's Meredith Kohl," the voice called. "I was checking to see if you have the store ready to put on the market. I can send our photographer up to take some shots and video."

"Uhm, yeah, sure. The store looks great," Blair said, sweeping her hair off her forehead.

Hanging up the phone, she bit her lip. Gazing across the store, seeing Nella gleefully preparing to open, Blair's heart sank a bit. Only in that moment, did she realize the impact that selling the store might have on Nella.

"It's time!" Nella called, clearly giddy about turning the sign.

"Nella," Blair started, needing to get the truth out into the open.

"Yes?" Nella bounced, her grin wide.

The life in Nella's eyes was so full of joy and excitement, Blair couldn't bear to rip it away. "I'm really glad you're here with me."

"Me too!" Nella squealed. "Three, two, one…"

The bubbly young woman turned the 'open' sign and spun to face Blair, clapping her hands together.

Blair smiled.

"Let's get this party started!" Nella drifted to the record player. Her selection made Blair laugh as cheerful rodents began crooning carols in an alarmingly pleasant fashion.

"You are going to keep me on my toes, aren't you Nella Swanson?" Blair said.

Nella smirked in response dancing through the displays as the jingle bells hanging on the door rang announcing their first guest.

The morning was just shy of chaos. The thermoses of cider, coffee and cocoa were swapped out more than once as the town and visitors made their way into the store. The flow was steady as people came to meet Blair and extol her grandparents' impact on the town and delight in the legacy of The Toy Chest marching on.

The cash register had hardly rung, but the check stand was filled with welcome presents and Blair received hugs from more strangers than she could recount in her life. While the store's bank account may have remained stagnant, Blair's heart was rich with accolades and memories of her grandparents.

"My stars, it is you," a lady pushed through the door causing the jingle bells to amp up their raucous chorus. "Blair Cooper!"

The woman's broad smile was backed up by her exuberance. The woman was exquisitely attired, though Blair's keen Manhattan eye recognized the ensemble was cobbled together with discount store brands and faux jewelry. The way the woman carried herself and her bubbly persona pulled off elegant, better than any label could.

With a welcoming giggle, Blair acknowledged, "I am."

"I babysat you when you were barely knee high. I babysat your mother, too," the woman shared. "Mary Kay Albright."

Blair's eyes brightened, "You used to set up easels in your backyard and would try to teach me to paint."

Mary Kay nodded, "I did. You weren't half bad, though as I recall, you preferred crafts. You would spend hours making sets for your dolls and even made a complete town for your brother's cars."

"I remember that. And you baked!" Blair snapped her fingers. "You used to help Mom and Grandma bake the gingerbread for our annual contest."

"I did. Your family was famous for your gingerbread houses, winning most years, until you kids grew up, at least," Mary Kay added.

Blair looked thoughtful, "Wow. Those are some fun memories."

Mary Kay looked around the store. With a nod, "You've made the store look even better than your grandparents did. I wouldn't have imagined that to be possible."

"Nella was a big help. I really tried to channel them as much as I could," Blair admitted.

"To think after all these years, Blair Cooper is back and slipping into her grandparents' shoes," Mary Kay said.

"Yeah," Blair bit her lip.

"Well, I am off. Let me know if you need anything while you settle in," Mary Kay offered and pressed in for an enthusiastic hug.

"Thank you, Mary Kay. It was really good to see you," Blair said and watched the woman leave the store.

Another figure outside the store caught Blair's eye. Stepping back into the street, he lined up a careful shot of the store with his camera. Blair's heart skipped a beat. Glancing at her watch, she suggested to Nella, "It's past lunchtime and the store seems to be quieting down a bit. Why don't you take off for lunch?"

Shrugging, Nella didn't argue. "You want anything? There's a great little shop with soups and salads."

"I might check it out in a bit. Thank you," Blair said.

Leaving just as the harried man pushed into the store, Nella glanced back at Blair who nervously welcomed the photographer.

The photographer looked at Blair expectantly as she watched for the door to close and Nella to walk the past the window.

"Hi, you must have been sent by Meredith," Blair said.

"I am," the photographer nodded, taking a visual tour of the store. "I have to say, this place looks great. I think it is going to photograph quite well."

Blair's eyes followed with his lens around the store. She swelled with a bit of pride before she remembered why he was there. "Help yourself, just, uh, make it quick," Blair offered a weak smile. She did not want to have to explain why he was there.

The man started with still photographs, taking images of the store, the cash stand and the festive décor. Switching to video, he repeated the process. Standing in the corner, slinking behind a display of stuffed animals, he captured Blair welcoming guests. To his delight, he videoed them making a purchase, taking care to avoid their faces in the shot.

When the shoppers left, he cut his recording. Stepping out from the display, he tapped his camera, "I think we have everything we need. You should be able to sell this place in no time, from its visuals, at least."

The door had swung open and another guest walked in just as the photographer made his declaration. Blair squeezed her eyes tight, unsure of who might have heard his comment.

Opening one eye, she saw Luke Marsten holding a box out in front of him.

Swallowing hard, she thanked the photographer and quickly ushered him out, "Thank you. Tell Meredith I'll talk to her later."

The photographer nodded and walked by Luke on the way out.

"Hello, Luke," Blair clapped her hands and smiled sheepishly as she walked out from behind the check stand.

Luke cocked his head to the side, "Sell this place?"

Blair began to confess when she saw what he was holding. A Christmas village version of The Toy Chest, handcrafted from his re-purposed wine barrels. Drawn to the piece, her eyes ran along it, a faithful recreation with the hand painted sign swinging from tiny patinaed brackets.

Her heart a lump in her throat, she choked, "Yeah. Marketing. Toying with an online marketplace idea, if you'll forgive the pun."

Luke's eyes raised into a wary stare, he relented, "Good idea. Even classic shops need a bit of modernizing."

Focused on the replica building he was holding, Blair asked, "What's that?"

Luke shook himself, "Oh, this? I started making this last year. I wanted to give it to your grandparents for Christmas, but it wasn't finished yet. I, uh, I wasn't able to get it to them."

Blair nodded in understanding.

"I figured, with the new Cooper in town opening the store, I would give it to you," Luke said, walking it to the check stand.

"Luke, this is beautiful," Blair gushed.

"Your grandmother liked Christmas villages. I thought this would make a good first piece of a new collection," Luke said, his voice trailing.

Blair smiled, "It's really nice and a great idea."

Their eyes met briefly as the jingle bells announced another visitor.

Blair and Luke's heads swiveled to the door, seeing the typically bouncy Nella stroll in looking rather flat. Forcing a flash of a smile, she averted her eyes from the pair.

"Nella…," Blair called, giving a quick glance to Luke. "What's wrong?"

Nella stopped and faced Blair and Luke. "The lay-offs are happening sooner than expected. The first third of the staff were just cut, final paychecks on Friday. My husband was part of the group."

Blair rushed forward to give her friend a hug, "Nella, I'm so sorry."

"At least I've got the store. It's going to be our saving's grace to eek through the rest of the year," Nella said.

Blair's heart plummeted to its lowest point since arriving in Evergreen.

Appreciating the hug, Nella shook off her melancholy. "Mixing with the customers is the best distraction right now," Nella said. "You still need to have lunch. Take off for a bit, I'll mind the store."

"You haven't had lunch?" Luke asked.

Blair shook her head, "No. Not yet."

"I was just about to meet with a chef to do a tasting for our upcoming holiday dinner pairings. Why don't you come along? There's always more than I can eat," Luke suggested.

"I don't know," Blair protested. "That sounds like more time away from the store than I should take. I really shouldn't."

"It'll be fine," Nella assured. "Most of the folks that were going to come in already have and with the news from the publishing house, I'd bet people are going to be a bit distracted this afternoon."

Blair looked at Luke who offered a nod of encouragement.

"Alright," Blair shrugged. "But I need to get back as soon as I can, just the same."

"I'll do what I can," Luke smirked. "Thanks for sharing your boss."

Nella nodded.

"Will you two stop calling me that?" Blair snapped as she headed to get her coat.

Luke spun to face Nella; his face twisted. "What do you think?"

Nella shrugged, "Poohbah?"

"President?" Luke suggested.

"Queen?" Nella added.

"Supreme leader?"

"Stop!" Blair scowled. "Just Blair or you're fired and you...you're whatever!" She flailed at Nella and then scoffed at Luke in a huff.

"Fine!" Nella relented.

Luke looked more reticent.

An angry glare changed his tune abruptly.

"Okay, okay," he laughed. "Come on, you are going to love the food that is being prepared as we speak." Glancing at his watch, he held his arm out for Blair to accompany him.

Accepting the gesture, she slipped her arm into his. With a wave, they left the shop in what Blair had come to learn, Nella's very capable hands.

Eight

The drive from town to the winery brought back a whole new flood of memories for Blair. Staring out the window, she said, a tinge of excitement in her voice, "I think we used to get our tree out here!"

Luke glanced over from his side of the truck, "Yeah, Cascade Tree Farm is right next to my winery."

"I have so many good memories out there. It's so beautiful," Blair said, admiring the scenery that blurred by as they entered the hills just outside of town.

"You seem to be pretty fond of Evergreen, how come I haven't seen you around?" Luke asked.

Blair froze at the question.

"I hope I wasn't being too forward," Luke said.

"No, it's alright," Blair assured. "I guess, after college, life just got busy. I got a job in New York. I didn't have hardly any vacation that first year and by the time my portfolio of business took off, I haven't had time for hardly anything other than work."

"Who is your boss, Scrooge? Everyone needs time off for the holidays," Luke said.

Blair laughed, "The people I work for are great. And we get a few days off for the holidays, but we usually have turn of the year projects we need to work on."

"But you're here, now," Luke said.

"Yeah," Blair nodded quietly. "I'm here now."

Luke pulled the truck into a long dirt drive nestled at the edge of the foothills. Driving past an endless sea of grapevines towards a modern farmhouse and a large barn.

Blair was amazed, "This is all yours?"

"Yeah, well, mine and the bank's," Luke said. "It's no Manhattan high rise, but I'll take my office view any day."

"It's beautiful!"

"Thank you," Luke beamed. "Come on, Chef Raul should be about set up in the tasting room."

Luke led Blair into through a heavy oak door into a rustic but elegant tasting room. Concrete slab floors were graced with blonde wood beams and a polished wood bar. Blair took a deep breath, the scent of fermenting grapes thick in the air. Pungent, yet strangely pleasant.

"I'll pour you something and then check on Raul," Luke said, sliding behind the bar and pulling down a pair of glasses. "We'll start with Pinot Gris. Nice and light and should match Raul's first course."

Blair took the glass to her lips. Hints of pear and honeysuckle tickled her nose. Taking a sip, she studied the color of the wine in her glass.

"What do you think?" Luke asked.

"I like it. It's nice and light," Blair said.

Luke leaned into the door behind the bar, giving a nod that he was there. Turning back to Blair, he said, "There's no oak, all stainless steel. So, you're tasting nothing but the grape."

Luke poured himself a glass and took a quick sip.

The door burst open and a man in a smock whirled into the tasting room, a plate in his hand. "Ah, you have a guest," Raul announced.

Luke nodded, "Chef Raul, this is Blair Cooper. Her grandparents owned The Toy Chest downtown."

"The sweetest people you could ever meet," Raul said. "I'm sorry for your loss. We all miss them."

"You knew my grandparents, too?" Blair asked.

"Of course. Every one within a hundred miles knew your grandparents. Even if they only swung through Evergreen once a year," Raul said, placing the plate down. Frowning he shrugged, "If I'd known, I would have made two plates."

"From what you sent me in your email, it sounded as though you were cooking up enough to feed a family," Luke said. Pulling a pair of forks from the shelf, he handed one to Blair. "You don't mind, do you? It's kind of a test kitchen thing."

Blair hesitated as she eyed the plate. Three pieces of asparagus wrapped in prosciutto lay next to three more stalks left bare. "One for the carnivores, one for the herbivores," Raul grinned. He watched excitedly as bites were sampled.

"This is really good, Raul. What's the sauce?" Luke asked.

"It is my secret, but you have a discerning palate," Raul said.

"Is this goat cheese on the prosciutto wrapped one?" Luke blurted.

Raul nodded.

"Excellent," Luke said.

"Lemon, honey, a hint of Dijon and...," Blair looked thoughtful. "And a little bit of chili."

Raul confirmed, "Spot on. Just a swipe of cayenne."

"Flavor, but not really heat," Luke said, giving the hors d'oeuvre another bite.

The chef spun away and retreated back into the kitchen.

Blair took the opportunity to wander around the tasting room. A variety of white and red wines were displayed. "You grow all these grapes?"

Luke scoffed, "No. Not on my bit of vineyard and the cool climate here. I have a few Pinot Gris, Pinot Noir and Riesling plots. Most of my grapes come the east side of the mountains."

"Was the Pinot Gris we had yours?" Blair asked.

"It was," Luke nodded, a hint of pride in his smile.

Raul burst through the doors once more, this time with two plates. Sliding one in front of each he announced, "Frisee salad and split duck breast."

"Ah," Luke said. moving behind the bar and producing a bottle of chardonnay. Pouring three modest glasses, he leaned against the counter as he watched Blair take a bite.

The look on her face said everything.

Raul grinned, "You like it?"

Blair nodded as Luke filled a forkful for himself.

"Chardonnay pomegranate vinaigrette," Raul shared.

"As usual, very good," Luke approved.

"Enjoy, the best is yet to come!" the chef scampered away and Blair resumed her investigation of the tasting room.

She paused at a display of wooden picture frames. Cobbled from the same wood used on the toy chests, Blair picked up a frame, studying the picture closely. "Is this you and my grandparents?"

Luke looked across the room and nodded, "Yeah. That was out in the vineyard for a grape stomp. They were always game for anything that was going on in the community."

Blair nodded thoughtfully and put the picture back.

"It's really cool, you coming out here to take on your grandparents' legacy. I guess you share that legacy now," Luke said.

The words dug into Blair's heart like a frozen dagger. Her part of the legacy was going to be a check. The idea made her wince.

"You opening the store is like a much needed breath of fresh air for the town," Luke said. "The energy driving in this morning…it was different. Better."

"How so?" Blair asked, cocking her head to the side.

"This town has been through a lot. The publishing house closing is like a dark cloud of doom. None of us know how and if we'll survive it," Luke said. "Even my winery. This place exists because there is a town nearby."

"It can't be that bad, the town won't just crumble away," Blair said.

"Wither. I think the word is wither. A few shops, restaurants, a tree farm and winery in the middle of nowhere…there would not be much there to keep Evergreen on the map," Luke said.

Blair scowled, "Oh, come on. There had to be industry before the publishing company."

Luke scoffed, "Yeah. A logging mill which shut down decades ago. The publishing house coming in saved Evergreen, and now here we are again."

The words were harsh but signaled to Blair that selling the toy store was sad, but the right thing to do.

"Your grandparents wouldn't have batted an eyelash. They would have whipped the town into shape and gotten them to focus on the Holiday Festival. The new year will take care of itself," Luke said.

Their attention was turned as Raul backed through the kitchen door with two plates and sat them down on the bar. "Sorry, I didn't split these. Cedar plank salmon and Wagyu beef medallion."

"Do we fight over who gets what?" Blair asked.

Luke eyed both dishes, "I don't know. I don't want to miss out on either."

Reluctantly, Blair waved her fork in the air, "I guess we can share."

"Well, here's a challenge. I now have to find two wines. Two distinct flavor profiles," Luke said. Snapping his fingers, he announced, "No. My Pinot Noir from two years ago. Light enough for the salmon and just bold enough for the beef."

Rushing to a door at the back of the tasting room, Luke disappeared. Within moments, he returned triumphantly with a bottle in hand. "I think this will do well," he said.

"I *do* have to go back to work, you know!" Blair protested.

"We haven't even had a glass of wine yet," Luke promised, opening the bottle.

Pouring into fresh glasses, he handed them out and sat back at the counter.

Blair cut a bite into the salmon. "Wow, Raul, you weren't kidding. You were saving the best for last. This is amazing."

"The steak is good too. You hardly need a knife to cut it," Luke said. "This is going to be the best holiday tasting ever."

Turning to Blair, he said, "You should come. My treat."

"I don't know," Blair said, knowing she wasn't likely to be in town by the time the tasting rolled around.

"You just need to make the all important decision…the fish or the beef," Luke pressed.

"I guess…salmon. It was really delightful," Blair noted.

Raul beamed.

"Well, there you have it. It's a date. I mean, it's a date on the calendar," Luke choked.

Raul's eyes bounced from Luke to Blair and back again. With a wave, he grabbed his wine glass and excused himself into the kitchen.

Blair pushed away from the counter. "Look, Luke, I have a boyfriend."

"A boyfriend," Luke's chin fell to his chest. "I hope you didn't think..."

Blair's face grew red and gushed, "Oh, no. I just thought I should be clear."

"Right," Luke nodded. "I mean, a date...on the calendar, is just a date. Not like a *date*."

"Yeah. A date on the calendar," Blair said, darting her eyes away as she finished her wine.

The room fell into awkward silence, the quiet somehow echoing off the concrete floors and high ceiling.

"Would you do me a favor?" Luke asked, twisting in his seat trying to break the mood. "I want to introduce the next vintage at the tasting. I need to check the barrel; would you sample it with me?"

Blair raised an eyebrow and studied Luke. "This isn't some kind of ploy, is it?"

Luke looked offended, "Madam, I am a gentleman."

"Alright. I'm putting a lot of faith in you," Blair said.

"Santa is watching, I wouldn't jeopardize that," Luke said. "Come on."

Following his lead, Blair walked through the tasting room and into a vast warehouse. She shrugged off a slight chill at the temperature change. Past pallets stacked with cases of wine, past a half dozen gleaming stainless-steel tanks and one beautiful wooden tank that stretched nearly to the ceiling, Luke led her to the back of the large open room.

Slipping through yet another door, they arrived in another vast room, equal to the one with the tanks. This room was lined with shelves and racks that reminded Blair of a giant, chilly library. The walls were lined with more pallets piled neatly with cases of wine. The racks assembled a sea of oak barrels, each labeled with notes scribbled on pages that looked indecipherable to Blair.

"So, this is where your barrels for your toy chests come from," Blair said.

Luke nodded, "At some point. Each barrel can be used effectively three times or so before the flavors are neutralized. Some turn them into planters, I turn them into toy chests."

Grasping two glasses and what looked like a turkey baster, Luke stopped in front of a barrel. "Would you mind?" Luke held out the glasses that Blair accepted.

Blair danced in place to generate heat.

"Sorry, I should have had you grab your coat. I get used to going back and forth," Luke said. "We won't be long."

With an odd-looking wrench, he pulled at a plug on the side of the barrel and with the siphon, pulled red liquid out. Squirting a sample in each glass, he set his tools aside.

Holding his glass in the light, he said, "This is what I am hoping to be this year's Christmas release."

Taking a sip, Blair followed suit.

"Mmm. Tastes like fruit with the slightest sour note, but not so much you pucker," Blair suggested.

Luke admired her assessment, "Might have to hire you for as my official taste tester. I was using Pinot Noir and Beaujolais grapes to invoke a cranberry essence."

"Perfect for the holidays," Blair nodded. "I think it is going to be a hit."

"Thanks for indulging me," Luke finished his sip and placed the bung back in the hole atop the barrel. Taking Blair's glass from her, he said, "I should get you back."

"I am eager to get back to the shop," Blair nodded. "Thank you, though. I don't think I would have stopped to enjoy lunch today, otherwise."

Luke smiled softly, "My pleasure."

Blair was anxious to get back to the toy store. While no longer famished, she wanted to get back to the people that visited. She relished the interactions more than she thought she would.

Initially opening the store was merely a chore to accelerate its sale and hopeful selling price. The more she was immersed in her grandparents' world, the more she genuinely enjoyed the experience. The romanticism of nostalgia was part of it. It consumed her the moment the driver hit the exit for Evergreen and intensified when Blair twisted the key into the lock of The Toy Chest for the first time.

She could have anticipated that. What threw her, as she gazed out the window watching the snow dusted rural scenery whisk by, was the real-world presence in the store itself. Greeting and meeting visitors, whether for the first time or who were long term customers of her grandparents.

Her cellphone pinged. Glancing down, she hit the message. The initial real estate mockup with the photographs taken that morning filled her screen. Feeling guilty, she turned the phone to ensure Luke didn't see the images.

"Boyfriend?" Luke asked as he slowed the truck entering Evergreen.

Blair clicked off her phone, "What? Oh, no. Just business stuff."

"Say, why didn't he come out here with you? I assumed you'd be taking over the store together," Luke asked.

His question met with a frown and silence. "I'm sorry. Overstepped again. Just a country boy without much by way of people skills," Luke said.

"No, I suppose it's a fair question. Todd is very serious about his work. He wouldn't come out just to…," Blair stuttered. "To open the doors."

"He'll come out eventually, right?" Luke asked, pulling the truck up to the curb outside the toy store.

"Yeah, sure. Eventually," Blair muttered. The question seemed so foreign to her. "Thanks again for the lunch and the tour of the winery."

Blair hopped out and closed the door behind her. Luke gave a little wave and drove away. Turning to the store, her head was a bit clouded. The thought of Todd coming to a place like Evergreen and staying was laughable. But then again, she thought that of herself as well.

Shaking her head, she was only more resolved to ensure the store made a positive impression so that it could sell, and she could move on.

Nine

Day melted into evening. A steady stream of customers came to visit, even Evergreen's mayor Martha Stowe came into say hello to Blair and gush over her fondness for her grandparents.

"And to see the Noelle…Cooper legacy live on, it is so exciting to see you take over the store," Mayor Stowe said.

"This was always a magical place. It is tough to imagine it without them here," Blair said.

The mayor smiled, "They *are* here. They are in the decades of love they poured into the community. They are here in you."

Blair froze and looked at the mayor. She winced slightly at the inadvertent metaphoric knife that twisted in her back.

"I just can't help but to think, that maybe, they were once in a generation," Blair responded meekly. "That maybe, *they* were the store."

"I don't believe that at all. Look at this place. You are your grandparents and then some," Mayor Stowe urged. "Look at how the town has reacted since you turned that sign to 'open'. You're a beacon of hope to a town that desperately needs it."

Blair blushed at the notion and seized at that weight of the burden resting on the store's shoulders.

Mayor Stowe placed her hand on Blair's arm and looked her square in the eyes, "You are going to do great things in this town. I just know it."

With a reassuring smile, the mayor walked out.

"Wow, Mayor Stowe really likes you," Nella said.

"For now," Blair mumbled.

"What?"

"Nothing," Blair shook her head. "She seems nice."

Nella agreed, "She is. She has a tough job to keep this town together, especially with the publishing house closing."

Blair nodded and straightened items around the store.

"So, how was lunch?" Nella popped up next to Blair.

Taken aback slightly, Blair responded, her voice flat, "It was good. Chef Raul made some excellent dishes.

Traditional for the holidays, but with his own spin on them."

"The food was good, sure. Chef Raul is a marvelous chef. How was *lunch*?" Nella pressed.

Blair frowned.

"Aw, come on. Luke Marsten may not be Manhattan chic, but he is not displeasing to the eye," Nella grinned.

"Oh, Luke. He was fine. He is very nice. A good craftsman and an excellent winemaker," Blair said.

"A good *craftsman*?" Nella scoffed. "You go to lunch with a hunk like Luke and you come back with 'he's a good craftsman'? But you had wine."

"Well, yes. It was tastings for the pairing the winery has coming up. We didn't even have a full glass in total," Blair defended. "I have a boyfriend, you know."

"You have a boyfriend?" Nella was agape.

Blair's lips were tight and her face indignant, "Yes. Todd. He is very successful. We have been dating for a while now."

Nella frowned, "How come Todd didn't come out here with you?"

"He's busy," Blair shrugged. Furrowing her brows, she muttered, "That's what Luke asked."

"Luke asked about your boyfriend?" Nella marveled.

"He also wondered why Todd didn't accompany me," Blair said.

"To your grandparents' store that you haven't visited since their passing to take it over and run it? Yeah, it's a worthy question," Nella pressed.

"He... oh!" Blair was cut off by the ringing of the jingle bells hung on the door. Grateful for the disruption in the conversation, she lunged in the direction of the guest.

Blair continued to dodge questions peppered by Nella about lunch at the winery and Todd back in Manhattan. Fortunately, the flow of visitors didn't let up enough to provide too much opportunity for personal talk.

When it was time to turn the sign to 'Closed' for the day, the two ladies leaned back.

"What a day!" Blair exclaimed.

"We had a lot of traffic," Nella nodded.

Blair looked at Nella, "It was wonderful, but so exhausting to be 'on' all day."

"It was. People were excited to meet you, and why shouldn't they be? They adored your grandparents, and you are just as wonderful," Nella cooed.

"Oh, I don't think I can compare to my grandparents," Blair waved off the idea.

"Don't sell yourself short. You were charming all day long. The people genuinely like you. *I* like you," Nella said. "Besides, you don't have to be compared to them. You just have to be you."

Blair blushed, "Well, thank you."

"Hey, my family has game night tomorrow night. I do believe you owe me a trial of that game you made with your grandparents," Nella said.

"Oh, I meant like you and me, while the store is slow," Blair said.

Nella laughed, "During Christmas? No. Tomorrow night. 7 o'clock, after the store closes. We'll have pizza and snacks."

"I don't...," Blair started. The cross look on Nella's face changed Blair's mind. "Fine. 7 o'clock. What can I bring?"

"The game of course," Nella grinned.

Blair looked at the clock. "Listen, you get out of here, see your family. I'll lock up."

"I'm paid by the hour, you know," Nella countered.

"I won't dock your time. I just, I just want to be here for a bit," Blair said.

Nella's face softened. "I understand. Have a good night, Blair."

"Goodnight, Nella," Blair said and watched her employee pull her things together and step out of the store.

Flipping the lock, Blair turned to face the interior of the store. Her hands in her back pockets, she breathed deep. It was a good day. She felt close to her family by being there. Not just her grandparents, but her parents and brother, too.

The people of Evergreen were as kind and gracious as she remembered. The town, the beautiful gem she always pictured. Even lunch with Luke was a lot of fun. Being in the foothills brought back a rush of images from sledding to picking out the Christmas tree to snowball fights with her brother.

Coming back to Evergreen was like coming home. More so than if she returned to their neighborhood in Seattle. Evergreen was where they spent their holidays and summers. It is where the richest memories of her childhood were forged. If she had a place where 'she grew up', it was Evergreen.

"Well, let's see how we did today," Blair said as she slid behind the register. The old machine was sturdy and functional but in need of a double-decade update.

Searching for something that would provide a report, she realized she would need to do it the old fashioned way. Opening the register, she pulled out the cash drawer. Counting the contents and subtracting the bank for change, she rummaged through the checks and credit slips. What little she knew about credit card processing, she knew this old method was three times as expensive as the new ways. "Not that I'm staying, but if I was, I think a tablet and a card swiper are necessary upgrades," Blair muttered.

When the daily count was taken, Blair found an old journal in the office. As she opened it, the last entry made her heart fall. It was the week before her grandmother passed, a mere month before her grandfather followed. With a shaky hand, Blair made her post under her grandmother's.

With a heavy sigh, she closed the ledger.

Shutting off the lights, but keeping the Christmas tree lit, Blair locked up the store. She took in a deep breath as her senses enveloped the quiet of the small town. It was a stark contrast to the city that never seemed this still. This peaceful.

Soft flakes drifted downward only adding to the atmosphere. It felt like Christmas. Evergreen was a warm holiday blanket draped over her shoulders. Figuratively, at least, as Blair shook off a chill.

It wasn't just her grandparents' toy shop. It was the entire town. Evergreen was a holiday gem with each shop and tree that lined the streets decorated with charm for the holidays.

Walking along, she considered this could be the last time she experienced this feeling. When would she ever travel to Evergreen, Washington again once the store sold?

She was happy to have the chance to soak in the Christmas spirit in the wonderous town once more.

Her phone buzzed against her side in the pocket, tickling her ribs. Pulling off her glove with her teeth, she swapped it for her phone.

"Hello," Blair called into it.

"Hey, how's it going out there in the boondocks?" Todd's voice rang into the phone.

"It's good. It has been so nice to be at the store and immersed in all things Evergreen," Blair said.

"Did the realtor come by?" Todd asked.

Blair nodded to herself, "The photographer came by and took a bunch of really great photos. The realtor has some contacts she is going to run the store through."

"Were you open all day?"

"I was. We had a ton of people come in," Blair said.

"You must have made quite a haul," Todd chuckled, his tone conveying tongue in cheek.

"If compliments paid the bills, we would have done well. We had heavy traffic all day, just not a lot of buyers. Even in Grandma's last day, the store outperformed my first day. I think I paid for Nella's time, I'm not sure much else," Blair admitted. "The publishing house is accelerating the layoffs; it's made the locals pretty tight with their pockets."

"Well, just more the reason to dump it quick and get out," Todd said.

"Yeah," Blair said reluctantly. "I suppose."

"When are you coming back? The realtor got the action shots, right?" Todd asked.

Blair hesitated as she reached the bed and breakfast. Half staring at the elegantly decorated home and half thinking about her response. "I think the potential buyers will want to see it in action."

"Aw come on, they don't need you for that. You've got that girl...Nelly," Todd pressed.

"Nella," Blair corrected. "I have a few other things I need to do before I take off."

"Well, don't get stuck out there," Todd scoffed.

"Oh, I didn't tell you. When I was digging through the backroom, I found a game I made when I was a kid," Blair said, her voice brightening.

"A game?"

"Yeah, you know, like a board game," Blair said.

"Hmm. That's nice," Todd murmured. "Look, it's late. I have a busy day tomorrow. Try to get your realtor to jump on it before that market completely tanks."

"Yeah, I will. Good night, Todd," Blair said softly.

"Good night," Todd said, and the phone went dead.

Blair stood outside the bed and breakfast. Outside, she felt numb. Not from the cold, but from the conversation with Todd and her feelings about the store.

Looking at the Holly Bough Bed and Breakfast, she admired how warm and friendly it looked inside. She could see movement through the windows. The house was active with kind and welcoming people reveling together.

Moving up the steps, she swung open the door, startled when a voice called behind her, "Hold the door!"

Turning back, she saw Luke Marsten high-stepping through the snow with his arms outstretched cradling a large box. Hitting the porch, he stomped the excess snow off of his boots and flashed a smile at Blair as he pushed through into the house, "Thank you."

Blair nodded as she slowly closed the door.

"You seemed pretty deep in thought, everything okay?" Luke asked, calling over his shoulder as he carried his package down the hallway to the kitchen.

"Yeah, I'm fine. Just admiring your Mom's house," Blair said. "I didn't even hear you pull up."

"I don't park up front. We like to keep that space open for guests," Luke said. "It does force me to choose the long, shoveled path or the more direct route through the snow."

A voice snapped from behind them, "You didn't leave tracks in my yard again, did you Luke Marsten?"

Luke pivoted slowly to face his mother, a broad grin swept across his face, "I brought you and your guests a case of Pinot Noir. Great with chocolate."

Loretta frowned, "We just received a big, mysterious box of chocolate today."

"I know," Luke was proud of his insider knowledge.

Softened, but undeterred, Loretta huffed, "But still, you know I like my guests to wake up with unblemished snow when they look out their window, unless kids are here to play in it, at least."

"And they will," Luke promised. "Supposed to snow tonight."

"Ms. Cooper, it sounds like your first day was a success. It sure was busy when Sam and I poked our heads in. I was surprised when you weren't there to say hello to," Loretta said, her words with a purposeful edge.

"I was shanghaied to a certain winery for lunch," Blair admitted.

Loretta swung back to Luke, "I didn't know you served lunch at the winery."

Luke rolled his eyes, a bit flustered, "Chef Raul was coming to sample the dishes for the holiday pairing. I knew there would be more than I could eat, and Nella said Blair hadn't taken time out for lunch."

Loretta nudged her son, "That was very kind of you."

"Just being friendly, like you taught me, Mom," Luke said. "But, it is time for me to end this inquisition and get back to my own home. Good night, you two. I'm going to say hi to Dad on the way out."

"Love you, son."

"Love you, too, Mom. Goodnight Blair."

The ladies watched Luke disappear through the doors to the living room where Sam Marsten was once more entertaining the guests.

"Would you like some dinner? We can continue our tradition of visiting with a glass of wine, if you like," Loretta asked, as a loud cheer erupted in the next room.

"What's going on in there?" Blair asked.

Loretta's eyes sparkled, "I think they're playing a game. Our other guests arrived with their children. Would you like to go in? I can make your dinner easy to eat."

"I do like games," Blair admitted, her eyes following the sound.

"You go on in, Sam will introduce you and you can join in," Loretta suggested.

Blair pushed into the room. Sam stood by the fireplace while the guests were in sofas positioned around the room, two young children sat on the floor at their parents' feet.

"Ah, Ms. Cooper! Come on in," Sam waved and nodded towards a high back chair on the opposite side of the fireplace as he. "Blair Cooper, meet Gil and Kerry Hubbard, their delightful children Joelle and Niles."

"Hi everyone!" Blair waved as she took her seat. "It sounds like you guys were having some fun. I was wondering if I might join?"

"Yes, please!" Joelle shouted as Niles giggled.

"I like games," Blair admitted.

"Blair is the proud new proprietor of The Toy Chest, the finest toy store north of Seattle," Sam announced.

Niles' eyes widened to saucers, "Toys?"

Gil laughed, "Well, we will definitely have to stop by. Visiting The Toy Chest has always been one of our holiday highlights."

"Did the Noelles retire?" Kerry asked. "I always likened them to Mr. and Mrs. Claus. Kind of thought they might have been there forever."

Blair bowed her head slightly, "They were my grandparents. They passed this year about a heart-breaking month apart."

"Oh, I am so sorry," Kerry cooed.

"It's okay. I had the same impression of them and couldn't picture a world without them in it either," Blair nodded. "So, back to fun and frivolity. What's the name of the game?"

Ten

Blair woke up the next morning feeling refreshed. She couldn't remember sleeping so soundly. Glancing at her phone, she realized she was running late to get the store opened.

Putting herself together as quickly as she could, she sprung from her room and glided down the steps. Once again, she was met by Loretta, a paper sack and to go cup of coffee in her hands.

"You are my hero," Blair gasped as she tugged on her coat and accepted the breakfast.

"Have a good day, dear."

"You, too, Loretta!" Blair called as she was already streaking across the porch.

As she made her way to town, she realized Luke was right. A fresh layer of snow had fallen. The town of Evergreen glistened in the wintry blanket laid down for it.

Blair reached the store just steps before Nella arrived. Slipping her key in the lock, she gave it a twist and held it open for Nella to step through.

"Good morning, Boss!" Nella cheerily rang. Seeing the scowl in Blair's brows, she corrected, "*Blair!*"

Blair softened and smiled, "Good morning, Nella."

"My kids are so excited you are coming over for game night. When they heard you were bringing over a game you made, Scott and I could hardly get them to bed. They began strategizing their own game ideas," Nella reported.

Blair laughed, "I'm glad I could inspire the next generation. I think my job is done."

"Oh, no. They need tutelage from a game master, that my dear girl, is you," Nella beamed.

Blair chuckled, "I don't know about that. I should probably check on the game to make sure everything is there and remember how to play."

"I can get the store open if you want to work on it," Nella offered. "No one is going to beat the doors down early in Evergreen."

Blair hesitated.

"If anyone exciting comes in, I'll let you know," Nella promised waving Blair on.

"Fine," Blair conceded and headed towards the office desk in the storeroom.

Finding the game, she set in on the desk. With an excited breath, she slid the lid open and set it aside. An unconscious smile crossed her face as she studied the contents inside. Sifting through the pieces, she remembered how much fun she and her family had putting it together and playing it.

The entire calendar gameboard made up an image of a Christmas village. Little doors and windows revealed one of the game pieces.

Blair picked up Santa's sleigh, a little pack of presents made out of an old velvet jewelry pouch sitting in the back. Her favorite piece was the Christmas tree, nearly a foot tall, it served as the centerpiece for the game. Memories flooded back as Blair was reminded of how much fun they had as a family.

The morning had its share of guests. Some would find their way back to Blair to say hello, most browsed, a few out of town visitors made purchases.

Blair had no idea how long she had spent cataloguing the game and making notes in its crude rule book to ensure it would be functional for Nella's family game night. A rap at her door stole her attention. Looking up from her desk, she saw two little faces peeking in at her.

"Hi, Joelle. Hi, Niles," Blair called. "What do you think of the store?"

"This is amazing!" the kids squealed.

"I've never known anyone who owned a toy store!" Niles exclaimed.

"*This*, is all yours," Joelle pointed out, being emphatic with her sentence.

Blair bobbed her head, "Yeah, kinda."

"Wow!" the kids' eyes grew large.

Gil and Kerry's heads loomed over their children's, "I hope they aren't bothering you. They wanted to say 'hello'."

"Not at all," Blair said, getting up from her desk. "It is a good interruption."

"Watcha working on?" Joelle asked, peering over the desk.

Blair chuckled, "That is a game I made with my family when I was probably about your age. I was fixing it up to play with my coworker Nella and her family."

"We should play that with Sam at the bed and breakfast. He likes games!" Niles suggested.

"I'll ask him!" Joelle offered.

"We did have fun playing that game last night, huh?" Blair smiled.

Blair walked them out of the office and took in the store.

"This store is wonderful. The glowing reviews from Sam and Loretta didn't do it justice," Kerry said.

"Thank you," Blair said. "It was my grandparents' vision. They built this place with love."

"It shows," Kerry nodded.

"We didn't mean to disturb you, I'm sure the kids have lots to look at," Gil said.

Blair shook her head, "No problem. You have a sweet family. It does the heart good to see kids so excited."

"We look forward to playing your game!" Joelle called as she raced to a display of an elaborate dollhouse that caught her attention. Niles followed suit taking off in the opposite direction, a little wave over his shoulder as his interest was captured by a remote-control dinosaur.

"We'll let you get back to your work. Nice to see you," Gil said.

"Nice to see you, too," Blair smiled.

"See you at the Holly Bough!" Kerry said as she was waved over by Joelle.

Blair leaned against the office doorframe, watching the family enjoy each other and the store. Her chest swelled as she realized this is what her grandparents enjoyed. Watching people visit and creating joy.

Her ever-spinning brain contemplated the guests at the B&B playing her game. Chewing her lip, she realized as fun as the game was around a kitchen table, it wasn't the right fit for casual evening play around the fireplace. They needed something they could play together from their seats across the room.

Cocking her head, she whirled and crashed into her office chair. Pulling out a sheet of paper, she grabbed a pencil and began scribbling furiously as the thoughts cascaded out of her head.

It was nearly lunchtime. Blair had hardly stepped out onto the floor as she was consumed by ever growing gameplay ideas.

The jingle bells announced a visitor as Nella greeted a well-attired businessman followed by a small, professionally dressed entourage.

The man paused as he slipped through the door. Pivoting his head, he took in the store, nodding his head as he did.

"Hello," Nella called.

"Good…," the man checked his watch as it had just ticked past noon, "Afternoon. Meredith Kohl sent me. She suggested I have a look around."

"Wonderful, The Toy Chest has a lot to offer," Nella said.

"Yes," the man nodded, scanning the store. "The place looks impressive."

Nella gushed, "Thank you. We like to embody the spirit of Evergreen."

"I see that," the man agreed.

"What can I help you find, is there a specific age group?" Nella asked.

"Oh, no. Just looking," the man replied as his team spanned out throughout the store. "About how many square feet would you say this space is?"

Nella frowned, "I don't…know."

"Updated wiring, that's good," one of the man's staff called out.

Blair heard the conversation and leaned out; eyes wide. Hopping up from behind her desk, she streaked out of her office.

"Hello, I'm Blair Cooper!" she made her way in front of the man.

"Ah, yes. The seller," the man said.

Blair nodded vigorously, "Yes, that's me. The seller of toys...store."

Guiding the man to the far corner of the store and away from Nella, Blair said aloud, "What can I help you with today?"

In a more hushed tone, Blair said "Welcome to Evergreen." Nella looked on as Blair escorted the visitors to the play area in the back of the store.

"Thank you, Ms. Cooper. My name is Bradley Marcom. I invest in properties that run along thoroughfares. Evergreen's location has piqued our interest," the man extended his hand.

"Nice to meet you, Mr. Marcom."

"Tell me, Ms. Cooper, how has business been? Not just for you, but for the other merchants along your block?" the man asked.

Blair shuffled as she responded, her voice hovering awkwardly just above a whisper, "The economy is tough this year, especially for the residents. From what I understand, visitor traffic and spending is consistent with previous years."

"I see," the man nodded. "Do you know the other owners?"

"Not well. I would suggest Meredith make contacts for you. It would be awkward for me to do so," Blair said.

"Of course," the man agreed.

Blair studied him for a moment, her eyes shifting to Nella greeting guests on the other side of the store. "If you don't mind me asking, what is your intention with the store? Do you sell toys?"

The entourage chuckled.

"Oh, no, Ms. Cooper, though that does sound quite charming and some days more fun, but wholly less profitable, I'm afraid," the man replied. "We create thoroughfare centers…truck stops, hotels, casinos…safe and first class stops for weary travelers."

Blair choked, "You're going to turn The Toy Chest into a rest stop?"

"Well, no, not in and of itself. It is a process, but as these towns go, they tend to fall pretty quickly. My company intends to have a toe hold. The good news for you, is your store gets current market rates. The others… won't be so fortunate," Marcom said.

"I see," Blair said, crestfallen.

"Meredith tells me you have a lucrative marketing career in New York. This will be the perfect way to close your estate claim with virtually no delay," Marcom added as he eyed Blair's trepidation.

Blair nodded absently, "Yeah, perfect."

"We have seen what we need from here, we're going to tour the town and head out. Your realtor will be in touch, Ms. Cooper," Mr. Marcom said as he and his staff turned on their heels and marched out of the store as abruptly as they had come in.

Nella finished up with a customer and jogged over to Blair who had become pale after Marcom's visit. "What was all that about?"

Blair's head snapped up, she looked a bit dazed as she focused on Nella and the words that she said.

"That, that was a businessman. Quite taken with the town of Evergreen, it would seem," Blair said.

"I've seen visitors taken with Evergreen before, they never appeared like that. They were a bit more Mr. Potter and a little light on festive," Nella observed.

"Yeah. Kind of reminded me of the people Todd works with," Blair mumbled, almost more to herself than to Nella.

"Do you mind if I take off for a bit? I was going to meet Scott for lunch. He's pretty down on himself and wanted my help with his resume," Nella asked.

"Sure," Blair nodded, "Absolutely. You know where to come if you want some 5th Avenue copy for his resume. I'm here to help."

Nella smiled as she put her hand on Blair's arm. "Thank you, we just might take you up on that. In today's job market, it will take some pretty special advertising. Scott might have to take a pay cut, but we are hoping with my job here at the toy store, we can make it work. Otherwise, we are going to have to consider packing up and moving south closer to Seattle," Nella said.

"But you guys love it here," Blair said.

"We do. I always pictured raising Sophie and Evan in Evergreen. I can't imagine them anywhere else," Nella said.

"Let me know how I can help," Blair said.

Watching Nella leave, Blair's heart sunk the lowest it had been since here arrival. She had no idea how difficult it would be to sell the store.

The jingle bells at the door rang, a welcome interruption to her gray thoughts. As a family with three children streamed in, each child streaking to a different part of the store, Blair lifted her head and strolled to greet them.

Absorbed in her guests, her spirits lifted dramatically. She lost track of time when Nella returned and started to help with visitors.

Over her shoulder, she called, "Why don't you go grab some lunch. I'll hold things together for a bit."

Blair hadn't realized how hungry she had become. With a nod, she finished with her last guest and grabbed her coat. With a quick wave to Nella, she pushed through the front door. The streets of Evergreen were a postcard of pre-holiday shopping. Light snow on the ground, twinkling lights and aromatic wreaths were joyous sentinels for the families bundled in their wool coats as they explored the town.

Finding the shop Nella had mentioned to her, she ducked inside and found a table. Ordering butternut squash soup and salad, she stared out at the families bustling about the sidewalks.

Chuckling to herself, she watched a man and woman walk by arm in arm. The woman gripped a shopping bag that Blair recognized as being from her shop. A boardgame she had recommended before she left protruded from the sack.

The game brought her to the request of the Hubbard children to lead game night. She tapped the table. She knew the game she had made with her brother and grandparents was more of a huddle around the table as opposed to lean back on the sofa by the fire kind of a game.

She began tinkering with ideas on how to make it fit for the setting. Excitedly, she asked the waitress for a pen she could borrow and began scribbling furiously on her napkin.

Pausing momentarily to marvel at the soup and appreciate the pomegranate seeds in the salad, her mind whirled faster than her pen could write as she sketched out a party game idea. When she was finished, the game didn't resemble the one she had made decades before, but she was proud of the result.

Reviewing her napkin notes, with scarcely a blank spot, Blair grinned. Nodding to herself, she was excited to share it with her friends at the bed and breakfast.

Just as she put her money down for the tip, a woman strode into the diner and made a beeline for Blair. Looking up, Blair smiled, "Mayor Stowe."

"Do you have a quick minute?"

"Sure," Blair nodded and pointed towards the empty seat across from her.

Mayor Stowe leaned across the table and looked intently at Blair, "So, every year, the day before Christmas Eve, your grandparents would put on a special event for area foster kids. I wanted to check and see if you would still be open to do that."

"Yes, yes, of course," Blair said, realizing she blurted out a promise she would struggle to keep.

"Nothing big, volunteers bring in treats and drinks. We scrounge up someone to play Santa Claus, take photos. Your grandparents usually had a modest gift for each of them from their stock," Mayor Stowe explained.

Blair rubbed her chin, "It sounds great. But what if we set up the store to run as it is? The kids get a budget and are empowered to buy for their siblings? We can still have Santa hand out presents to each."

"Help them get the joy of *giving* at Christmas," the mayor grinned.

"Exactly," Blair said.

"I like it," Mayor Stowe approved. "Thank you so much, Blair. I'll let the foster committee know and work out the details."

"Sounds good," Blair said as the two women rose from their seats.

Mayor Stowe spun back towards Blair, the slightest frown wrinkling her forehead, "There was a contingent of businessmen poking around town today. I hear they were particularly interested in your store. Do you know what that was about?"

"They were...inquiring about my intentions with the store," Blair admitted.

"And what did you tell them?"

"I told them I was focused on the holidays and it was a tough year for everyone in Evergreen," Blair said.

"That it is. I don't know how, but I am confident brighter days are ahead of us," the mayor said. "See you around, Blair."

"Bye," Blair said softly. Giving the waitress a friendly wave, she left the diner and retreated to the toy store.

As she walked along the sidewalk, she was struck with the realization that she had just committed to staying in Evergreen until the day before Christmas Eve.

"How do I keep doing that?" Blair muttered to herself, kicking the snow with her feet. "Just keep agreeing to things when I know I am supposed to be leaving. 'Hey,

Blair. Your grandparents used to host a Fourth of July picnic'... 'Sure, I'll do that'."

Head down, she didn't see the mass in front of her until it was too late. Progress impeded; her head was firmly planted into the thick plush of a wool coat. Reluctantly and completely embarrassed, Blair slowly raised her head up.

"You," she quipped.

"Me," Luke Marsten nodded.

Blair's cheeks glowed red, "I am so sorry, just a lot on my mind."

"I gathered, what with a full conversation going on with yourself," Luke grinned.

"You heard that, huh?" Blair's cheeks turned fiery.

Pursing his lips, Luke answered, "You were speaking out loud."

"I guess I was," Blair said sheepishly.

"Anything you want to talk about? I understand when you converse with another person, the response feedback is very different than talking with just yourself," Luke offered.

Blair breathed deep, "No. No, I'm going to go back to work and see if I can locate my pride somewhere. I think I left it in the office."

"Well, I'm a good listener, offer stands," Luke said.

"Thank you," Blair said, her hand on the toy store door.

Luke nodded farewell and continued down the sidewalk. Blair stared after him for just a moment. She watched him greet almost every person he walked by. Life in Evergreen was certainly different than Manhattan.

Eleven

Blair was strangely nervous yet excited to visit Nella and her family for game night. The sale of The Toy Chest loomed over her head, she welcomed the distraction, even if for an evening.

What surprised her, as she stood outside the quaint bungalow home of her friend and employee, was the excitement to share her family's game with the Swansons.

The door swung open, Nella smiled and ushered Blair in as two little faces appeared on either side of her.

"Hi Sophie and Evan," Blair grinned.

Their eyes grew wide as they saw the bag Blair was holding. "Is that the game?" Evan blurted.

"We can't wait to play, come on!" Sophie urged, grasping Blair's freehand and pulling her down the hall.

"I'm sorry," Nella apologized.

Casting a glance over her shoulder, Blair replied, "It's okay. I'm excited too!"

Sophie deposited Blair into a chair at the kitchen table next to hers.

"Hello, Blair," Scott welcomed.

Blair set her bag on the table and smiled at Nella's husband, "Thanks for letting me crash game night."

"It's not every night we get to play a game with its creator," Scott beamed.

Blair was sheepish, "It's never been shared outside the family before. It hasn't been played in two decades."

"A treat indeed," Scott said, circling to take Blair's coat for her.

"Thank you," Blair said.

Nella put a platter in the center of the table and doled out plates, "I hope pizza is okay."

"Are you kidding? It's a game night staple!" Blair exclaimed. "I hope you don't mind I brought treats. Gotta snack while you play!"

"The kids won't argue, that's for sure," Nella said. Turning to her kids, she raised a brow, "You both washed, right?"

Evan melted out of his chair and raced to wash up.

When the young boy returned, the Swansons stretched their arms out along the table and grasped hands.

Sophie grinned at Blair as she held her hand out for Blair. With a smile, Blair accepted her tiny hand and held Nella's on the other side while Scott said grace.

Watching Nella's family interact warmed Blair's heart. Not a speck of despair was in the air despite the news of Scott's job. Blair knew they were in dire shape but to see them, you would never know.

When the pizza was cleared, Blair poured candy-shell chocolates into bowls and divvied them as she placed the makeshift game box on the table. With a broad smile, she lifted the cover and set it aside.

"This is Countdown to Christmas!" Blair's eyes glistened as she unveiled the contents.

The game board, crafted by her grandfather held was made from cardboard folded in half, trimmed to the size of the gift box. Hand-drawn and painted to emulate Santa's village, a tall paper tree erected in the center of the board..

Blair and the Swansons giggled through two rounds of game play. The second time through, Blair had a distant look in her eye.

Picking up on her friend's distraction, Nella cocked her head, "What?"

"I just had an idea, a bit more complicated than this, but I think would be a lot of fun," Blair said.

"We should play it our next game night. Scott and I invite friends over," Nella said. Biting her lip, she added, "We'll need another adult…"

Scott started to offer a suggestion, but Nella shushed him. Taking the hint, he bowed his head and backed down.

"Well, I had a great night. Thank you so much," Blair said.

"Thank you for sharing the game, we had a blast!" Nella said.

"Yeah we did!" Evan said.

Sophie, looking a bit sleepy, slid over and wrapped her arms around Blair.

"I think you were a hit," Scott said.

Nella walked Blair out. "You have such a sweet family," Blair said.

"Yeah, they're pretty special," Nella nodded.

"See you tomorrow," Blair said.

"Bright and early, boss!" Nella gleamed.

Blair chuckled and walked down the steps.

As Blair walked towards the bed and breakfast, she glanced at her phone. It had been buzzing in her coat pocket. Todd's face was on the screen.

"Hi, Todd!" Blair called into it.

"Where have you been? I was starting to get worried," Todd exclaimed.

"I'm sorry. I had my ringer on vibrate, I didn't get the calls," Blair said. "I was at Nella's house with her family."

"Your worker?"

Blair looked to the sky before responding, "Well, yes, she does work at the store."

"Any updates from the realtor?" Todd asked.

"Actually, she sent a prospective buyer up today. He wants to purchase several properties, using the toy store as a catalyst," Blair reported.

"That's great!"

Blair paused, wrinkling her nose, "Sort of. I think they plan on mowing everything down and putting in a big highway travel center."

"Who cares what they do with it once it's theirs?" Todd scoffed.

Blair chewed her lip, "I kind of do. I just imagined someone putting the same love into that space that my grandparents did."

"Sounds like the town could use whatever boost it can get. Like you said, with the publishing house closing down, the travel center would at least provide jobs," Todd countered. "Even your toy store couldn't do that. Besides, what choice do you have? Your life is in New York, now. You have your new marketing campaign that sounds like is going to take you to Paris for travel."

"You're right. The nostalgia of everything just gets my head a little clouded," Blair admitted.

"That's okay, Blair. You're human. You have a connection with those memories. But they are memories of someone else's dream, your grandparents'," Todd consoled.

Blair hesitated, standing outside the bed and breakfast, "It looks like I'm going to be here until the day before Christmas Eve."

"What? For the real estate investor?"

"For a charity event my grandparents used to host. I agreed to run it this year," Blair said.

The phone went quiet. Todd's voice finally came through again, "Why would you do that? You're going to miss my company's Christmas party."

"I know. I'm sorry. It is for a good cause," Blair pleaded.

"You *are* going to be back Christmas Eve, right?" Todd asked. "I got reservations on the terrace in Rockefeller Center. It was going to be a surprise, but it sounds like I need to give you some incentive to come home."

"That sounds great," Blair said, a little bristled by Todd's irritation with her stay. "I am coming home. This has just been a bigger emotional deal than I thought."

"I know. I know. I suppose I can even understand it. But that is why you need the rational thinking even more to help keep you centered," Todd suggested.

"I suppose you're right," Blair sighed. "It's been a long day, I am going to head in to the bed and breakfast and I know it's late for you. Good night, Todd."

"Good night, Blair."

Blair stared at the phone as the call ended. With a deep breath, she ascended the steps onto the porch and reached for the bed and breakfast door. She almost expected a laden Luke Marsten to barrel up behind her. This evening, she entered alone.

The house had gone quiet for the evening with the lights dimmed. The Christmas tree was still lit and the fire in the wood stove stoked. Hanging up her coat, she walked towards the stove to warm up.

"Hello, dear," a voice in one of the wingback chairs startled her.

"Loretta," Blair gasped. "I wasn't sure anyone was up."

"Most of the household retreated just a few minutes ago. The Hubbards had gone sledding today, so the little ones were exhausted. Made for an early night," Loretta shared. "Have a seat. Can I get you some cocoa or tea? I was just about to pour myself a cup."

"Tea sounds nice," Blair nodded.

"Take a load off, I'll be right back," Loretta said and scurried towards the kitchen.

Blair settled into the chair and leaned towards the fire. The living room was so peaceful washed in the glow of the Christmas tree and radiance of the flames in the wood stove.

Loretta handed her a cup. "It's nice, isn't it? Being in here when the house has fallen quiet."

"It is," Blair nodded.

"I hear you are taking the reins on the foster Christmas party," Loretta noted.

Blair smiled, "Word travels fast. I am."

"Evergreen is a small community with big hearts and equally sizable tongues," Loretta grinned.

"It sounds like a great event, I am happy to do what I can," Blair said.

Loretta looked over her cup, "So, you'll be staying a while longer."

"Oh, yes. If my room is still available," Blair said.

"It is yours for as long as you care to stay with us," Loretta said.

"Thank you," Blair said. "A part of me would love to stay forever."

Blair saw Loretta cock her head as she absorbed the comment, and corrected, "I mean, I can't stay in a bed and breakfast forever, can I?"

"No, I suppose not," Loretta smiled. "Well, I am going to take this weary body upstairs. Good night, Blair."

"Good night, Loretta," Blair said, sipping her tea as she watched the hotelier walk away.

Leaning back in her chair, Blair cupped the mug and curled her legs under her, enjoying the fire.

Twelve

Blair slid the key into the lock. The mechanical clicks had become inviting, like opening to the first page of a new book. Each day at the store in Evergreen, was like a new chapter of a Christmas story.

Flipping on the lights, The Toy Chest once again came to life.

Blair straightened the candy canes and prepped the table for the coffee, cocoa and cider. No sooner had the treat station been tidied, Kris backed her way into the store with two thermoses full of hot beverages.

"Good morning, Kris," Blair sang.

"Good morning, Blair. We have cranberry bars and chocolate dipped candy canes coming for the treats today," Kris announced.

"That sounds amazing, thank you," Blair beamed.

Kris spun, frowning, "Hey, there were some people in suits poking around yesterday, not just my shop but others. Know anything about them?"

Blair shrugged, "They came in. Asking what my plans were after taking it over from my grandparents."

"That's curious. They asked if I had thought about selling, especially with the publishing house closing," Kris said.

"What did you tell them?"

"I told them I wasn't interested and that I had faith in Evergreen to pull through," Kris said. "The man in charge said it would take a Christmas miracle and they laughed and walked out."

"What are we going to do? It will be tough to keep the shops afloat once the publisher closes," Blair asked.

Kris stood still, "I really don't know. It is going to be tough. The holidays will float most of us for a while, but without the local traffic we'll start dropping one by one. You must be horrified, being new to this whole thing."

"It's weighing on me," Blair nodded.

Kris offered a broad smile, "You'll be fine. Your grandparents made it through many a tough time. I'll be back with the rest of the treats."

Blair watched Kris walk out of the store. She knew her store wasn't to blame for the town's struggles, but she did fear selling would be a catalyst that would accelerate the domino effect throughout Main Street.

The door swung open again, this time a chipper Nella danced into the toy shop. "Good morning!" she sang. "You were a hit last night. The kids loved your game. So did Scott and I."

"It was fun," Blair said. "Thank you for letting me join you."

"You still up for round two?" Nella asked, taking her coat off and heading to hang it in the back room.

"I'd like that," Blair said.

As Nella reappeared from the storeroom, she pondered, "We still need another player. Scott has a few friends from work…"

Her thoughts were broken up when the jingle bells on the front door chimed. Luke Marsten wheeled in carrying a toy chest.

Nella's eyes widened as Blair launched herself towards her, "No, no, no!"

It was too late. Nella met Luke at the front of the store, "Luke, are you free tomorrow night?"

Luke frowned as he set the toy chest down, "Yeah, I think so. Why?"

"Scott and I wanted to invite you over to game night," Nella grinned, watching Blair scowl in her peripheral vision.

"That sounds great. I'll bring the wine," Luke offered.

Blair crossed her arms in a huff as she glared at Nella. Her glare melting into a forced smile as Luke turned his attention to her. "I had a special order for a toy chest," he revealed his new creation.

"It's the manger scene with Santa Claus waiting in line behind the three wise men. I like it," Blair said.

"Well, they could have bought it directly from me, but I know how important it is that we support all of our small businesses. So, I told them I sold exclusively through you," Luke said.

"That's very thoughtful, Luke. Thank you. I have much the same philosophy," Blair said.

Luke peeled away, "I've got to run. They should be by before noon to pick it up."

Blair nodded.

Luke turned to Nella, "I'll see you and Scott at game night!"

As the winery owner and craftsman left, Blair looked at Nella.

"What? We needed a fourth player!" Nella grinned.

"I have a boyfriend. I don't want to send mixed messages," Blair said.

Nella scrunched her nose, "It's not a date. It's boardgames with friends. When do we get to meet this boyfriend of yours, anyway? Is he coming out for Christmas?"

Blair was desperate to change the conversation, the jingle of bells gave her just that opportunity as she welcomed a family into the store.

The kids darted towards the displays filled with the latest toys while the parents marveled at the wide selection the toy store had to offer.

It warmed Blair's heart to see the family's joy as they browsed the store.

"Hey guys!" Nella called.

"Hi Nella," the woman said. "I guess we're in the same boat, huh?"

"With a lot of folks around here. Scott is already looking for a new job, but it's tough to find anything local," Nella said.

"Dave had to widen his search area too. Looks like a long commute," the woman said.

"Mommy! Come look!" a little voice called from behind a shelf.

"That looks so cool!" the mother cooed. "That might be a bit out of range this year, I'm afraid."

"I'll ask Santa for it!" the boy said.

"Yeah," the mother sighed. "You can ask Santa."

A little girl careened around the corner, a talking stuffed toy in her grips. Showing it to her parents, the conversation was much the same.

"Hey, guys! Those things are so cool. But, you know what my brother and I loved best at Christmas? A gift we could share and play together," Blair called, bringing them to a section of games and less expensive toys.

"And these, these are classics. You know why they're called classics?" Blair handed a toy to each child. Their eyes wide as they inspected the items as she they shook their heads.

"These have been around since before your parents were even born," Blair said.

"I even had that exact train," the father said.

"They are called classics because they never get old. Kids never get tired of them. They end up on their shelves sometimes so long, that they give them to their kids," Blair said. "The stuff up front is cool, but it's kind of like trying bubble gum ice cream. You try it once, but you're ready for chocolate or vanilla the next time through."

The girl grinned, "I like them swirled!"

"Me too," Blair smiled back.

The parents shot Blair a thankful look. A new problem was already swirling through Blair's head. As the children made wish list selections more in line with what their parents could afford, they thanked Blair and Nella as they left with warm cups of cocoa and candy canes.

"I think you saved the day," Nella beamed.

"Yeah," Blair's mind was distant as she chewed on her lip. "We need to make some changes. Will you help me?"

"Sure...," Nella looked at Blair with trepidation.

Moving to the front of the store, she declared as she began removing items from the shelf, "We need to move these displays around. Put some of these higher priced items in the back and pull more affordable options up front."

"I'm no marketing major, but isn't that the opposite of how you're supposed to lay out a store?" Nella asked.

"Not in a town with sweet people where most of them have gotten laid off," Blair said, carrying an armload of expensive remote-controlled drones towards the back of the store.

Nella scooped up an armload of toys from the back and brought them up front to fill in the openings made by Blair. "I love this idea. These toys are so much more classic than the new ones. They spark such nostalgia," Nella called.

"I think they are every bit as fun," Blair defended.

"More so," Nella agreed, stepping back to take in the display she was creating. "Besides, they are way more postcard worthy than electronic gadgets."

Blair joined Nella, preparing to scoop up another load of digital toys. "These really do bring back memories," she said, admiring Nella's work with the new display.

"I'm glad you're my boss. You give me a sense that things are going to be alright around here," Nella shared.

Blair winced, closing her eyes tight for a moment before continuing with her load. "I'm glad you are here, too."

Kris walked in with fresh thermoses and studied the display swaps. "I like the new displays, they're charming. Kind of makes the store seem that much more magical when you walk in," the coffee shop owner said. "But don't most stores put the new, more expensive stuff up first?"

Nella grinned at Blair.

"Thanks, Kris," Blair said, returning from her new electronic toy section in the back of the store.

"The Evergreen Holiday Festival kicks off tonight with the town tree lighting. We close the shop and run a booth. Stop by, I've got special cocoas and peppermint mochas," Kris said.

Blair took a deep breath, a sparkle in her eyes, "I remember the tree lighting. It was a magical night when I was a kid. I'll be there."

"Good, stop by, coffee is on me," Kris said.

"You don't have to do that," Blair protested.

"You're my best customer," Kris said, cheer in her voice.

Blair relented, "Alright, I'll see you tonight."

Blair and Nella completed the front to back swap. Stepping back, they looked at the store. "It really is more charming, isn't it?" Nella mused.

"It is," Blair agreed.

Wooden trains and trucks, endearing dolls, spirographs and classic bookshelf games dominated the store front. "Straight out of Santa's workshop," Blair added.

The jingle bells signaled the arrival of another guest, both Blair and Nella turned to welcome them.

"Hi, Hank," Nella said.

"Hello, Nella," the man smiled. "And you must be Ms. Cooper."

"I am," Blair acknowledged. "Blair Cooper."

The man stepped back and smiled, "I remember you from your visits with your parents, though it has been some time. Welcome back to Evergreen. My name is Hank Martin. I own…owned the print house."

"It's a pleasure. Sorry to see it go," Blair said.

"We all are. A sign of the times, I suppose. We had been a specialty shop for that last decade or so for a larger publisher, it was the only thing that kept us going this long. With me retiring, long overdue, I might add, the publisher decided it was time to consolidate," Hank said.

"Isn't there anything that could be done to save it?" Blair asked.

Hank shook his head sadly, "No. They kept it going well beyond what they should have. The only reason they did was for me."

Blair offered a sullen nod.

Hank glanced around the store, "You've done a remarkable job here. I'm glad not everything will change around here, I just wish I could have done more for the workers and their families."

"I know you do," Nella acknowledged.

"I'm not supposed to say anything, but there is a Christmas bonus coming this week to everyone at the publishing house. Won't change any lives but might put a present under a tree or a ham on the dinner table," Hank said.

Nella's eyes lit up with the notion, "Anything helps."

"Between us, if you will, Nella," Hank asked.

"Of course," Nella nodded.

"Now, I came in here to pick up a toy chest," Hank said.

"That was for you?" Blair asked.

Hank nodded, "It was. I commissioned Luke Marsten for it. He does good work; his wine isn't half bad either. Like to get a toy chest for each of the grandkids. He demanded I purchase it through a local merchant, and I applaud him for that. The shop owners of Evergreen have always taken care of one another and that shouldn't change."

The elderly man held out his credit card for Blair to ring in the register.

"I'll connect with Luke on the others, I hope it helps you with the store," Hank said.

Blair and Nella followed Hank out to his SUV and slid the toy chest in the back.

"Will we see you at the tree lighting tonight, Hank?" Nella asked.

"I wouldn't miss it," Hank replied climbing into his vehicle.

The ladies watched the man drive away.

"He's nice," Blair remarked as they walked back into the store.

"He is a great man. Scott loved working for him. Everyone there did. That is probably why no one heeded his warnings to start looking for other jobs. As long as he was there, no one was leaving," Nella explained.

Blair nodded thoughtfully.

Nella grinned, "Kind of like you, boss!"

Blair shook her head and sighed.

Thirteen

As night descended on Evergreen, the streets grew busier. Main Street was blocked off and turned into a massive pedestrian thoroughfare and booths lined the spaces typically used for parking alongside the shops.

School choirs and bands began to play carols as families streamed into the tiny town. The quaint foothills town had morphed into a bustling Christmas village in mere hours.

Nella's family stopped at the shop as they beckoned Blair to join them. Agreeing, Blair locked up the toy store and wrapped her coat tight as she willingly followed the excited lead of Sophie and Evan.

Blair recognized that the streets were filled with many more revelers than lived in Evergreen. Families and couples browsed the stands of homemade wares, treats and crafts. Main Street had become a quaint boutique shopping mall with displays of jewelry, artwork, scarves and candles.

Sophie and Evan were halted by a friendly elf who gave each of them a candy cane.

"Thanks for letting me tag along," Blair said.

Nella wrapped her arms around Scott's, "You are most welcome as part of the Swanson family anytime."

"How are things at the store?" Scott asked.

"Receipts are down over last year, or really any year in the past decade according to Grandma's records," Blair admitted, "It is a lot of fun, though."

"Well, it sounds as though you are doing great things," Scott said, shooting Nella a knowing glance.

"I couldn't do it without your wife," Blair gushed.

Scott gave Nella a squeeze.

"Ooh, chestnuts!" Blair spied. "My treat!"

In a flash, Blair was scurrying to the stand doling out paper sacks stuffed with roasted chestnuts. Slapping a handful of bills into the purveyor's hand so that she could pass the warm treats to the Swansons.

"I haven't had these since…since the last Christmas I was in Evergreen," Blair declared, digging into her own bag.

"There's Kris!" Nella called, pulling her family to the coffee kiosk.

"Hi, guys! Are you having fun?" Kris asked.

"We have chestnuts!" Evan squealed.

Kris' eyes widened, "You do! I was planning on getting a bag later."

"You can have my bag. Evan and I can share," Sophie held her bag of chestnuts in front of her.

"That is awfully nice. I'll grab a sack during the tree lighting," Kris said. Looking at Nella and Scott, "You two raised them well."

Scott rubbed Evan on the head, "They're pretty good kids."

Kris looked at Blair, "I owe you a coffee."

"Nonsense," Blair shook her head. "It is the season to support small businesses. I will have one of those peppermint mochas you teased and whatever the Swansons want."

"You don't have to do that," Nella said.

The look on Blair's face suggested that she insisted.

Hands full of treats, Blair followed the Swansons to the tree lighting. The mass crowd began to gather in a large semicircle around a stage built directly in front of the tree.

Blair held her cup and the bag of chestnuts in one hand as she reached in with her other. Fumbling for a nut, she juggled it in the air, swinging to try and regain her grip. To her dismay, her arm slammed into another reveler, launching the chestnut high airborne.

Blair looked up to see who she crashed into. To her amazement, a hand sliced through the air and snatched the rogue treat. With a knowing nod, she grimaced.

The grinning face of Luke Marsten stood before her.

"I am so sorry," Blair said.

"Quite alright. I'm glad I was able to save your little friend here," Luke chuckled.

Looking at the Swansons, he asked, "Mind if I watch the tree lighting with you?"

"Not at all," Nella said. "Your latest toy chest was beautiful."

"You like that? Mr. Martin says he wants to buy a few more," Luke said.

Blair looked up, "He seemed pretty happy with it. It was a stunning piece of work."

"Ooh, there's Mayor Stowe," Scott called, a hand on each of his children's shoulders while Nella nuzzled in close.

Taking the podium, the mayor looked out at the crowd, "This is a challenging Christmas for many of you. I have seen the town pull together, supporting one another. It gives me great hope, reassuring me that I know Evergreen and her people will be alright. In this season of Christmas, seeing you all gathered with our guests is truly a splendid sight. But you didn't come here to see me blabber on. We have a Christmas tree to light!"

Spinning, she faced the tree. Holding her hands high in the air, she brought them down like a great conductor. When her hands descended past her chest, the lights when on and the band started playing. The lights on the two and a half story tall tree were brilliant, each strand winding its way up the thick boughs until it reached the star at the top, twinkling brightly.

When the band hit the chorus, the crowd began to sing along.

The Swansons hugged as they sang. Luke smiled at Blair, who caught up in the moment, couldn't resist a return smile. When the song was over, Mayor Stowe reminded the crowd to visit the booths and for those taking part in the snowman building contest to head to the side of the stage where several ten-foot sections of snow were sectioned off.

Sophie snaked between Luke and Blair, grabbing each of their hands, "Come on, you have to come with us!"

Blair looked around at Nella and then at Luke for an exit, but Evan joined Sophie in insistence. Sophie stopped in front of one of the sections and announced, "This one's yours! We'll be right next to you!"

Luke and Blair looked at each other. Shrugging, Luke smiled, "I guess we're building a snowman."

"I guess we are," Blair smiled back.

"I'll get going on the bottom," Luke said, dropping to his knees and quickly rolling snow into a large ball.

Blair set forward on the upper snowballs. Placing the first two together, she began crafting the head while Luke set to searching for limbs. Part of the contest was scurrying around the festival to locate items to adorn the snowmen. They could be recycled or repurposed items, clothing you brought to the tree lighting or items you purchased at the festival.

Blair had the idea of recreating the scene the best they could. Once Luke fashioned arms he borrowed from hockey sticks outside of the community center, Blair gave their snowman a bag of chestnuts and mocha from Kris' stand.

Taking off her own scarf, she wrapped it around the snowman's neck. Luke used change from his pocket to craft a gleaming smile and pucks for gaping eyes. Pulling a wool hat from his pocket, he set it on top of the snowman.

Stepping back, the pair admired their handiwork.

"Not bad," Luke approved.

"I agree. It is a pretty fine snowman if I say so myself," Blair said.

Time was called and the judges began making their rounds. Blair greeted the Swansons and admired their family of snow people, adorable in their own right, if a bit roughly crafted. The judges lingered between their two stations. They clearly liked the effort to build multiple snow people and the whimsy of the facial features the Swansons built. They were also taken with the festival items used in Blair and Luke's station.

Blair got the sense that the decision was leaning towards them. Glancing over at Evan and Sophie squeezing their hands together in anticipation, Blair suddenly had an inspiration.

As the judges began to make their announcement, Blair cast a sheepish glance at Luke. "Forgive me for this," she hissed.

Luke frowned, "Wha...?"

Blair edged her shoulder into Luke's ribs and gave him a shove. His calves catching on the timber used to section off each snowman creation station, Luke stumbled back. Flailing, he crashed right into their snowman toppling it over.

Landing in a heap of snowman parts, Luke looked up at Blair whose mittens concealed her expression. It was unclear whether she was stifling a laugh or gasp as she covered her mouth with her hands.

"Oh, no!" she cried as she leapt into the snow to help him up. Sophie and Evan giggled at the wild sight.

With little recourse, the judges moved their impending ribbon to the Swanson's station. Sophie and Evan's giggles turned to jubilant cheers, jumping up and down as they were declared the winners.

Luke brushed himself off as Blair dusted snow off his shoulders. "I'm so sorry about that," she whispered with a mischievous smile. Feeling bad for her snowman after the judge's decision had been levied, she straightened the snowman to a semblance of order.

Running to Sophie and Evan, she gave them huge congratulatory high-fives. "Congratulations, guys! I love your snow family!" Blair said. Nella and Scott stood proudly next to their children while choking on giggles at Blair and Luke's folly.

Blair leaned into Luke, ice crystals clinging to the tail of his wool coat, "I think I owe you a hot cocoa after that."

"I could go for cocoa," Luke nodded.

"We'll see you all tomorrow?" Blair suggested.

Nella nodded as she huddled with her family for a victory photo.

"That was fun," Blair said to Luke.

"It was," the winemaker nodded. "Right up to the point when you pushed me into the snowman. You could have just kicked it or something."

Blair pursed her lips, "It had to be an accident."

"I see," Luke mused, scratching his chin. "No harm done, and the right team won."

"About that cocoa…," Blair said, slipping into line at Kris' stand once more.

Kris smiled as the two made their way to the front, "Back for more?"

"This one is more of a penance purchase," Blair admitted.

"I see. On who's part?" Kris asked.

"Mine," Blair confessed. "We had a little incident at the snowman building contest."

Kris laughed, "Drama at the snowman contest…I'm sorry I missed out."

"It was all fun and games until some toy shop owner pushed me into our own snowman," Luke explained.

"It sounds like you deserve your cocoa," Kris said handing them their hot chocolates.

"Thanks, Kris!" Blair waved as the next family moved up to place their orders.

Blair and Luke walked through Main Street; their pace leisurely as they took in the scene. Couples walked hand in hand. Families moved like an amoeba from station to station as children led their parents along the festival booths.

"Is it how you remembered it?" Luke asked.

"It's like being in Santa's village. Each shop decorated to the nines, each booth decked with garland and evergreen. It's magical," Blair said. "Yeah, pretty much just as I remembered it."

"What about your mom and dad and brother? Have they been back?" Luke asked.

"My mom and dad came back a few times. They moved to take care of my other grandparents and they haven't been able to get away much," Blair said. "My brother is career military. He doesn't often get to call when he goes on vacation."

Luke nodded, "I'm grateful for his service."

"I'm real proud of him," Blair said.

"Did he like it here?" Luke asked.

"He did," Blair nodded. "The whole family did. But, we all had to make a living."

Luke laughed, "Yeah, I don't think I would ever call making a living in Evergreen an easy task. But I would call it a rewarding one."

"How about you? Always have plans to start a winery in the middle of nowhere?" Blair asked.

Luke paused in front of the town Christmas tree, admiring the lights and decorations. "My folks moved here and bought the Bed and Breakfast, well, about since the last time you visited. I came out to help them move. I loved it, but I had my own life in Seattle. I got hired by a big tech firm in Seattle and didn't really love what I was doing. Sold some really overpriced stock and bought the winery."

"Wow. You just planted some grapes and...?" Blair started.

Luke let out a laugh, "Oh, no. I took a complete bath, nearly lost everything, twice! When I started, this was a piece of dirt, an old ranch house and a dilapidated barn. I took a few viticulture and enology courses while in college, I had weird electives. I purchased grapes for my first few bottlings, lost money on each. But I started to realize I was losing less and less each year and gaining a following. Then my own grapes started coming in and that's where I am today."

"That's amazing, Luke. To work so hard for what you wanted," Blair said.

Luke grinned, "Hard and fun."

Blair took a long look at the tree and the families enjoying the Christmas village together. The choirs stopped and the evening was winding down. As her attention retuned to Luke, she swung face to face with him. For a moment, they looked in each other's eyes, the lights of the tree reflecting a dazzling scene.

"I uh, I should be going," Blair said, bowing her head down and creating space between the two. "Busiest time of the year for a toy store."

"Of course. Thanks for letting me tag along, even if our snowman partnership ended a bit abruptly," Luke said.

Blair nodded, "I guess I'll see you tomorrow night?"

"Game night! Looking forward to it," Luke said. "See you tomorrow night."

Luke stood by the tree as he watched Blair make her way down Main Street headed towards the bed and breakfast.

Fourteen

Blair waved at Kris and Jessica as she walked past the coffee shop. Deep in thought, she pulled up abruptly as she was surprised to see the real estate investor and his assistants waiting outside the toy store door.

She studied them for a moment before striding forward with her key. "Mr. Marcom, did we have an appointment this morning?"

"No, Ms. Cooper. I was hoping to discuss some business with you this morning," Bradley Marcom said, nudging towards the store and out of the chilly morning air.

"Come on in, coffee, cider and cocoa should be arriving soon," Blair said. She looked around the sidewalk, hoping to dispense with the businessman before Nella arrived.

Marcom and his pair of assistants accepted Blair welcoming them inside. "I'm sorry for the early morning intrusion, our investors are hoping to have the first property under wraps before Christmas. That, puts you in remarkable favor for terms," Marcom reported.

He studied Blair for a moment before moving on, "I can see you have an emotional attachment to this store and your realtor confesses you have an admirable job in New York in which to return to. I will make this quick and give you some time to ponder unless you wish to sign today, in which I am prepared to offer you a handsome cash bonus."

The real estate investor held out a portfolio for Blair to review. The first page summarized the deal. The figure was enough to make Blair swallow hard.

"As you can see, we are not taking into consideration that the major employer in this town is shuttering and instead are offering you full value for the property with a five-year appreciation," Marcom said. "Add to that, the bonus should you sign today, and you have a very generous windfall."

"Thank you. This is very generous," Blair said, taking in the numbers on the page. "Can I have some time to consult with my financial advisor?"

"You may. I will extend the offer for the signing bonus to the end of day," Mr. Marcom said. With a nod, he ushered his companions out of the toy store, holding the door open for Nella as she arrived for the day.

Nella unwrapped from her coat and asked, "What was that about?"

"More interest in what happens when the publishing house closes, I suppose," Blair said.

"The vultures are circling. They smell a town in trouble and swoop in quick, don't they?" Nell scoffed.

"I suppose they do," Blair offered a sullen nod.

Nella set her purse down and hung her coat up. "You and Luke seemed to get along well."

Blair laughed, "We had fun. I'm not sure what happened at the end of the snowman building contest, but we had fun."

"The kids had a blast, thank you," Nella added. "Scott and I are excited for game night."

"Me too," Blair said, her mind was whirring in the background. "Would you mind opening the store? I have something I need to sort through."

"Yeah, of course!" Nella shrugged.

"Thank you," Blair grabbed her coat and the folder, rushing out of the store.

Dialing Todd, she pulled the summary sheet from the folder.

"Hey, Babe! How's it going in the boondocks?" Todd's voice called.

Blair was taken aback for a moment, shaking it off, she replied, "The town is great. I'll have to come as a guest in the future. I forgot how much I loved it here."

"You'll have to send me some pics, it sounds…quaint," Todd said.

"Listen, that real estate investor came in this morning. He offered full market plus five year growth. If I signed today, I get a twenty-thousand dollar bonus," Blair said.

"That's great! Nice job," Todd said. "Does that mean you can come back sooner? In time for my office party?"

"I don't think it changes my return trip," Blair admitted.

"Well, sign away and we'll celebrate when you get back," Todd said.

"It's just...," Blair started.

Todd cut her off, "I have to get into my next meeting. Congrats! We'll talk later."

Blair was stunned, staring at the phone that fell silent. She wanted to talk about her reservations but was left to mull them alone. Part of her knew Todd was right. Her life was on the other side of the country.

Heading back into the store, she shuffled, head drooping.

"Well, that's not the face of tonight's game master," Nella called out. "Is something wrong?"

Blair lifted her head and stared at Nella. Nella deserved to know. "There's something I need to tell you," Blair started.

Nella studied Blair as the shop owner fought for words. Before the right ones found their way to her lips, Nella's phone rang.

"Oh, sorry. It's Scott. Hang on," Nella held up a finger. "Hey hon!"

Blair ambled away, browsing her own store. She was in particular drawn to the displays of classic toys she and Nella put together. Looking at the toys and games she and her brother played as a child filled her heart with warmth. They created so many wonderful memories.

"I'm sorry. Scott wanted to make sure we had everything for tonight. I think he's excited for grown up game night," Nella said. "You were saying?"

Blair looked at Nella. She beamed through kind eyes at Blair.

"I, uhm. I'm nervous about the game I made," Blair spat, startled and confused with the words that tumbled out.

Nella laughed, "Oh, I'm sure it's brilliant. We all loved the kid's game. Besides, we have back up games if needed, but I have a suspicion that yours will be great!"

"You're so sweet, Nella. I don't think I deserved to have found such a great friend in taking over the store," Blair said.

"Life's funny that way. The All-Mighty pits people together for a reason. I have to tell you; I was nervous to meet you. I wasn't sure what was going to happen to the store," Nella admitted.

Blair pursed her lips and nodded.

The door jingle bells chimed, and Luke pushed his way in. "Mr. Martin finalized his order. He has four more of these coming in. He's going to pay for them all today, if that's alright. He is visiting his other grandchildren in January, so I'll have a little time to get them finished," Luke shared, setting the toy box down near the register.

"You've created heirlooms that will be in that family for generations, Luke. These are beautiful!" Blair admired the latest chest. This one had a soldier kneeling to hug his son next to the Christmas tree with his wife's hand on the soldier's shoulder. "I love this."

"Since each is custom, he offered a higher price. With your 45% they should help out the store quite a bit," Luke said.

Blair was struck. She hadn't contemplated the impact of Luke selling his crafts through the store. The scale of Hank Martin's purchase for his grandchildren magnified the impact.

"Luke, I am happy to have Mr. Martin pick the chests up here, but I can't accept the money. You deserve every cent," Blair said.

Luke grinned, his voice cheery, "Nonsense. This is how local economies work. If you didn't buy coffee from Kris, I didn't sell through you, the farmers didn't supply me with grapes…it all comes together to make the town run. It's how I know we'll survive the publishing house closing."

Luke glanced at Nella who paled slightly at the reminder. He cast a reassuring nod, "We will."

His confidence produced a smile on Nella's lips.

"Well, I have a lot of work to do. Along with the holiday tasting, I have toy chests to design," Luke gave a quick wave and headed out the door.

Nella picked up the invoice on the chest. Her eyes widened, "Wow. This is like a full month's revenue, outside of the holiday shopping season, at least."

Blair looked at the sheet. The number made her only feel more guilty about the news she was hiding.

"Scott having any luck?" Blair asked.

Nella froze, her perpetually happy face fell as she shook her head, "No. I'm sure things will get better in January. We just have to get through the next few weeks."

"I wish there was something more I could do," Blair said, not realizing the trap she had just set for herself.

"Having the store to lean on is everything, Blair. You coming to town was a blessing," Nella beamed, the smile that she typically wore once again gracing her lips.

Blair turned away and squeezed her eyes shut. Every positive cast towards her and the toy store just dug the icicle stabbing her in the chest even deeper. She knew that she was the one digging it in.

Fifteen

Blair closed the shop promptly and arrived at Nella's home laden with snacks for game night. She was surprised Nella asked her to come over so early and even more surprised when she met her at the door with an apron in hand.

"How sloppy does game night get around here?" Blair asked, a raised brow eyeing the kitchen garment.

"You were telling me about missing holiday traditions with your grandmother and mother. I thought you might want to join Sophie, Evan and I in making some Christmas cookies," Nella suggested.

Blair's eyes lit, "That sounds fun."

"Here, let me help you with this stuff," Nella said, grabbing the bags of snack food. "Is that the new game?"

"It is," Blair nodded.

"I'm excited to try it," Nella said, leading Blair towards the kitchen.

"Me too," Blair admitted, a hint of reservation dripping from her words. Seeing the kids with their aprons donned and chef hats, she called, "Hi, guys!"

"Hi, Blair!"

"What do we have going on in here?" Blair asked, setting the game down and slipping the apron on.

"We're making sugar cookies and shortbread cookies," Sophie declared.

Evan pointed towards a pan they had just prepared, "Shortbread is daddy's favorite!"

"They are pretty good," Blair nodded. "Which is yours?"

"We like sugar cookies!" the kids cried in unison.

Blair went to the sink to wash up, Nella set the snack food bags down and explained, "I got them started on the shortbread cookies. Would you help Sophie with the sugar cookie batter?"

"Sure," Blair nodded.

Scott walked into the kitchen, coffee cup in hand, "Oh, hi, Blair!"

"Hi, Scott."

"We sure are excited to play your game. I'm glad you were able to come early and help with the cookies. Nella always says it is a fun part of the holiday. It looks like work to me. Well appreciated, mind you, but work nonetheless," Scott said.

Blair laughed, "The making and baking is not so bad, clean up is the rougher part. But she's right. There is something fun about getting together, especially with family...and friends to make Christmas cookies. It's been a while for me. I miss it."

Scott emptied the last of the coffee from the pot into his mug, "Well, back at it for me. I treat my job search like my fulltime job, now. See you in a bit!"

He paused to nuzzle his kids, not minding the sprinkles of flour he picked up while doing do so.

"Alright!" Nella said, producing bowls and utensils for Blair and Sophie. Hearing a knock at the door, she ran off, soon followed by a couple all bundled from the cold.

"Nana and Papa!" the kids cried. Hopping off their stools, they careened around the kitchen island and gave floury hugs.

"Blair, these are my parents Bill and Barb Jones," Nella announced.

"It's nice to meet you," Blair waved across the counter.

Barb smiled at Blair, "We've met. Your mother and I would volunteer at the Christmas Village together. It was years ago, mind you, and you would have been quite young. I'm sorry to hear about your grandparents. They helped furnish many a Christmas for our grandchildren over the years. Wonderful people."

"Thank you," Blair nodded.

"Well, I'm going to wash up and see if can't help these whippersnappers make some cookies!" Barb rubbed her palms together excitedly.

"I'm going to poke in and say hi to Scott. It's nice to see you, Blair," Bill said.

Just as the last cookie sheet was slid into the oven, a rap at the door stole their attention. Nella was elbow deep in the sink scrubbing the mixing bowls. Looking over her shoulder, she asked, "Would you mind grabbing the door?"

"Sure," Blair shrugged as she closed the oven.

Wiping her hands on her apron, she wrenched the handle on the door and swung it open. Luke Marsten stood on the porch; several bottles of wine cradled in his arms. Eying Blair's apron and adorned glittery sprinkles from a wild round of cookie making, he couldn't resist a grin.

"Hello, Blair."

"Hello, Luke," Blair answered meekly as she wiped hair away her forehead with the back of her hand, leaving a duty swath of flour in its wake.

Luke sauntered in, followed by Blair who closed the door.

"Hi gang!" Luke called as he walked into the kitchen.

Setting the bottles of wine down, he handed one directly to Barb, "This is for you and Bill. Won't cut you out of game night imbibement."

"This is my favorite! Thank you, Luke," Barb accepted the bottle.

"Sophie and Evan, here is some kid-friendly cider I made," Luke slid a bottle towards the kids.

Nella called from the sink, "Just washing up from cookies. We'll dive into game night momentarily."

Luke nodded, observing the cookie creations. "Wow! You guys did great!"

Sophie blushed and pointed to a row on the cooling rack, "These are mine. Would you like to try one?"

Luke feigned shock at the question, "Would I? You bet! Which one, do you suppose?"

Sophie reviewed her wares, "That one!"

"Ok," Luke grabbed the cookie Sophie pointed out. With a keen eye, he studied the cookie. He held it up to the light, swirled it around, sniffed it and took a tentative bite, looking very thoughtful as he did so.

"What are you doing?" Sophie gasped.

Luke cocked his head towards her, "What? This is how people taste my wine, I figured they had a good reason for it."

"You're silly!" Sophie giggled.

"You know, this is an excellent cookie. Well-balanced, it's a snowman, so... well-bodied, delightful notes of sugar, flour and butter. Well done. I give it a 98 on the Marsten scale. Just don't tell my Mom, that's the highest score she ever got," Luke declared.

Evan and Sophie laughed.

"Kiddos, I think it's time we find Grandpa. We have a whole line up of Christmas cartoons to watch!" Barb declared to her grandchildren. Snatching her bottle of wine, she hugged it close to her chest and winked, "You guys try and keep it down in here!"

Ushering the children away, Barb disappeared down the hall as Nella put the last dish away. Blair whipped out her dips, chips and candies, divvying them into small bowls Nella set out for her while Luke worked the cork on a bottle of wine.

"I love making Christmas cookies with the kids, but an evening of playing games with my adult friends sampling some of the finest wine sounds divine!" Nella said. "I'll let Scott know we're ready and we can have some fun!"

Blair and Luke looked awkwardly across the kitchen island from one another.

"Wine?" Luke asked, breaking the stand-off.

"Yes!" Blair breathed.

"This probably isn't as luxurious as Christmas in Manhattan, but you seem to be having fun," Luke observed, handing her a glass of Pinot Noir.

Blair looked over the rim of the garnet liquid filled glass, wondering if there was a note of hidden implication in the question. "I am. While this whole trip…situation… was unexpected, it has been a nice reminder of life outside the bustle," Blair admitted.

Luke raised his glass, "To life outside the bustle."

Blair lifted her wine, "*Salut.*"

"Salut!" Luke toasted. With a grin, he studied Blair, the white streak of flour still splashed across her forehead. "Do you mind?" he asked, stretching across the counter to delicately wipe the remnants of cookie making away with a kitchen towel.

Blair blushed with the attention as well as the realization she must have looked pretty silly.

"Hey, are you guys getting started without us?" Nella teased as she led Scott into the kitchen.

"Making sure the wine was up to standards, worthy of prestigious game night," Luke joked.

"And…?" Nella pressed.

Luke looked at Blair for a verdict.

Blair raised her glass, "Exquisite!"

"Alright!" Scott accepted a glass from Luke. "Let's play!"

Nella and Scott grabbed the snack bowls while Blair began setting up the game.

Luke eyed the game pieces laid out on the table. The crude, yet appealing design piqued his interest. "Did you make this?"

"I did," Blair smiled, shuffling nervously in her seat. Reaching across the table to set up the remaining pieces.

"When did you have time to work on this?" Luke asked.

"I had a few slower moments at the store and late nights in my room at the Holly Bough," Blair admitted. "I would have liked to have gotten some of these printed instead of hand sketched, but I didn't have time for that. I did liberate a handful of pieces from games and toys around the shop to improvise."

"It's gorgeous!" Nella said.

"Thank you. I was inspired by the Christmas tree at the Holly Bough and how Mrs. Marsten has each person take their hand at decorating it," Blair said., settling into her seat. With a deep breath, Blair unveiled the rules of the game, "So, here's how we play..."

The foursome surrounded the table and once the kinks of learning a new game were smoothed out, lost themselves in a relaxing evening that served as respite from stressful and challenging times. Each person at the table had life stressors that weighed on them. For that evening, the concerns and burdens melted away.

Nella placed her pawn across the threshold triumphantly, "This is really fun!"

"Sure, you won twice in a row," Scott scoffed. "But it is fun."

"Strategy, my dear, you need to be more strategic," Nella teased, placing a tender hand on her husband's shoulder.

Luke admired the game set up, "I can't believe you put this together in a couple of days."

"It's a bit rough," Blair wrinkled her nose. "I took the concepts of the original game I created with my family and added a few twists to up the challenge."

"Well, you did good, thanks for sharing it," Luke said as they collected their pieces.

"Ready to dive into the stack of games Nella brought out?" Blair asked.

Scott shrugged, "I'm good playing this. Besides, I'm devising a tactic to take Nella down!"

"Bring it on, slugger!" Nella said.

"Let's do it!" Luke agreed, rolling up his sleeves for another game.

Blair passed out game pieces as Luke refreshed their glasses.

"You must play a lot in New York," Nella suggested.

Blair paused, her head tilted slightly to the side as she contemplated the question. "No," she shook her head and scrunched her nose, "I don't know that I've ever had a game night in New York. Kind of sad really."

Luke handed her glass back, "To making up for well-deserved lost time, then. To game nights!"

"To game nights!" they all cheered.

As the next game got underway, Luke tossed a soft question to Blair, "So, what do you do for fun in Manhattan?"

Blair chewed on her lip as she contemplated how to make her move. When she confidently placed her meeple, she looked at Luke and replied, "Lots of dinner and cocktail engagements? Most seem to have some kind of work connection either mine or Todd's."

"It sounds so elegant," Nella muses, resting her chin on the hands.

"Kind of," Blair nodded. "I mean, I guess it is. Lavish dinners on a corporate card, dressed to the nines. But it's funny sometimes. I can be in a city so big, so vast, meeting so many people and yet, there is a weird feeling of not being connected. Not intimate gatherings like this. This is nice."

"Our rickety dining table is as metropolitan as Evergreen gets," Nella laughed.

Blair rested her hands on the table, "I don't know, it's quaint. Approachable. Welcoming. Comfortable, and in a good way."

"Sounds like you're describing a quilt," Nella scoffed.

"There are nice luxuries in Evergreen, like Luke's winery," Blair suggested.

Luke sat up straight in his chair and puffed his chest out, "My place is luxurious, hmm? I really need you to do my marketing for me."

Blair laughed, "Look at the town this time of year. It's like living in a Norman Rockwell painting and I say that as an enormous compliment. People yearn to be in a place like this."

"Never mind my winery, Mayor Stowe needs to hire you to market the town," Luke said.

"Well, she's Evergreen's now. She belongs here," Nella said.

Blair cringed at the notion and just offered a weak smile. Luke eyed her as she did so.

Returning the table's focus to the game, Luke declared, "I've got you all right where I want you!"

Moving his game piece, he leaned back confidently, feeling he had sealed the game in his favor. Blair took her turn, reviewing all of the possibilities. Suddenly, her eyes widened, a grin crossing her lips. Countering Luke, she put herself in position to win the game.

Running the table one more round, Blair held on, just edging out Luke.

"One more round?" Luke asked.

"I would love to," Nella said. "But I have two babies that need to get ready for bed. The last time I walked past, all four of them, including my parents, were asleep with Rudolph running in the background."

"Could only imagine what their dreams must be like," Scott wondered.

"This was really fun, thank you," Luke said.

"Let's do it again soon, maybe right after Christmas?" Scott suggested.

Nella grabbed her phone, "Yeah. Let's put a date on the calendar!"

Blair paled as Luke studied her for a response, "Yeah, I, uh, sure. Toss out some dates and we'll see if we can make it work."

Nella snapped up from her calendar on her phone, "I guess we don't have to set it now. We can zero in on a date later."

"You know where to find me. After the holidays, things get pretty slow around the winery," Luke said.

"So, it's settled. Soon," Scott said cheerily.

Luke began helping Blair put her game pieces in her makeshift box.

"Go ahead and leave the dishes on the table. I need to dispense with the remaining cookie items, but I don't want to raise a ruckus with the little ones," Nella said. She glared at Luke and Blair before they could speak, "And, yes. I'm sure. You two have a good night."

"Thanks again!" Blair said, picking up her game.

Luke held his arms out towards the door, "I'll walk you out."

Stopping at the coat rack, Luke helped Blair into hers before donning his own. Pulling their collars tight, they made their way into the chilly night.

Snow drifted down, sparkling off the streetlights. As the flakes cascaded over the homes aglow with Christmas lights, it only made the scene more charming.

"Well, that was a fun night," Luke said, hands stuffed in his jacket pockets.

"It was. Nella and Scott are a sweet couple. They have a great family," Blair said.

Luke nodded, shuffling along the path. "Your game, wow. I didn't know what to expect. It was a blast."

Blair looked at Luke to see if he was teasing her. His eyes were sincere. "Thank you. It would have been better with something other than cardboard cutout pieces and a real board," she said.

"The fact that you put that together in your spare time was impressive," Luke added.

"Thank you," Blair said. "Playing with the game I created with my family just kind of inspired me."

"You must be a great marketer. You're creative and connect with your audience," Luke said.

Blair shot Luke a confused look.

"Come on, you must be used to receiving compliments on your work," Luke pressed.

"It's a demanding industry. Even when people like your work, it is balanced with how effective it is. Clicks, sales, ratings...those are the compliments that matter on Madison Avenue," Blair said.

As they rounded the corner of the street the bed and breakfast was located on, Blair admired a family of snowmen set up alongside the sidewalk, "Aw, they look so sweet, peaceful amidst the new falling snow."

Luke shot a mischievous grin. With a sudden shift of his hips, he sent Blair tumbling towards one of the snowmen. At the last second, his arm flashed out and caught hers, moments before she crash headlong into the snow.

Blair's eyes took the shape of saucers in her surprise.

Pulling her gently upright, they ended up chest to chest. Blair looked up at Luke and for a moment, was breathless and silent, looking into his eyes. The moment was broken as he released a laugh, "I'm sorry. I was just teasing, trying to make up for the other night."

"You… are kind of a brat," Blair declared, smacking Luke on the chest. "What if you didn't catch me? Some poor child would wake up in the morning to the tragic death of their beloved snowman."

"I was going to catch you," Luke defended. Looking thoughtfully, he admitted, "I hadn't thought of if I didn't. Snow parts everywhere. Your prints all over the scene. You would be implicated in a very rare Evergreen crime investigation."

Blair tilted her head and pursed her lips but couldn't resist a laugh herself. "You're impossible."

They lingered, face to face, in the falling snow for a moment before Blair shook herself and nudged her head towards the bed and breakfast, "I should be…"

"Yeah," Luke nodded.

Taking a step away, they turned and continued their walk.

"You didn't have to walk me back, you know," Blair said.

"I don't mind. I love an excuse to walk the streets at night, especially this time of year. It is so quiet. So peaceful," Luke admitted.

"It is," Blair agreed.

Stepping up on the porch, she turned back, "Thank you again for my gallant escort."

"Milady," Luke bowed and watched her enter the bed and breakfast. As the door closed, he cursed himself, "Milady? What was I thinking?"

Sixteen

Blair had a bounce in her step as she opened The Toy Chest. Turning the key and flipping on the lights was almost beginning to feel natural. Turning on the record player filling the store with Christmas carols transported her back to a time that was calmer and warmer.

Buzzing around the store, she prided over minor adjustments to the displays, making sure the store was magical for the day's guests. She wanted the store to look fit for Santa's village in the North Pole.

Hearing the jingle bells chime at the door, she whirled expecting to see Kris or Jessica with the coffee shop supplies. She was surprised to see Nella burst through. The effervescent cheeriness that typically shone around her missing, replaced by a fervor of excitement, but not the good kind.

"What is it?" Blair asked.

"Mr. Martin, the factory owner, he fell ill. The board decided to shutter the factory early. All remaining employees have been laid off," Nella announced.

"Oh, no!" Blair gasped. "Is Mr. Martin going to be okay? He seems like such a nice man."

Nella frowned, "I'm not sure. The family is keeping Mayor Stowe in the loop, they know how much the town reveres him."

"All those families…," Blair shook her head.

"We all knew it was going to be a financially bleak holiday. Closing early will only make it worse," Nella said.

Blair leaned on a rack. "Nella, I am so sorry. It has to be so tough on everyone."

"I'm just grateful I have a job to go to. Not just for the paycheck, which I desperately need, but for the happy distraction. You can't walk into The Toy Chest and stay blue," Nella bounced back into her cheery self.

"Yeah," Blair said, her voice trailing.

Nella put her things in the office and smiled, "Last night was a blast!"

"It was fun," Blair nodded. "Thank you for having us…me."

Nella studied Blair for a moment, contemplating her hasty repeal of words. "We can't wait for our next game night. Scott and I are hoping we can make it a regular thing," Nella said.

"Yeah, that would be great," Blair said. Welcoming the interruption, she lunged to help Jessica open the door as she lugged two large thermoses.

"Good morning, ladies!" Jessica called as she swung into the store.

"Hi Jess!" Nella and Blair chimed.

"Did you hear about the publishing house? It's been eerily quiet and empty this morning," Jessica said.

Nella nodded, "Yes, a lot of the people Scott worked with were hoping to hang on until the new year."

"I wish there was something we could do," Blair said softly.

"You're helping Kris, that's for sure," Jessica said. "I'll be back with the treats!"

Blair watched Jessica walk out. Staring out the window, she could see the streets were quiet. The tourists would come, starting their day later than the locals. Main Street was usually active by this time of day with employees headed to the printing house.

Nella observed Blair's concern. Bouncing over, she placed a hand on her boss' shoulder, "The best thing we can do is to do our part in making this a great Christmas for the people of Evergreen. It's not like you can give everyone jobs."

The last sentence struck Blair, snapping her head, she drank in the thought, "Find everyone jobs, that would be a fix."

Nella lost her sparkle for just a moment as the reality struck her. For her husband to find a job in the pay scale he had at the print house, they would likely have to move from Evergreen.

"I'll be right back; I need to make a quick call!" Blair said excitedly.

Disappearing into the back as Nella helped Jessica who had returned with the day's treat trays, Blair shuffled through her papers.

Finding the card she had slid under the mat on the desk, she dialed the number.

"Meredith Kohl," the realtor's voice sang through the phone.

"Meredith, I think it is time to move the transaction forward. What do we have to do?" Blair asked.

"Unless you have adjustments to the offer, you can have your attorney or financial advisor review it. Sign it and I'll send a courier to pick it up. If you want, we can have the documents converted to digital and you can sign them that way," the realtor said.

"Would you? I'd like to send a copy to New York for review. Thanks, Meredith!" Blair said. Sliding the card back under the mat, she pushed back from the desk. Her heart was aflutter in erratic directions. She felt like she was doing her part for the people of Evergreen, yet turning her back on her grandparents and their store.

Looking out at Nella, she knew her toy store salary wasn't enough to support her family. If the developer could sweep in and rehire most of the town, they could stay in the place they wanted to call home, even if it required a few changes.

With a new resolve, she strode forward determined to do what Nella had suggested. Help make this season a wonderful Christmas for the people of Evergreen.

"You want a latte, Nella? I'm buying!" Blair called, grabbing her wallet.

Nella grinned, "Peppermint mocha?"

"You bet!" Blair replied, pushing out into the cold street.

Without taking time to put her coat on, she hustled into the sanctuary of the coffee shop. She was surprised when she didn't have to wait in line. Placing her order, she wandered the shop. She hoped there was a place for Kris in Marcom's plans.

The Christmas carols playing over the speakers brought her back into a festive mood between the whir of the coffee grinder and woosh of the frothing machine.

Two ladies entered the shop, their gleeful conversation bringing more light into the store.

"Mrs. Albright!" Blair recognized. "Good morning!"

"Good morning, dear. Please, it is Mary Kay," the older woman insisted. "This is my friend June Kennedy. June, this is Blair Cooper, the Noelle's granddaughter."

"This whippersnapper? You had a brother, right?" June asked.

"Derek," Blair nodded.

The woman gave Blair a stern glare, "You two used to career dangerously close to my rose bushes on those sleds of yours!"

"That may have been us," Blair scrunched her nose. Quickly, she soothed, "That was a long time ago."

June burst into a broad smile, "I miss that. It was nice seeing young ones having fun in the snow after my own kids grew up and moved out."

"Your coffees are ready!" Jessica called out.

Blair nodded a thank you and turned back to Mary Kay. "You said something about a gingerbread contest. Whatever happened to that?"

"The publishing house used to host it. They sort of stopped doing that when they got purchased. No longer a necessary budget item, I suppose," Mary Kay said.

"Why don't we put one on anyway? It would be a boost to town spirit!" Blair suggested.

Mary Kay looked thoughtful, "That would be a wonderful idea. June, you can get space at the Community Center, can't you?"

"I can," June replied. "And the ladies' auxiliary could bake the gingerbread pieces."

"I'll buy the supplies!" Blair bounced excitedly.

Kris stepped out from behind the counter, "I'll connect you with my supplier, I'm sure they can give you a discount. We'll bring cider and cocoa."

Blair beamed. Seeing her spur of the moment idea blossom to something bigger, so fast filled her with warmth. It felt good to be part of the community, even if it was in passing for one final holiday season.

Sliding into a booth, the four women began plotting the event.

By the time Blair was ready to leave the coffee shop, she ordered a fresh peppermint mocha for Nella, refusing Kris' insistence it was on the house, she stuffed a wad of bills in the tip jar and gave Jessica a wink.

Dancing her way back to the toy store, Blair sheepishly handed Nella her hot mocha.

"I was beginning to worry, but I know how running errands in Evergreen can be," Nella grinned. "Thank you."

"My pleasure," Blair said. Her eyes widened, "We are going to host the town gingerbread contest!"

Nella looked surprised, "We haven't had one of those in years, that's a great idea!"

Frowning, Nella glanced around the store.

"Oh, not here. Mary Kay Albright and June Kennedy are arranging for it to be held at the community center and are even assembling a baking crew!" Blair announced.

"Wow, this is so fun!" Nella looked at Blair and grasped her hands. "You are such a blessing to this town."

Blair gave Nella a hug, "I'm happy to be here. We can't control the future, but we can make the most of the holiday!"

Blair pulled away, "Listen, I need to get going on the marketing for the event since we don't have much notice. Mind if I slip into the back?"

Nella glanced around the quiet toy store, "I think I'll manage."

Nodding, Blair hurried off.

Applying her marketing trade craft, she built post cards, tent cards, posters, banners and digital marketing. Leaning back, she admired her work.

Sending the digital notices to Mayor Stowe and posting on every social media engine she could think of, Blair chewed her lip. Leaning out of the office, she called, "Nella...where can I get this stuff printed?"

Nella hopped into view, "Nowhere with short turn around. I mean, the publishing house has printers, but it's shut down."

Blair looked contemplative for a moment, "Is there any way to get in touch with Mr. Martin?"

"Yeah, I think his number is on the toy chest orders from Luke," Nella said. As the front door jingle bells rang, she said, "I'll find it while you visit with our guest."

Blair rose out of the office chair and scurried down the aisles, "Hi, welcome to The Toy Chest!"

A man with grey hair and rosy cheeks flashed a smile, his eyes darted about the store. Frowning, he said, "I've been shopping at this store for decades. It has been tradition that I find something from Evergreen to send to my daughter as a Christmas present."

"That sounds like a wonderful tradition. You must have bought from my grandparents in the past," Blair said.

The man studied Blair, "Lovely people, your grandparents. They were in no small part one of the reasons the tradition started in the first place. Trouble is, it was easy when my daughter was young. She is married now, I'm afraid I may have come to an impasse with the tradition."

Blair put her hands on her hips and thought about his dilemma. "No kids of her own?" she asked.

"Not yet. That would present an easy tweak on the tradition," the man admitted. "I really want something special. I just can't think of it."

"Special as in sweet memento or special as in enduring statement for holidays to come special?" Blair asked, her mind formulating a solution.

The man looked at Blair with hopeful eyes.

Leading the man to the display of holiday ornaments, they took in the assortment. Blair presented baubles for the tree and stockings. As she whirled with a stocking, she toppled a wiseman on the Nativity set that Luke delivered.

"Enduring, statement forever that she could pass down to her own children someday," Blair breathed as she righted the wise man figure and stepped back.

The man's eyes widened, "That is perfect!"

"Handcrafted by a local artisan. It's beautiful, isn't it?" Blair said.

"It is. Thank you. You have made my holiday, from a shopping perspective, at least," the man beamed. "You will do well with your grandparents' legacy."

Blair looked at him thoughtfully.

"I have Mr. Martin's number. If you'd like, I can wrap up the set," Nella offered.

"That would be great, thank you," Blair said. Turning to the man, she smiled, "Merry Christmas!"

"Merry Christmas. Thank you, again," the man was fervent in his gratitude.

"My pleasure. Now, I must see about hosting the town's gingerbread contest. If your family is near, they are welcome," Blair said and hurried back to the office.

Mr. Martin was waiting for Blair as she pulled up to the front of the publishing house.

"Thank you so much for meeting me and doing this," Blair exclaimed as he welcomed her into the lobby and closed the doors behind them. "I wasn't sure I should trouble you. I hope you are feeling better.

"It is no bother. I am happy to help and it's a wonderful idea," Mr. Martin said. His eyes worked their way around the offices. "Sad to see this all go. Kind of strange without the flurry of activity. The board, it seems, was ready for any excuse to execute the shutdown. A little touch of the common cold and I may have as well been on my death bed. Come on, I'll give you a tour and then we can work on your prints."

Waving Blair along, he said, "The first floor is the press floor. Jackets, hardcover embossing, covers, interior pages all have their lines. In the old days, each piece of text was line placed. Nowadays, these are like big office printers where multiple books can queue."

Leading Blair upstairs, Mr. Martin continued, "These are all of the offices – sales, marketing, graphic design."

Moving up to the final floor, Mr. Martin paused outside a large office that overlooked the hills. His name was still in a placard on the door. "And these were the executive offices and meeting rooms. This place was an extension of home. My wife would call and get mad as I lost track of time the same as she would a husband tinkering in the garage."

"You built something really special, Mr. Martin," Blair said.

"I did," Mr. Martin conceded. "It was rough in the beginning. A boutique press. As we landed large education accounts we were able to grow quickly. We had some pretty good years. Then technology changed, bookstores closed…that's when I had to integrate with a large publishing house. They wanted access to our clients, not the shop. My deal was as long as I was here, the office and staff would be as well."

"You had a great run and helped give so many families jobs and memories in Evergreen," Blair said.

"Devil in the details. I held off retirement for years, much to my wife's dismay, just to hold this thing off a little longer. But, we knew this day would eventually come," Mr. Martin said. "Enough of memory lane, let's get your gingerbread contest to the presses! We can print everything on your list, even the posters and banners."

"That's wonderful. And thank you for sharing your story," Blair said.

"Thank you for listening to the nostalgic ramblings of an old man," Mr. Martin said. "Here, you can use my computer. It can connect to our entire system. I'll head down and get the machine and materials ready."

Blair nodded, sliding behind his desk. Placing her hands on the massive mahogany piece of furniture, she flipped the switch on the monitor and woke up Mr. Martin's computer by wiggling the mouse. The machine brought to life, she inserted her files.

When she input all of the print requests, Blair walked downstairs. Following the sounds of the machines whirring to life, the smell of inks permeating the air, she stood in the corner of the first floor production room.

She watched Mr. Martin glide from machine to machine. The man was certainly in his element. He followed the media through the process and inspected each output. Holding up a flier, he admired the design and scrutinized the quality before approvingly placing them in neat stacks.

When the machines had completed their tasks, the room once again fell silent. Mr. Martin ran his hands along the presses while his eyes moved around the room. There was a hint of sadness in his gaze, but there was a lot of pride as well.

As his eyes worked their way to the end of the room, he saw Blair.

Blair blushed, "I didn't want to disturb you."

"Not at all," Mr. Martin beamed. "Your printing is done. You did all this?"

Blair nodded.

"You do beautiful work. It is like a story on each page," Mr. Martin held up a poster. "This looks like Evergreen." A gingerbread town covered in snow with pine tree covered hills in the backdrop looked very much like the town of Evergreen itself, only made with cookies.

"Thank you," Blair said, joining Mr. Martin. "Thank you, again, for doing this."

"Thank you for bringing some joy back to this town. I didn't intend for all this hardship and the early shutdown right before the holidays was most certainly not my call," Mr. Martin said.

Blair nodded, "The town knows that. Your employees are very fond of you."

"I'm fond of them, too," Mr. Martin said. He looked around, the building fallen eerily quiet.

Finding protective folders for the print items, they packaged Blair's wares and headed towards the lobby, switching lights off as they went.

Blair could see Mr. Martin's heart was heavy when the last light was switched off and they stood outside the front door, his key in the lock.

"Had a good run," he said softly. Turning to Blair, he fished a card out of his pocket. "If there is ever anything I can do for you, don't hesitate to call. That's my personal number on there."

"Thank you, Mr. Martin. Merry Christmas!" Blair said.

"Merry Christmas!" Mr. Martin cast a glance at the building as he made his way to the car. With a sigh, he opened his door. Giving a wave to Blair, he disappeared inside.

Seventeen

Blair left the publishing house and working in tandem with Mayor Stowe and Mary Kay Albright, painted the town hotspots with posters, flyers, and counter tents for the gingerbread contest.

The last two sites were the coffee shop and her toy store. With the coffee shop bolstering the most traffic in town, she left most of the postcards and flyers there. On her own shop door and at the register, she put the final posters.

Mayor Stowe commissioned her maintenance crew to hang a banner on Main Street and one above the community center doors.

Entering the store, Blair found Nella straightening the shelves, humming to Christmas carols. "How was the day?"

Nella looked at Blair, "Quiet. The locals really appreciate the lower priced items up front. Most admitted to being afraid to bring their children in, knowing there wasn't much in their budgets this year. They didn't want to get their hopes up for things they knew weren't going to happen."

"We have a new Nativity," Blair noticed.

Nella nodded, "I told Luke one sold and the gentleman who came in earlier must have told his friends, because we had requests for two more sets."

"Wow," Blair nodded. "Good for Luke!"

Blair looked at the receipts. They were half us much as the year prior for the same day.

"Thanks for letting me run around. Hank Martin is such a nice gentleman," Blair declared.

"You're the boss, so…you can take off pretty much anytime you want and yes, yes he is," Nella said.

"I had no idea what to expect when I came to Evergreen this year. It has been so different and so much more than I ever anticipated," Blair admitted.

"What did you expect?" Nella asked.

Blair closed her eyes and opened them slowly. "I think I expected…a charming, though forgotten town, an old toy store, equally oozing with charm, but well past its prime."

Nella stopped, stunned, "That was brashly honest."

Blair suddenly paled, trying to reel back her impression.

"I get why that would be how Evergreen and The Toy Chest would seem that way, but now that you've been here, how would you describe it from your Madison Avenue perspective?" Nella asked.

Blair was pensive, "Evergreen isn't just a place on the map, it is a community that embraces all who step within its township as family, visitors and locals alike. For a special treat, visit at Christmas time when the shops and streets are easily mistaken for a Bavarian outpost or even Santa's village itself."

Nella was agape, "That is the most accurate and beautiful description of Evergreen I have ever heard. You should send that to Mayor Stowe."

"Maybe I will," Blair chuckled. Looking at Nella, "It's people like you, like Mary Kay, Mr. Martin, Kris, Loretta...*you* make this town special."

"Aww, that's so sweet," Nella gushed.

"Alright, my dear. Let's lock up and get you home to your sweeties," Blair suggested.

Nella began closing down the store, "You know, Sophie and Evan were asking when you and Luke were going to come over again. They want to play games with you."

"That sounds nice," Blair admitted. "Let's say, as soon as I can. You guys are coming to the gingerbread contest, right?"

"Yeah. I think my kiddos might win again," Nella grinned.

Blair laughed, "They probably will!"

When the register was cleared, Blair snatched the vacuum away from Nella, "Go home. That's an order!"

Nella smiled and saluted, "Yes, boss!"

Grabbing her things, Nella prepared to leave. "See you tomorrow!" Blair called.

"See you tomorrow, Blair!" Nella disappeared into the night.

Blair finished tidying up for the night and reporting their numbers. She sighed, Nella was spot on, they were fifty percent lower from sales the year before. Taking over the store in a struggling town was a losing proposition.

She would work hard to give the town a wonderful holiday and return home to New York feeling she had done what she could. Locking up and shutting down the lights, she walked back to the bed and breakfast.

There was something about returning to the Holly Bough Bed and Breakfast that felt like coming home. It was such a warm and friendly environment. The Christmas lights washed with the craftsman lighting, candles and fireplace was visually welcoming. The scents of the home were equally powerful. Holiday aromas of evergreen, pomegranate and hints of cinnamon permeated the air. The crackle of the fire and sounds of laughter completed the homey and festive environment.

The ever gallant Sam Marsten taking her coat and gracious Loretta greeting her in the hall added to the ambiance offered by the boutique residence.

"Hi, dear!" Loretta cooed. "Let me get you fixed up with something to eat and drink."

The bed and breakfast proprietor led Blair into the kitchen. "Tonight, we had cranberry-chile chicken, one of our holiday favorites," Loretta shared.

"Sounds fantastic. I'm not going to pull any punches, I'm famished!" Blair exclaimed.

"You won't go hungry here, I assure you," Loretta shared. "Grab the glasses, wine is on the table. Help yourself and pour a little for me, will you?"

Blair grabbed the glasses. She recognized the red wine from Luke's winery. "I've tasted this one. It's a good one," she declared, enthusiastically.

"One of my favorites, too," Loretta admitted.

Loretta brought a plate to the table and sat down next to Blair. "I heard you are heading the revival of the gingerbread contest, that's great!"

"I was inspired by Mary Kay Albright and some memories of my brother and I having a wonderful time at the contest," Blair said.

"You are a light in our little town cast in a bit of a fog," Loretta eloquated.

"I'm just happy to be here," Blair ducked her head towards her plate of food.

Loretta laughed, "Lots of people are happy to *be* here. You are *living* the Evergreen way."

Scooping a forkful of cranberry chicken, Blair said, "I will take that as a very big compliment."

"As intended, my dear," Loretta cooed.

When Blair was finished, they took their wine glasses to the living room. Sam and their guests were fully engaged in a card game. Loretta and Blair book-ended the doorway and watched the families play together.

Blair smiled at the interactions between the siblings. They would support each other, coach each other, tease each other all at the same time. The glances of affection towards their parents while they played together were precious.

Families, once strangers, mingled around the living room. Conversations that would never have otherwise found their voice if not for assembling to play a game at a quaint bed and breakfast in the snowy foothills of a little Christmas village. The setting at Christmas only made the scene more beautiful.

"What's it like here the rest of the year?" Blair asked.

Loretta looked at Blair, "The daily activities change. Families go hiking, kayaking or rafting. Couples come for quiet retreats. Writers book weeks at a time to finish their manuscripts. Nighttime is much like this, though usually around the firepit out back. The games change from cards and charades to horseshoes and corn hole. The treats from Christmas cookies to s'mores."

"Sounds nice," Blair said.

"Don't get me wrong, Christmas is a magical time of year," Loretta added. "There is nothing else quite like it. The anticipation the children have, the carols, the decorations, the traditions. Christmas is special. Life here at the Holly Bough, aside from raising Luke, has been a blessing."

Blair admired the warm look that enveloped Loretta as she reflected on her bed and breakfast. The moment was shattered by a buzzing in her pocket. Sliding out her phone, she looked at the screen. "Excuse me," she said to Loretta who nodded.

Scampering into the kitchen, away from the families having fun in the living room, Blair answered, "Hello."

"Blair, it's Candace Barrows, with Lorent," the voice answered back.

"Candace, it's a pleasure to connect," Blair responded, suddenly aware she wasn't sure if she was supposed to call her 'Candace' or 'Ms. Barrows'.

"I hope I'm not interrupting anything," Candace said. "I know Mr. Lorent said we could kick things off in January, but I wanted to get a head start before the holidays, so that we may make a positive impression with him and the board."

"Okay, what do you have in mind?" Blair asked.

"I was hoping we could meet at your offices in New York. I'd like to have some storyboards ready to present," Candace said.

Blair frowned at the phone, hating to say anything but the words 'yes' to a request from anyone at Lorent, "I'm sorry. That won't be possible. I am across the country…on business."

"Hmm. I see. I thought Lorent was your priority after completing your last assignment," Candace said, her voice terse.

"Just using the window to close out a few outstanding items so that my full, one hundred percent attention is on Lorent," Blair sang.

"Very well, working remotely will have to do. We could conference call a few hours today to get the boards done. I could have them printed here and have them waiting in the boardroom for their return after the New Year holiday," Candace said.

Blair hit the mute button and sighed. She knew to do a project such as this one to Lorent's standards, she would need to work through Christmas. Fortunately, she sketched out several preliminary ideas on the plane flight out to Washington. "Sure, that should not be a problem…," Blair started.

"Blair…Blair…are you still there?" Candace called into the phone.

Blair gasped and fumbled for the mute button, "I'm sorry. Yes, it should not be a problem. They will only be preliminary."

"Prefect. I knew I could count on you," Candace said. "Happy holidays!"

"Merry Christmas," Blair said, but the phone had already fallen silent.

A wave of anxiety washed over Blair. Closing her eyes tight, she knew she would need to devote all of her free time to working on the boards. She could sketch on her laptop and send Candace digital proofs. There was a lot of work to be done.

Blair said goodnight to Loretta, Sam and the guests and headed up to her room. Sliding behind the writing desk, she pulled out her laptop and situated herself to work on the storyboards for Lorent.

As she laid her fingers on the keyboard, Blair thought deeply, trying to conjure up the mindset for work. Her eyes drifted towards the window, peering outside as snowfall gently drifted down, shining off the Christmas lights strung from the roof. It was a scene that reminded her of her childhood.

She pictured a scene with snow falling, silver and blue elements dazzling as Lorent's product family was displayed on a sheet of ice. Grinning to herself, it was not at all the original plan she had. A man and woman, dressed elegantly in Paris, New York and Monaco drawn only closer together by the allure of Lorent. She liked her new plan better. It was different. Nothing Lorent had used before.

Before she could dive into her new storyboard concept, her phone rang. Blair hesitated to answer. "I already feel stressed enough," she muttered, suddenly finding it odd that was the thought that went through her head.

"Hi, Todd," she relented.

"Blair, how's it going in the great wide wilderness?"

The quip was somewhat friendlier than the last, so Blair let it slide. "It's nice," she admitted. "I got to work on a project with the owner of that publishing house that is shutting down."

"Like a marketing plan? For liquidation?" Todd asked.

Blair laughed, "No, nothing like that. I am hosting a gingerbread contest for the town. I'd like to give something back to them they're missing during this hard time."

The phone went silent.

"A gingerbread contest? You're hosting it? How do you have the funds and the time to do that?" Todd asked.

"I don't know, really. I know that's not what 'my finance guy' boyfriend wants to hear. Things move a little slower out here, though the days are long with evening events almost every night. Some of the contest items are supported by other members in the community. What the store can't afford, I'll pay for myself," Blair said. "It makes me feel a little better about having to sell."

"I get that, I guess," Todd conceded. "What is that doing for your timeline coming home?"

"No change, just another event to squeeze in while I'm here," Blair said. "Though Lorent called. Candace Barrows wanted to meet in New York to complete storyboards for her to have in Paris by New Year's."

"How is that going to work?"

"I told her I could provide everything they needed remotely, and she and I could video chat as needed," Blair said.

"Blair, are you sure about this? I agree with Candace Barrows, maybe it is time you came home. You said it yourself, this is a client of a lifetime. The store sale is in your realtor's hands. I'm sure people there would understand," Todd pressed.

"I'm getting there, I just need a little more time. I really can manage the account from here," Blair defended.

Todd pressed, "Your future is here. Maybe even Paris. I tell you what. Come home. Spend Christmas in Manhattan. I'll take some time off afterwards. We can fly to Paris over New Year's and inspire you as you work on the Lorent campaign."

Blair was stunned, "You never take time off work."

"This is important to you. You're important to me," Todd said.

"That's very sweet," Blair said.

"Well…what do you say? Do I book our flights?"

Blair paused, staring at the phone, "Let me sleep on it. I am way too exhausted to be making major plans. And my brain is on a new concept for the Lorent campaign."

"See, this is perfect. You'll get to shape the final vision in the cities that sing Lorent elegance," Todd said.

"Actually," Blair admitted. "The inspiration came right from the window of this little bed and breakfast."

Todd sighed, "Pack that inspiration and hop on a flight."

"We'll see. Good night, Todd."

"Good night, Blair.

Blair hung up and stared at her phone. Her attention soon swung her gaze back to the gentle snow outside her window. It snowed in New York, but it never seemed as peaceful and calm as it did drifting outside her window in Evergreen. She remembered as a girl watching the snow fall and felt much the same then. An overwhelming sense of contentment fell over her.

Looking at the Christmas lights and reflecting on the conversation with Todd, she tried to get her mind back on the Lorent account. The snow and ice concept excited her, but a different thought began tugging on her mind. She pictured snow people racing to complete their ensemble for the Christmas pageant.

Blair knew she had work to do, but she pushed her laptop away and began scribbling furiously in a notepad. Not of cosmetics and perfumes, but of snowmen and families playing together. She was suddenly inspired to leave the town of Evergreen with a gift, if she could figure out how to get it finished in time for Christmas.

Eighteen

Despite not getting a lot of sleep, Blair strode to open The Toy Chest with a bounce in her step. She forced herself to sketch out the basics of her new idea for Lorent while her mind kept straying towards the snowman game.

Sliding her key into the door, she swung it open and hurried into the store. Flipping on lights and getting Christmas carols playing, she pulled out her laptop and notes.

She woke with what she thought might have been the missing mechanic for the game and wanted to get the concept on paper to see if she could make it work. She had a few ideas in mind to get it put together with a little help before Christmas.

Scribbling furiously, she worked on her notes and diagrams while flipping on her laptop. She tried to force herself to open the Lorent account information, but as she looked at what she had just laid out, she grinned. Picking up the phone, she made a hasty call.

Nella found Blair humming happily behind her laptop as she arrived at the toy store. Despite dark circles under her eyes, the toy shop owner seemed in joyful spirits.

"Whatcha working on?" Nella asked as she peered into the office.

"A little surprise for the town. I hope to unveil it at the gingerbread contest," Blair said, looking up from her computer.

"The days before Christmas are starting to get busy. I think it is a good thing though, cheery distractions," Nella mused. "You want me to kick off opening the store so that you can finish up your mystery project?"

"Do you mind? I shouldn't be long, though I may have to run an errand later," Blair said.

"Not at all. You're the boss...like figure," Nella grinned.

Blair smiled and focused on her computer, helping her ideas to form digital life.

She didn't know how long she had been buried in her work when Nella gently rapped on her door. "Someone has requested your presence," Nella announced.

Peering over Nella's shoulder, Luke's smiling face bobbed.

"Hey, Luke," Blair turned her head.

"Hey," Luke bobbed his head. "I was wondering if I could borrow you for a bit."

Nella shrugged. The store traffic was steady but not overwhelming.

Blair looked confused, but not at the request as much as her own jumbled to-do list. "I just finished up something and need to run an errand…"

"Great!" Luke bounced on his feet a bit. "I'll drive you."

Frowning, Blair replied, "Yeah. Okay. As long as it doesn't take too long."

Luke shifted his lips nervously, and replied rather non-convincingly, "Probably not too long."

"You're good?" Blair asked.

Nella nodded.

"Alright. For a little while. What's this about?" Blair asked, grabbing her coat and a zip drive from her computer.

"You'll see," Luke mischievously avoided answering. With a raised brow, he inspected Blair's feet, "What shoe size are you? Ah, never mind."

Blair cast a look over her shoulder towards Nella who just grinned and shrugged. Reluctantly, she followed Luke, though her own mission on the way gave her a boost of haste.

Luke helped Blair into the passenger seat of his truck. As he slid behind the wheel, he looked at Blair and asked, "Where to?"

"The publishing house," Blair said, her voice flat.

"The publishing house?" Luke frowned. "I'm sorry to say it's closed."

"I know," Blair grinned, "I can be mysterious too!"

"Very well," Luke turned the key in the ignition.

Driving to the publishing house, Luke parked out front. Once again, Mr. Martin was waiting out front and excitedly waved them in.

"Hi, Mr. Martin!"

"Hello, Luke. Blair, I didn't know you had a partner in this?" Mr. Martin asked.

Luke flexed the lapels on his coat, "I'm the transportation end of the operation."

Mr. Martin laughed, "I see. Nice to see you. My grandchildren, and I believe their parents, are going to be thrilled with those toy boxes. They are something."

"Thank you. I hope so," Luke said. "I thought you were going out of town?"

"For round two of the holiday. I am happy to say, round one is in our home in beautiful Evergreen," Mr. Martin said.

"Thank you so much for doing this, Mr. Martin," Blair said.

The retired publisher looked at Blair, "To give a little back to the people of Evergreen, I am overjoyed to be a part of it. You just make me ponder whether I left the game with a little reserve still in the tank. I enjoy coming here and spinning up the presses."

"I was surprised you had all the capabilities that I needed," Blair said.

"Oh, sure. We could create the full marketing package for book launches and academic programs. We made everything from bookmarks to boxes to dynamic charts," Mr. Martin said, a great deal of pride in his voice.

Luke frowned, "Dynamic charts?"

"Yeah, you know…like where you take multiple layers of cardstock print material and you can spin the outer edges to reveal information in various boxes when the tabs correlate," Mr. Martin said.

Luke's eyes widened, "I know, I had one on the solar system. When I moved the tab to each planet, the boxes would change to show that planet's specs like how big it was and how far away from the sun or earth."

"That's right. We might have even made that one," Mr. Martin gleamed. Turning to Blair, Mr. Martin nodded towards the stairs leading to his office, "You know the drill by, now. Feel free to use my computer. I'm sure there are some on this level, but I'd be darned if I know what the passwords are."

Blair nodded, holding the zip drive in the air.

When she disappeared, Mr. Martin turned towards Luke, "So, you and Ms. Cooper seem quite chummy."

"She has a boyfriend," Luke stated, rocking back on his heels, his hands burrowing into his coat pockets.

Mr. Martin seemed to not be convinced, "Hmph!"

Flipping on the machines that Blair was going to need, Mr. Martin wandered around the print room locating the stock for the machines.

"Hmph?" Luke questioned the old publisher.

"There's an affinity between you two," Mr. Martin said, loading a tray with cardboard stock.

Luke frowned, "We're friendly…we're friends."

"Mm…hmm," Mr. Martin said as he mashed a glowing green button on a machine. "I've seen enough budding relationships in my time overseeing staff over the years to recognize it."

"Flattering as that might be, I feel there are more complications with this one," Luke said.

Mr. Martin stopped and eyed Luke who just shrugged and shook his head.

Taking the hint, that Luke knew more than he about Blair, he focused on getting the machines ready. Within minutes, the first one's green light began blinking and the press came to life as the scrolls began to spin.

Mr. Martin followed the line as the cardstock weaved its way through the various belts and rollers until it spit out a sheet in the end tray. Mr. Martin held it up, studying the print before walking to a screen attached to the machine, made a few fine adjustments and hit a button. Repeating the process, he nodded with satisfaction and hit yet another button as the machine began whirring out sheet after sheet of the media.

Luke sauntered over to peek at the finished product as Mr. Martin moved on to tend to the next machine.

"It's a game," Blair announced, nearly making Luke jump. "I came up with it last night and I thought it would be a nice send off from m…Mr. Martin for the community."

Luke held up the stock that he realized would be for the game box. Astonished, he turned to Blair, "You came up with this last night?"

"Yeah," Blair nodded, a broad smile crossing her lips.

"This is incredible. It looks like a game you'd find in your toy store," Luke said.

Blair tilted her head, "You think? I just purchased some stock artwork and cobbled it all together."

"It looks great," Luke nodded.

"Thanks. I hope it plays great," Blair said.

"If it is anything like what we played the other night, it will be fantastic," Luke said.

They followed the various machines to where Mr. Martin was fiddling with particularly complicated looking machine. "This is the computer-aided router. This will make the cut-outs you needed."

Blair picked up a sheet and punched a playing piece out, "This is so cool."

"Yeah. You can do that with just about anything. We even have a 3-D printer. You'd need a cast model, the computer will scan it and then layer material to create an exact facsimile," Mr. Martin beamed.

Blair admired the joy and passion the man had for his work, "You really kept up with the times."

"Had to stay relevant for as long as we could," the publisher admitted.

"Well, this is all turning out fantastic. Thank you," Blair said.

Mr. Martin looked directly at Blair, "Thank you for putting this together for the town. And for taking over your grandparents' shop. The more icons we lose around here, the harder it will be for Evergreen to keep its identity and not become just another small town rest stop along the highway."

"I'm glad to do what I can. The future…is a bit harder to understand," Blair said.

Luke cast her a glance as the words clamored around the print shop room.

"Well, that's the last piece to print. I have assembly tables over there. If we all roll up our sleeves, it shouldn't take long to put all this together," Mr. Martin suggested as he carried a stack of cardboard sheets of meeples to a row of tables.

Blair set up the order of materials and the trio soon picked up a rhythm of packaging items together into a box. Mr. Martin found a stack of shipping boxes the finished products were placed in. When five containers were filled, they stepped back and appreciated their effort.

"That is a game for every household in Evergreen, with a few to spare," Mr. Martin said. "Just one request. May I take one for my family?"

"Of course! I'd be honored," Blair said. "Thank you again for opening up the shop and donating the materials."

"My sincerest pleasure," Mr. Martin said, grabbing a game box.

Luke found a handcart and stacked the shipping containers on board and wheeled it behind Mr. Martin as he led them back out of the publishing house. After loading the containers in the back of Luke's truck, they waved goodbye to Mr. Martin.

Blair turned to Luke, "Thank you for your help."

"Glad to. You and Mr. Martin are doing a nice thing," Luke said.

"Pales to what the people of Evergreen really need," Blair shrugged.

"What they need most now is hope and compassion and community. This is a gesture of all of that," Luke said. Climbing in the truck, he asked, "Where are we going to take all of these?"

"I figured the community center. The town could give them out at the gingerbread contest," Blair suggested.

Luke scrunched his face, "How about, you give them out at The Toy Chest? It would bring people downtown and along the shops. It would be a symbol of the legacy that your grandparents' left behind."

Blair gushed, "I don't want it to be about me."

"It won't be. I mean, there will be an element of you and there should be. It will be about the town. The small shops that struggled this season. Think about it, a toy store giving away games. A pretty good one, too," Luke grinned.

"I'll think about it," Blair said.

"Good," Luke started the truck. "Now for *my* phase of the journey."

Blair shot Luke a curious look but relented to see where he was going to take her. She was surprised when Luke started to drive out of town. "Should I be worried?" she scowled.

Luke chuckled, "Nope. We're not going far, in fact, here we are."

Just outside of downtown Evergreen was a ring of trees strung with Christmas lights. Several booths were set up within the ring of trees as families bundled up walked hand in hand or drinking cocoa on the edge of a clearing.

Blair looked thoughtful, straining her memory, "I've been here before..."

"Come on," Luke urged, climbing out of the truck.

As they neared the clearing, Blair began to recognize where Luke had taken her. Her eyes lit, "We're going skating?"

"You any good?" Luke asked.

"It's been a while. I skated once at Rockefeller the first year I was in New York, but not since," Blair said. "How about you? Come out here often?"

Luke shook his head. "No. Always wanted to. Thought it would be a nice Burl Ives moment."

Blair cocked her head, "That's 'Holly Jolly' and Sam the Snowman. I think you mean Currier and Ives."

"Yeah, the Christmas cards," Luke nodded sheepishly.

Finding the skate rental booth, they ordered their sizes. Spying a bench overlooking the frozen pond, they watched the skaters. Graceful ones streamed through bands of the slow and unsteady. Couples held hands as they made their loops. Parents guided their children grasping their mitten clad palms.

Blair watched Luke as his large frame tried to balance on the blades of his skates. She cast a scrutinizing glance at his wobbly on-land form. "Are you going to be alright?"

"Yeah, just need to get to the ice," Luke said, spreading his arms out to improve his balance as he tiptoed to the edge of the pond. Instinctively, Blair caught his arm to steady him as he hit the ice.

Luke grinned and to Blair's surprise, he glided gracefully out onto the ice. Following, Blair pushed off, her blades slicing along the surface catching up to him.

"I thought you hadn't done this?" she asked.

"I haven't skated *here*," Luke said, skillfully spinning to face her as he skated backwards. "Played a little hockey back in high school, though."

Blair cocked her head confused, "You looked a little wonky when you laced up."

"Oh, yeah!" Luke laughed. "Never did get the hang of walking in skates. My teammates used to laugh at me. Gave my opponents false confidence, though!"

Blair's eyes widened as a father and daughter tumbled in their path. Grabbing Luke's hand, she spun him around and away from the impending collision. The sudden change in direction spun them. Clinging to each other, they fought to control their momentum until they were still. Face to face, they looked at each other, their hearts racing as the father apologized and thanked them for their quick avoidance maneuver.

Blair looked up at Luke, her hands clasping his jacket. His arms had wrapped around her as they had taken evasive action.

"Nice save," Luke said, his voice soft.

Letting go of her grip on his jacket, Luke released her from his arms. Grasping her hand, he spun her away and pulled her along as they resumed their circuit around the pond, this time with all eyes forward.

Catching up to the father and daughter, they slowed. "You guys alright?" Luke asked.

The father looked sheepish while the young girl looked up, "Dad's not very good at this. But I like that he's trying!"

Luke and Blair laughed as they skated forward. Blair liked the grip Luke had on her hand, but reluctantly withdrew it.

Nineteen

Blair and Luke traded in their skates for cups of cocoa. Slowly walking a little trail that weaved through the lit trees and encircled the pond, they watched the skaters. Blair recognized several families as Evergreen residents. When she and Luke rented their skates, she overheard the booth attendant let families know they could skate for free if they couldn't afford it.

Quietly, Blair marveled at the people of Evergreen. Many, if not all, had lost their jobs. While they had to be under unyielding pressure and stress, they didn't let it suppress their holiday spirit. Their drive to enjoy their time together as families, couples and community was inspiring.

As she enjoyed the quaintness, she was torn. She knew she was doing the right thing by selling and allowing the developers to build and create jobs to replace the ones they lost. A part of her was concerned that the Christmas village of Evergreen might not ever be the same afterwards.

"It's nice out here, thank you for taking me," Blair said, looking up at Luke.

"It was fun," Luke nodded.

"I know there are things like skating and parks with lit trees in New York. When I first moved there, I sought each experience out," Blair said, looking nostalgic.

Luke slowed his walk as they rounded the far end of the pond. "It sounds nice. I've never been, but the images of New York at Christmas have their appeal."

"Life in the city. Most cities, I think, takes hold. There is such a frenzy to survive. Competition and opportunity are equally abundant. You perform well, scrap your way to make a name for yourself, but you know there are a thousand similarly qualified applicants nipping at your heels, ready to replace you. It can take the fun out of things. Work becomes paramount so that you can keep up with the rent," Blair sighed.

"You must be excited, then to…move into the small town haven of Evergreen," Luke studied Blair and her response.

Blair froze. Squeezing her eyes tight, she turned away.

Collecting herself, she opened her eyes and faced Luke.

"Luke," she sighed. "I'm not moving to Evergreen. The store…I came to sign for it. And then sell it."

Luke observed Blair quietly for a moment.

To Blair's surprise, Luke nodded.

Raising an eyebrow and cocking her head to the side, she looked at him.

"I know," Luke admitted.

"You know?" Blair asked.

"You have evaded questions regarding the store and your future and moving to Evergreen since you arrived," Luke shared.

Blair was astonished, "I...I didn't mean to mislead anyone. The realtor wanted me to make the shop look serviceable. And then Nella arrived wanting to work and the next thing you know..."

"You're skating around a pond on a non-date with a stranger three thousand miles away from your real home," Luke smiled.

"Yeah," Blair nodded. "It's just being here. Being part of the community..."

"Evergreen has its effect on people," Luke shrugged. "Trust me. I had no intention of moving back once I left. I felt pulled, drawn."

"There is a real estate developer. He wants to buy the store, buy more properties along Main Street. It can provide jobs for those that lost theirs due to the closing of the publishing house," Blair said. "It will be different, but people can make a living. Families like Nella's won't have to move from their homes."

Luke looked dubious, "Buy properties along Main Street and do what with them?"

Blair shook her head and said in almost a whisper, "Make a travel center."

Luke choked, "A travel center…like a truck stop?"

"Sort of, but…," Blair started.

"That would fundamentally change Evergreen. Forever," Luke scoffed and took a step away from Blair. "I thought you'd sell to maybe someone who wanted to keep it a toy store. I never imagined it would be the catalyst for paving over Evergreen."

Blair stared at the lights hung on the tree as evening seeped in early in the winter sky. "I can't control what people do with the property once they purchase it," Blair defended.

"But you can elect not to sell it to buyers where their intentions are known," Luke snapped.

"The town needs jobs. I need to get back to New York. What else can I do?" Blair gasped.

"That's why you made the game. You felt guilty. Like somehow that token would make up for selling," Luke said.

"For leaving," Blair corrected.

They both fell silent for a moment.

"What should I do?" Blair pleaded.

"I can't tell you that," Luke said. "You need to do what is right for you."

He looked into Blair's eyes; the sparkle that had lit them had vanished just as the sun hid beyond the western ridge. "I should get you back," he said quietly.

"Luke!" Blair breathed, placing her hand on his chest. Looking up, she fought for the right words to say or a fragment of inspiration in his eyes, but they too had lost their shine. Dulled, vacant, they had already taken several steps back.

"I see the conflict in you. I've been there before myself. You need to decide whether your life is in Manhattan or here in Evergreen," Luke said. Without waiting for a response, he began walking her back to his truck.

The ride back to the shop was quiet. The air hung heavy amidst the painfully obvious lack of cheeriness Luke had typically displayed. Even as he helped Blair unload the cartons of games, he barely said anything more than the simplest of responses.

He waved to Nella, shot a glance at Blair and walked away.

"What happened between you two?" Nella gaped as she took in the scene.

"The truth," Blair said softly. "If you want to go home to your family, I can finish up here."

Nella frowned at Blair, "You're sure? You need to talk, I can stay..."

Blair shook her head, "No. I need time to think."

"Scott got a job offer," Nella said.

"He did?" Blair's affect instantly improved.

Nella nodded and then her head drooped, "It's over two hours away. We'd have to move."

"Oh," Blair said, crestfallen once again.

"It's just the start of the search, we'll see what turns up," Nella shrugged. "See you tomorrow, Blair."

"Goodnight, Nella."

As Blair watched Nella leave, even the joyful Christmas tunes over the store's record player and jubilant trappings of the store did little to lift her spirits. While she shared the same concerns Luke did about Evergreen, she was more concerned about families like Nella's being forced to leave their homes.

Twenty

Blair sat at the writing desk in her room. Her head in her hands, her mind felt like it physically ached. Her trip to Evergreen was supposed to be a simple task, but it opened up such a complicated and convoluted trove of competing thoughts, questions and dilemmas.

When her phone rang, she reluctantly lifted her head. In truth, she didn't want to talk to anyone unless they held the magical answers for her. Seeing Candace Barrow's name pop up in her screen did not encourage her to pick it up.

Relenting, she hit the answer button, "Hello, Candace."

"Blair, I was hoping to have something from you today," the Lorent Communication Director snapped.

"I've…made strides. I played with some designs, even worked with a local print ship to review some artwork.

I have a few adjustments to make and I will put them into a digital portfolio for you," Blair said. Her mind reeling as she had in fact done those things, but not for the cosmetics giant.

"Hmm. Sounds promising, but if I can't see it myself, I can't present it, now can I?" Candace said. "Why don't you fire off what you have so far, and we can review it while on the phone right now."

Blair responded meekly, "I'm really not ready to do that. I am playing with taking the campaign in a new direction. I wanted to be satisfied myself before I shared it."

Candace paused on her end of the phone. "You are making me very concerned, Ms. Cooper. How about you walk me through this new direction of yours," Candace demanded.

"Every big cosmetics and fragrance company uses elegant dates. Luxury vehicles, art galleries, elegant gowns to market their products," Blair started.

Candace cut her off, "That's because we offer a luxury item. We are a luxury brand."

"What if we take that elegance and make it more approachable," Blair suggested. "Instead of gold and champagne as imagery, we use silver and blue. Ice and snow."

"We aren't selling peppermint sticks, Ms. Cooper," Candace snapped.

"Think about Christmas. An ice skating rink surrounded by lit trees. Snow gently blowing across the ice revealing Lorent's newest products. Classy, yet different from everyone else," Blair suggested.

"Go on, I'm listening. I am starting to understand the color palette, but what is the message?" Candace urged. "I encourage you to go back and look at the other campaigns that we have done. Pearls, diamonds and champagne. Gold gowns and elegant nights out, that is our brand persona. That is the industry image tested and true for decades."

"That's the point. Set Lorent apart. Shake up the market, reinvigorate. Let busy mothers feel as glamorous watching movies during date nights at home as much as the elegant gown images of stepping out of the luxury vehicle in front of the exclusive restaurant or event," Blair said.

"That isn't our audience," Candace said, the tone in her voice clearly inflecting she was unhappy with Blair's concept.

"The numbers show it is," Blair countered. "Sixty-four percent of Lorent sales are purchased in the suburbs by married women with children. Another twenty percent that are in urban markets are in brackets that are on the lower end of the economic scale for that geography. These are everyday women that want to feel glamorous and in fact do when they wear Lorent products. We won't divorce ourselves from the elegance, we'll weave the two together. Help Mom feel like she is in that gown in a ballroom even when she is in the living room with jeans on."

"I don't know. I can run it by Mr. Lorent, but I warn you, it might cost you the account. I'm open to reviewing your concept, but I'll need a complete storyboard by tomorrow," Candace said, and the phone went dead.

"She's nice," Blair mumbled, staring at the phone.

Scraping her hair out of her face, she opened up her laptop. She breathed deep. She created most of what she shared with Candace on the fly while on the phone. Other than the ice concept and color palettes, she had done nothing on the campaign.

Looking at the clock, she knew she had a long night ahead of her. With Candace several time zones ahead of her, Blair cursed, "What is she, a vampire?"

Staring at the computer screen, she was flustered. She had worked her entire career for this moment. She should be excited to sink her teeth into the project. Instead, she found herself thinking about the store and the town of Evergreen. She thought about her walk with Luke and the difficult conversation they had.

She wondered where things stood between them as Luke was clearly unhappy with sale of the store. She thought of Nella and her family on the precipice of moving away from the home that they love.

Opening the files on Lorent, she began clicking through the images and lining them up on a series of slides for the storyboard. She pictured a Christmas village with husbands and wives, boyfriends and girlfriends walking hand in hand. The men soaking in the radiance of their loved ones as they window shopped, the hint of Lorent fragrance clinging to their coats.

Blair typed furiously at the scene, reflecting on all of the Christmas romance movies she watched and putting those scenes in her head to convey warmth and romance and elegance that she could tie to Lorent.

She barely realized she had done so; Blair opened a second folder. A Christmas village theme with a family making their way through the town enjoying all things Christmas from snowmen to ice skating to cups of cocoa and candy canes. Built around a giant Christmas tree, sleigh bells ringing on horse drawn carriages, bake shops with gingerbread and even a toy shop filled the page.

As she worked through the details and set the objective, Blair felt as though she were forging ahead on her assignment, making sound progress. When she pushed back and took a sip of tea which had long since cooled, she was stunned with what she had created.

Seeing the tab below for Lorent, she was hovering over the second tab she had worked so feverishly on. She had sketched together another game.

Hitting the Lorent tab, she swallowed hard. While she had made some progress, there was a whole night's worth of work to get the storyboards ready to send to Candace.

With a heavy sigh, Blair pushed away from her desk. Swirling the tea cup, she realized she was going to need a lot more than tepid tea to get her through the night. Tiptoeing down the stairs, she made her way into the kitchen and stared at the coffee pot.

As Blair began fiddling in the cupboards, a soft voice called from behind her, "Need something dear?"

Blair spun, her hands to her chest, "Loretta. I'm so sorry. Did I wake you?"

"Years of being a mother, I am afraid it is a virtuous curse. But don't mind that. I'm happy to assist," Loretta said.

"I was trying to make some coffee," Blair said, casting a glance at the coffee maker.

"Now *that* is an easy matter to resolve," Loretta said. Pulling out a drawer, she revealed a filter and began scooping beans into the sieve. "Well, now that's doing its job, what's troubling you?"

"Who says I'm troubled?" Blair countered.

"That dour expression in the wee hours of the night searching for coffee for starters," Loretta declared.

Blair looked at the bed and breakfast proprietor like a child that had been caught stealing Christmas cookies. "Yes, I suppose that is a fair deduction," she admitted.

"So…?" Loretta pressed.

Blair scrunched her nose, "It's complicated."

"If it wasn't, it wouldn't be keeping you up, now would it?" Loretta cooed.

Blair hesitated.

"My worlds from the east and west coast collided and now they are tearing me apart," Blair admitted.

Loretta studied Blair, with a sympathetic raise of her eyebrow, she asked, "Boy trouble?"

Blair scoffed, "That is the least of my worries. No, it is much more than that."

"Hmm," Loretta thought. "Change is always difficult."

"It's not just that. My own changes are one thing. I can manage those, I think. It is other changes and the ripple effects that those changes have on others. Those are the complicating elements that are keeping me up," Blair shared.

"Care to talk about it? Sometimes sharing your thoughts can help you discover you already have the answers locked somewhere inside," Loretta suggested.

Blair looked as though she wanted to talk, but she was not sure how even sweet Loretta might take the position Blair found herself in with respect to Evergreen and the real estate and The Toy Chest.

"Then again, there is always one confidant that has helped me through tough times," Loretta said.

Blair looked questioningly at Loretta.

"Pray on it dear," Loretta said. "When times are tough and answers are unclear, I pray on it."

"Oh, I haven't prayed for years. Since I was a kid," Blair said.

"It's never too late," Loretta assured. "Well, here's your coffee. Don't stay up too late. I find sleeping on a problem can deliver better results than slaving on it when you are deathly tired. Good night, Blair."

"Good night, Loretta."

Blair grabbed her cup, shut off the kitchen lights and headed back upstairs.

Retreating to her room, she shut the door carefully to not make a sound. Sitting behind her desk, both hands wrapped around the coffee, she curled her legs into her chair. Staring out the window at the nighttime flurry sparkling in the Christmas lights, she closed her eyes describing her problem to the heavenly host.

Twenty One

Blair woke, crumpled and hunched over her desk. Pushing herself up, she looked at her computer screen. Aside from a couple of sentences and thousands of 'k's from sleeping on the keyboard, she had not gotten very far into her Lorent storyboard. Glancing at her coffee, she saw that she hadn't made it very far into that, either.

Picking up her phone, she confirmed, night had slipped by and her alarm was about to alert her to a new day. Pulling her hair back and rubbing her eyes, she leaned back in the desk chair.

With a heavy sigh, she grabbed her cold coffee cup and turned the bottom towards the ceiling while she drained the mug in one fuel-injected gulp. She had no magical overnight interventions, inspirations or answers to her questions. Prayers tried but as of yet, unmet.

Shaking the multitude of kinks that she endured from the horrendous sleeping position, Blair cracked her knuckles, stretched a few sitting yoga poses and bellied up to her laptop.

With rejuvenated speed and focus, she hammered out her Lorent storyboard draft. Glancing at the time, up against Candace's imposed deadline, Blair reviewed her presentation. It was considerably rougher than what she would like to present, especially to a client like Lorent.

Blair's finger hovered over the send key. Reluctantly, she pressed it. Her heart sank, "Well, there goes my career."

A soft knock at the door almost made Blair jump.

"Yes?" Blair called.

"It's Loretta."

"Coming!" Blair said, getting up from her desk and crossing the room to open the door.

The charming hotelier stood in the hallway with a tray held out in front of her. "You didn't come down for your breakfast, so I figured your late night had persisted," Loretta said.

"Late night turned in to frantic morning," Blair admitted. "I had to take care of a few things from back in New York. Thank you for this."

"No problem," Loretta pushed through and set the tray down on Blair's writing desk. Spinning, she gave Blair a once over. With a grin, she observed, "My stars, I haven't seen a look like that since my less reverent days of my youth."

"That bad, huh?" Blair yawned.

"No worse than Mary after travelling all night and sleeping in a hay barn, I suppose," Loretta quipped.

"Hopefully I don't smell like I slept with animals," Blair grimaced.

"Nothing a nice warm shower won't fix," Loretta smiled.

Blair looked at Loretta, "I took your advice last night."

Loretta eyed Blair, "Which part, surely not the get a goodnight sleep part. Otherwise, I need to get better at giving advice."

Blair laughed, "I prayed on my…issues. And then promptly fell asleep at my desk."

"Good," Loretta looked pleased.

"No revelations, sadly," Blair admitted.

"Well, those things tend to come in time," Loretta promised.

"I hope so," Blair took a sip of hot coffee that she enjoyed definitively more than the cold cup. "I think I turned in a career ender this morning."

Loretta looked serious, "There is a season for all things. You just have to be ready to accept that it is fall when the leaves let go or winter when the snow falls, whether you think you're ready for that season or not."

Blair looked at Loretta through her cloudy, troubled-sleep vision, "Yeah. I guess you're right. Are you coming to the gingerbread contest today?"

"That's right. You have another full plate today. I wouldn't miss it for the world. The ladies have been talking about it all week. I haven't seen them so excited in a long time," Loretta confessed. "It is a wonderful thing you are doing. You injected new life into a town that was struggling. Quite the addition to our little Christmas hamlet."

"I don't know that I have done anything too special. Just listening to the town and helping continue some traditions, that's all," Blair protested.

"Delivering love, care and hope to an entire community sounds pretty special to me," Loretta said. "I'll leave you to your breakfast and see you at the community center this afternoon."

"Thank you, Loretta," Blair said.

Loretta winked and shut the door behind her.

Glancing at the breakfast plate, Blair excitedly dove in. She wasn't much of a breakfast eater, but her weary body craved fuel.

Blair and Nella shut The Toy Chest down, leaving the lights and music playing, hanging a sign saying that they'll reopen after the gingerbread contest.

Arriving at the community center, they were in awe with how quickly the Ladies' Auxiliary put the building together. The stage was adorned with several decorated trees, each with its own theme, each beautiful.

A giant gingerbread house and several gingerbread people dominated the rest of the stage. Around the room, evergreen boughs, candy canes and stars dressed the large room.

Blair found Mary Kay, lording over the décor. "Mary Kay, this is astounding!"

Mary Kay smiled and looked around, "It is quite beautiful."

"How did you put all this together?" Blair was amazed.

"I'd like to say the ladies and I are just that efficient," Mary Kay said. "Truth be told, the elementary school used much of this for their Christmas program last week."

"Well, how can we help?" Blair asked.

Mary Kay glanced out at the vast empty space in front of the stage. "Younger souls such as you and Nella might be better equipped to set up the tables than my haggard old troop," Mary Kay admitted.

"Very well," Blair said. With a nod, she and Nella placed their things down and began tackling their part of the set up.

As they labored to set up the first table, they were surprised when two more tables were heaved behind them. Spinning, they found Luke and Scott, each with a table tucked under their arms.

"Honey, what are you doing here?" Nella bounced and gave her husband a hug when they had all set down their tables.

"The kids and I were going to come for the contest of course, but I got a call that suggested you might be able to use some help in advance," Scott said.

Nella frowned, "Where are the kids?"

"With my mom," Luke said, offering a quick smile before retreating to grab another table.

"The supplies are here!" Mary Kay called from the community center doors.

"Why don't you two work with the building materials, Luke and I will set up the tables," Scott offered.

Blair and Nella nodded and began orchestrating the placement of the deliveries. As Luke and Scott placed a table down, a lady from the auxiliary would quickly roll out festive table covering, ready to move on to the next.

With time to spare the volunteers stood in front of the stage, taking in their efforts while toasting mugs of candy cane-laced cocoa. Several contestant stations were arranged around the room where they would work back to back. The audience could move around the room from station to station to watch the gingerbread builders create.

"We did good," Mary Kay said, hoisting a mug in the air, her eyes locked on Blair.

"We did," Blair nodded.

Mayor Stowe popped her head through the doors on the far end of the room, "Are you ready for this?"

Blair glanced at her watch, "They're early."

Mary Kay smiled, "They're excited."

"Let's do this!" Blair exclaimed.

Mayor Stowe pushed open the door.

Luke hurried to help her usher people in while Nella's family selected their prize crafting station right in front of the stage.

Blair started to wander away from the spotlight herself, when Mary Kay grabbed her sleeve and yanked her back with surprising strength for an older woman. "Oh, no. Your idea, you are up here with me," Mary Kay declared.

Blair looked momentarily horrified but the mixed pleasantness and determination in Mary Kay's look incited Blair to comply.

Mayor Stowe joined the ladies on stage as the community center quickly filled up. Wrinkling her nose, she said, "You know, one thing we didn't determine was judges."

Blair looked stunned at the oversight.

Mary Kay just grinned, "I think the three of us *are* the judges."

As the room filled and the flow of new arrivals slowed, Mayor Stowe walked up to a hastily placed microphone patched into fixed speakers hanging from the community center walls.

With a big smile, Mayor Stowe called into the microphone, "Hello, Evergreen! It is so good to see the people of our town and our guests we get to share the season with come to what is really a revival of a forgotten event. Welcome to the great Evergreen Gingerbread House Build-off! This event, which involved many kind and capable hands, was largely spearheaded by these two lovely ladies beside me. Mary Kay Albright of the Evergreen Ladies' Auxiliary and Blair Cooper, proprietor of The Toy Chest!"

Mayor Stowe began clapping as she cast appreciative glances at the women sharing the stage with her. The crowded community center attendees joined her in applause.

Mary Kay stepped to the microphone, "I echo Mayor Stowe in welcoming you all to this cherished event. While my ladies and I helped put her vision together, this was all Blair's doing. Blair…"

The vacated microphone waited for a resistant Blair to step up. Realizing there was little choice with all eyes on her, she walked up to the microphone. "Merry Christmas, everyone! We are so excited to have you here and see what marvels you will have prepared over the next three hours starting…now!" Blair called into the microphone.

A monitor had been placed behind her with a counting down clock for all contestants to see.

"The rules are simple," Blair continued as the participants started taking stock of their wares. "You may use any of the ingredients and tools placed at your station. You are welcome to share with your fellow participants if you like. Other than that, build the best gingerbread display and have fun!"

Blair gladly descended from the stage, her face a few shades of crimson. Greeting people as she slipped into the crowd she watched the contestants dive into their opening tasks.

Stopping at Nella's table, her eyes grew wide, "Hi, Sophie and Evan. I'm excited to see what you're building."

"Hi, Blair!" Sophie looked up from her task of sorting by colors.

"Blair!" Evan smiled. His small hands wrapped around an icing bag. "I'm helping Dad with the walls. He calls it 'Mordor'."

"Mortar, buddy," Scott said.

Evan nodded at his dad and turned back to Blair, "When are you coming back over to play games?"

"I don't know. Maybe soon?" Blair glanced at Nella and shot her a wink. "Good luck, guys!"

Blair wandered the room, flowing in a circuit with the other delighted attendees. She greeted each table of contestants which included visitors and residents alike.

She reached one table with more helpers packed behind it than any other. A frenetic older man in a Santa hat did his best to retain order amongst his minions. "Mr. Martin?"

"Blair! How nice to see you. Wonderful event. Great turn out, too!" Mr. Martin beamed.

"Well, we had world class marketing materials," Blair quipped.

"That we did," Mr. Martin nodded.

Blair asked, "Who is the band of helpers you have there?"

"These are my grandchildren who could make it for Christmas day," Mr. Martin beamed and one by one, introduced them to Blair.

"It is wonderful to meet you all. Good luck and Merry Christmas!" Blair said.

As she continued to make her way around the room, she came to a table that gave her pause. It was already taking impressive shape. Looking up from the design, she found a familiar face smiling at her. "What do you think, so far?"

Blair looked at Loretta, "I think to this point, you might be the team to beat, but there is a long way to go."

Sam held up a gingerbread wall as a row of icing was carefully lined along its edge to steady the next piece, "This is fun. With all due respect, without the skillful Cooper kids to battle, I'm feeling pretty good about our chances."

Blair laughed, "I think you might have even licked us with what you have going on there. You're a talented bunch yourselves."

Looking up, she locked eyes with Luke as he finished a row of icing mortar. "When Mom says come to the community center and help, you come to the community center and strap on an apron," Luke shrugged.

Blair's eyes smiled back at Luke's, "Good luck, Luke…Marsten family."

Mayor Stowe bumped into Blair as she was moving against the grain. Eyeing the unspoken interaction between Blair and Luke, she cautioned, "Hey, no favorites here, Judge Blair."

"Judge, huh?" Sam Marsten perked up, offering Blair his most charming smile.

"Mr. Marsten, I run a clean competition, I warn you," Blair scowled eliciting laughter from the Marsten family and Mayor Stowe.

"This one is going to have my job at some point in the future, I assure you," Mayor Stowe chuckled.

"I don't know about that. I think I am content enough to partner with a wonderful mayor such as yourself," Blair conceded.

Mayor Stowe snapped her head, "See?"

"I think I'll focus on the earnest task of deciding which of these amazing displays is worthy of the highest honor today," Blair said. With a wave, she continued her rounds observing the other contestants.

Blair made her way around the room. She met guests from out of town who dove into the contest as a family and recently laid off workers who brought their families in as a much needed bit of holiday fun and a healthy distraction.

Blair admired the families, especially those she met that had been employed at the publishing house. Everyone seemed so cheery. Blair tried to imagine the stress on those families. Families like Nella's. You wouldn't know it by looking at the faces around the room. There were no furrowed brows and pensive reflections, just joy and laughter.

Families cheered each other on. They cheered their neighbors. They cheered the guests from out of town.

Blair took a step back to absorb the entire scene. The event was more than she could have ever expected. A figure sneaked through the crowd and stood next to her.

"Pretty impressive."

Blair turned to see Mayor Stowe standing beside her.

"It is," Blair nodded.

"I think your event is quite the success," Mayor Stowe said.

Blair looked at the mayor, "It's more than I could have ever expected. It's wonderful to see everyone so happy."

"It warms the heart," Mayor Stowe nodded. "Being a mayor of a small town like Evergreen is kind of like being a parent. You feel the pain and concern of the community. You get to feel their joy as well. Christmas in Evergreen is the most wonderful feeling. This year has definitely had a different feel. Like a Christmas without snow. It's still a magical time, but somehow, something is just... a bit off."

"I'm glad I could help bring a slight bit of respite, even if for a moment," Blair breathed softly.

"You have been a light in our community this year. Just like your grandparents were," Mayor Stowe said, giving Blair an appreciative smile before continuing her rounds.

As Blair overlooked the crowd, the scent of ginger and cinnamon heavy in the air, she eyed a few other contemplative observers. Husbands and wives, parents stepped back from their own family's creative toils to take the moment in. See the smiles on their children's faces, to soak in the giggles as their ginger creations began to take shape.

Blair noticed that if she looked carefully enough, through the veil of the moment, she could see wisps of concern. Re-entering the fray at their table with their children, those concerns would wipe away, if only for a moment.

Deciding to follow the community's lead, she allowed her own concerns to be put on hold as she enjoyed the afternoon. Ignoring the vibrations emitting from her phone, she didn't want any possible negativity from Candace or unsolicited advice from Todd to steal the moment.

As the phone kept ringing, she glanced at it to see 'Call from Candace Barrows' on the screen. Moments later, her assistant Ann Marie was displayed. Blair sighed and ignored the call. With a grimace, she turned the phone off completely and allowed herself to be absorbed into the event.

From across the room, Luke leaned between his parents as he helped steady a repair on a faulty roof panel.

Using some fresh icing, they were able to stave off a potential disaster. Pulling away to allow his mother to return to her decorating, he glanced up and through the crowd.

He watched as Blair interacted with the crowd, flittering through, greeting each guest like a butterfly stopping to test flowers in a field. He didn't think she had missed a soul as she made her way around the participants' tables.

There was a genuineness about her visits, taking time to connect with each person who attended.

"She's quite the special woman, isn't she?" Loretta's voice crashed Luke's thoughts.

He shook himself from his gaze, "Hmm? Who is?"

Loretta glared at her son, "Don't play dumb, it doesn't suit you."

"She has a boyfriend and a life in New York," Luke said.

"Life in New York? She's here now, isn't she?" Loretta asked.

"I'd imagine without the publishing house and relying only on tourists, keeping a toy store or any small business will be quite difficult around here," Luke said, sprinkling a confectioner's sugar snow fall gently over the roof and trees of their gingerbread scene.

Loretta studied her son, "I can't say I haven't thought about the impact it would have on the Holly Bough. Just another storm to weather."

"Imagine crossing the country just in time for that storm to hit, might be cause to return home," Luke muttered.

"You think she isn't staying?" Sam asked.

"I think anyone who had a life and successful career who found themselves in a situation that could crash all round them would have to at least consider their options," Luke said. "Can we follow hers and everyone else's lead and enjoy the contest?"

He picked up a slab of yet unused gingerbread and took a defiantly crunchy bite. When met with disapproving glares from his parents, he shrugged, "What? I haven't eaten."

Mayor Stowe waved Blair and Mary Kay up to the stage as the monitor counter clicked off the final ten seconds of the gingerbread contest timer.

"Wow, that was a lot of fun!" the mayor clapped. "Let's give a huge round of applause to the two who spearheaded putting this together, Blair Cooper and Mary Kay Albright!"

The audience burst into an enormous uproar of applause and cheers.

"Now, for the big moment," Mayor Stowe said, pacing the stage, making eye contact with each contestant. "I must say, and I think the other judges…I think you all will agree…each of the displays is amazing and unique. You should all be very proud of yourselves. Each contestant gets a voucher for free coffee or cocoa for each team member at the Evergreen Cafe. The third place winners get a gift certificate for The Toy Chest, second place receives a gift certificate for dinner at Natalie's Diner and first place gets not only two tickets for the Holiday Wine Pairing at Marsten Winery but also receives the honor of turning on the town Christmas tree lights for the Christmas Eve town carols."

The mayor cast a glance at Blair and Mary Kay who nodded to confirm their results.

"Third place goes to the Martin family! We loved your unique take on Santa's village," Mayor Stowe called out. Mr. Martin's grandchildren squealed with delight. "Second place did receive one first place vote and it goes to the Marstens of the Holly Bough Bed and Breakfast. Your retelling of the Nativity caught the eye of the judges for beautiful design but also for hitting the real heart of the season. Great job!"

Mayor Stowe clapped along with the crowd as Sam and Loretta sandwiched Luke in a hug while he rolled his eyes sheepishly at the response.

"And, our first place winners, travelling all the way up from Camas, Washington…a what…four and a half hour drive with good weather?" Mayor Stowe mused. "The Schulstad family! We loved your recreation of Main Street Evergreen decked out for the holidays! It was beautifully crafted and a wonderful sentiment for what makes our community so special, in particular at Christmas! We will see you at the town tree on Christmas eve! Well done, everyone!"

The mayor turned to Blair and Mary Kay, thanking them one last time for their efforts.

Mary Kay and Blair exchanged quick hugs themselves before descending the stage steps and mingling with the crowd. Blair sought out Nella's family to high five the kids on their efforts.

Mr. Martin congratulated Blair again for her efforts in hosting an inspirational event and she applauded his family for their place in the contest. Mayor Stowe had her maintenance department coming to clean up and transport the entries to a window display they had set up at town hall. Blair funneled towards the exit, finding herself in step with the Marstens.

"What a lovely event!" Loretta cooed.

"Another second place," Sam cracked to the ire of his wife.

"I loved what you guys put together. It is the true meaning of Christmas, after all," Blair lauded.

Luke took a step out of reach from his mother when he replied, "I liked what the winning family did. Especially this year, celebrating Evergreen was a nice touch."

Loretta started to glare but then softened, "It was. Towns like ours can be like children. You want them to stay the way they are, but there is always a chance they have other ideas for their future. I think we'd all like Evergreen to stay the same forever. Sometimes it is about appreciating what you have while you have it."

Blair was shocked at Loretta's poignant and somewhat prophetic sentiment. As they walked down Main Street themselves, Blair studied the quaint town.

"It would be a shame for this to go away. I think every state needs an Evergreen to call home for the holidays. A little respite from the busy and chaos of the cities," Sam remarked.

"You never know, Pops. Nothing stays the same forever," Luke said.

Sam grumbled at the comment.

"This place is special," Blair said softly as they reached The Toy Chest.

"Will you make it to the Holly Bough for dinner?" Loretta asked Blair.

Blair shook her head, "I'll probably be in after the store closes."

"Very well. I'll have your plate ready," Loretta smiled. With a little gleam in her eye, she added, "And our customary wine glasses as well."

"Thanks," Blair said, slipping her key into the lock.

"Nice event today," Luke said, hands shoved in his pockets. "I'll see you around."

Turning, he continued to walk with his parents towards their bed and breakfast. The sight to Blair was Christmas card worthy, especially as a light flurry started to fall around them. They were a family so full of life and love.

The Swansons swept in behind her. Scott and the kids just stopped to give Nella hugs before they continued home.

"Great job, Blair! Everyone had a wonderful time," Nella said.

"Thank you," Blair said. "It was nice to see families have fun without additional pressures on their shoulders."

"There were a lot of families from the publishing house there," Nella admitted. "It is a tough holiday for most of us."

Blair nodded, "I know."

Nella surprised Blair and wrapped her in a big hug. "Any season, even a rough one, where you get to make a great friend is a good one!"

"Thank you, Nella," Blair's tone was soft. "I feel the same."

Blair watched as the young woman skipped her way to the back room to put her coat and purse away.

Twenty Two

The afternoon was busy with attendees from the gingerbread contest descending on Main Street, mostly out of town guests to Evergreen shopped, sipped and dined among the shops.

One very excited family came in. Mr. Martin had given his winning gift certificate to a family that he knew was hit particularly hard from the publishing house closing. Nella entertained the children in the play area while Blair helped the parents maximize their spending, ringing everything up at cost to keep them within the gift certificate value but still find suitable gifts to put under the tree.

As the afternoon wore on, most shoppers were attendees of the gingerbread contest. Blair enjoyed the day with Nella and their guests. The lack of phone interruptions made her day that much more enjoyable. With a gasp and a chuckle, she pulled her phone from her pocket realizing she never turned it back on from the contest.

When the phone booted, she was presented with a barrage of notices. With a gulp and a sigh, she began sorting through the messages. Blair wasn't surprised to see that most were alternating pings by Candace and her assistant Ann Marie.

Wanting to get as much insight before taking on Candace, Blair dialed Ann Marie.

"Where have you been?" Ann Marie gasped. "Candace Barlow has been calling you and me and Roberta…"

"Candace called Roberta?" Blair asked. Wincing, she had been so involved with events in Evergreen, she hadn't stopped to think what her boss might think. Taking vacation days, she hadn't used since she started with the advertising firm, Blair discounted her boss' approval while she was away.

"She did. Several times," Ann Marie hissed.

Blair stared at the wall trying not to imagine her boss' reaction to being called by Candace and more so, her incomplete storyboarding. "How did she react?"

"She stomped down to my cubicle to see if I could get a hold of you and spun away muttering something about if you mess up the Lorent opportunity to not bother coming back," Ann Marie reported.

"I see," Blair sighed. "Any idea exactly what Candace is after?"

"She said she needed to talk to you right away about your storyboards and if they were some kind of a joke or maybe you sent the wrong file. She arranged for the

Lorent board to see a preview before they broke for the holidays," Ann Marie said. "It sounds like she has her own internal issues she is trying to get in front of and was hoping to use your campaign to accomplish that. I gotta say, I looked at what you sent, it isn't like you. I mean, I like the concept, but I have never seen you submit a file this..."

"Rushed?" Blair said.

"Messy," Ann Marie admitted. "Roberta is fuming."

Blair pushed her hair back, "I better call Candace."

"Good luck!" Ann Marie called.

Blair stared at her phone for several minutes before reluctantly hitting the call button. In one ring, a voice snapped, "Where have you been? I have been trying to get a hold of you. Your office couldn't locate you...I hope this isn't how you operate!"

"Hello, Candace," Blair breathed. "I apologize that I had other commitments. Please keep in mind, we were supposed to officially begin in January. I have been working while tending to family matters."

"Your official work with Lorent begins January second, but your work for Lorent begins the moment the agreement is made. I want to provide an update to the board prior to their holiday break. This is important for me...for the company," Candace spat. "What could be more important than the largest account of your lifetime?"

"Uhm...," Blair started but was quickly cut off.

"Never mind that," Candace said. "I am as concerned about the quality of work. Is this really what you would have me present to Mr. Lorent and the board?"

Blair stammered, "Given the time constraints and the limited tools I have to work with on the road…when are you presenting?"

"Seven P.M. Paris time," Candace declared.

"That's ten o'clock my time. That was hours ago," Blair frowned.

"Exactly! When I couldn't get a hold of you, I had to go forward with that ragamuffin storyboard package you sent me," Candace said. "Frankly, I was embarrassed. I am only grateful that I objected to hiring you in the first place, something I was sure to point out at the board meeting."

Blair's head fell, "I see."

"I had to present one of the least complete, untidy, least professional presentations I have seen in the entirety of my career at Lorent," Candace went on.

Blair's heart sunk as the words from the rant hit home.

"For some reason that I certainly cannot fathom, Lorent loved it. The board did as well. The concept at least. They saw glimmers of a raw but unique perspective they are eager to explore with you. The quality of work was notably well below expectations and that did raise concern for the board," Candace shared.

"I'm glad they liked it," Blair said, her voice soft.

The phone went quiet for a moment. "Can I ask you something? Do you want this account? I have never worked with an agent so…apathetic," Candace asked.

"I have worked my entire adult life for this opportunity," Blair admitted.

"But…?" Candace pressed.

Blair swallowed, "Nothing. I am excited to take on the opportunity with my full and complete attention when I return to New York."

"Good. I certainly hope that return is soon, because I did promise the board a freshened package when they return from holiday," Candace said. The phone went dead.

Blair flopped in her office chair; her eyes fixated on the calendar hanging on the wall. Her grandmother had already filled in the events in Evergreen through the holiday season. Even though it had been years since the family gathered there for the holidays, her grandmother had the second Sunday marked to prep their guest rooms for Blair, her brother and her parents in the event they somehow showed up for the holidays.

The sting of tears stabbed at her eyes. She wondered how life got so complicated, so important that it overtook being together for Christmas. Her parents visited throughout the year, but they stopped coming for Christmas. Her brother Derek, being deployed for many of those years, had the only reasonable excuse. For Blair, she didn't want to miss a day on the calendar when she might be able to impress her boss so that she might land an account like Lorent.

Staring at her grandmother's notes, she squeezed her eyes tight, "I'm sorry I didn't come back more."

She didn't have time to lament for long as her phone buzzed yet again. Rolling her head back, she muttered, "Might as well get this over with too."

Hitting the answer button, she called, "Hello, Roberta!"

"Where have you been? Candace Barrows from Lorent has been on the warpath to get a hold of you! So have I and Ann Marie!" Blair's boss railed into the phone.

"I know," Blair admitted. "I just spoke to Candace."

"And?"

"Lorent and the board love the concept but felt the presentation was a bit raw?" Blair said.

"Raw?" Roberta yelled into the phone. "You have done better, more complete work on the discount mattress warehouse campaign. And I mean by a lot!"

"I know. I have been managing some issues for my family," Blair said.

The phone was quiet for just a moment. "I know. And I reluctantly signed off on your little hiatus thinking engagement with Lorent wouldn't begin until the new year. This, this is something else," Roberta said. "I think you need to come back to Manhattan straight away where you can have the agency's full resources."

"I'll be home soon," Blair said. "I'll be back by Christmas and can be in the office on the twenty-sixth."

"Blair, it is one thing to win an account like Lorent. It is death in this industry to fail a client like Lorent. Not just for you, for all of us," Roberta warned.

Blair nodded despite being on a phone thousands of miles away, "I know. I won't let you down."

"I know you won't. We all get distracted from time to time. This is not one of those times to be distracted, Blair!" Roberta urged.

"I'll see you on the twenty-sixth," Blair promised.

"Alright. Merry Christmas, Blair. We're all counting on you," Roberta said.

"Merry Christmas, Roberta," Blair hung up the phone. She stared at the screen, not feeling any better.

Setting the phone down, she wanted nothing more but to go out into the store and mingle with guests. It had become an unusual respite for her. She was quite certain there was a time that she would have called that work.

Pushing away from her desk, the ringer on her phone began playing a tune. With a heavy sigh, she muttered, "Might as well get this call out of the way, too."

"Hey, Blair!"

"Don't you mean 'where have I been?'" Blair breathed.

"What do you mean?" Todd asked.

"Just seems everyone from New York has been starting their conversations with me like that," Blair said.

"Maybe that's a sign," Todd suggested.

Blair looked out at the shop watching Nella help a customer, "Maybe it is."

"Well, then come home," Todd said.

"I have the foster party I promised to run," Blair said.

"Don't you have staff for that? That…Nelly?" Todd suggested.

Blair scowled, "Nella. It isn't her responsibility."

"Yeah, but does it really matter who is there as long as the kids get their event?" Todd pressed.

"It matters to me," Blair said, her voice resolute.

"Is everything okay?" Todd asked.

Blair hesitated, "Just dealing with stuff from work. Lorent likes my work, just not up to my usual design standards which got Roberta in a tizzy."

"What did she say?"

Blair's hesitation even more profound, "She suggested I come where the full weight of the firm will be at my disposal."

"Well, there you have it. You'll come home. We'll have some champagne rink side at Rockefeller. You'll get your project together and we'll fly it to Paris ourselves," Todd suggested.

"I'll think about it. It is looking more and more like that might be the solution," Blair breathed.

"I've already mapped out some flights and places to stay. I'll email you what I found," Todd said.

"Sounds good. Thanks, Todd," Blair said. Shutting her phone off, she tossed it on the desk, unable to bear another call.

Blair gazed out onto the toy store floor where Nella was gleefully showing a family around. She wanted to go out there herself, but felt she'd just be a buzzkill. Instead, she watched from her seat in the office. A little girl's eyes widened as she found a stuffed puppy dog. Sprinting towards it, pure joy lighting up her face as she plucked it from the shelf and gave it a giant hug.

Just as her mood was starting to change, her phone buzzed against. Recognizing it as a call from her realtor, she picked the phone up and chucked it in her desk drawer.

Sliding away from her desk, Blair straightened her clothes and marched defiantly into the store. Kneeling down, she handed the girl a candy cane as her parents came to pull her away from the stuffed puppy. With a nod, he handed the animal off to Blair as the child was distracted. Ringing it up and putting it in a big bag concealed under a sea of tissue, she handed it to the parents on their way out.

"The look over here technique. Well played, boss," Nella gleamed.

Blair scowled, "I thought we agreed to dispense with the whole 'boss' thing?"

Nella laughed, "I know, it's just so catchy!"

"I don't think so," Blair grumbled.

"Seriously, is everything okay?" Nella asked.

Blair looked deep into her friend's eyes. She wanted to open up to her about her real intentions with the store. The last thing families needed before the holidays were to lose hope. At least Nella and her family had hope going into Christmas. She didn't want her news to rip that hope away.

"Just been a long day," Blair said.

"You want to take off? I can cover," Nella said.

Blair smiled, "No. At this moment, there is no place I would rather be."

Twenty Three

Like the town of Evergreen itself, Blair's day was a series of hills and valleys. Facilitating the gingerbread contest was a highlight, sandwiching the drama of her New York responsibilities with the joy of working the floor at the toy shop.

Walking up to the Holly Bough Bed and Breakfast was another highlight of her day. Making her entrance at night had a bright side, she was able to the see the grand old house turned hotel in all its Christmas splendor.

Pulling the door open, she was greeted by Sam and Loretta like clockwork. Sam took her coat and invited her to join the other guests in the parlor after she had her dinner and Loretta was quick to whisk her into the kitchen.

Blair didn't wait for them to sit down at the table before she poured her and Loretta each a small glass of wine.

"Long day?" Loretta asked as she prepared Blair's dinner.

"You could say that," Blair nodded.

"Cheers," Loretta paused her work and raised her glass.

Blair raised hers and took a sip, "Salud!"

As Loretta returned to preparations, Blair laughed, "I almost said it was good to be home."

Loretta smiled, "You're welcome to call the Holly Bough home any time."

"You spoiling me like you do, I am very tempted," Blair said.

Loretta led the way to the table and set the plate down in front of Blair, "I think that was the best gingerbread contest we ever had."

Blair rolled her eyes as she looked up from her plate of chicken and dumpling soup. "You're kind. We threw it together pretty last minute. I remember events in the past that had music and had mini contests, tastings...way more involved than what we cobbled," Blair argued.

"True, they were more grand. But I am not sure I attended one that meant as much to the town as this one," Loretta mused over the rim of her wine glass.

"Thank you. That was the very impact we were hoping for," Blair said. "Thank you for dinner, by the way. This is delicious."

"I really like the sage in it," Loretta said. "Sam and Luke always find a way to ruin it with hot sauce."

Blair laughed, "My dad and brother would have done the same."

"So, tell me about your day. I can see the weariness. It is different from carrying a big event and running a toy store," Loretta asked.

Blair looked across the table. Loretta reminded her of her mother. She had an astuteness that she could pick up trouble in people's affect even though they were never spoken of.

"Just work and unfinished business in New York," Blair said, circling her spoon in her soup.

"That must be tough. Running the store for the first time, during the holidays, at that. The events and still carry burdens from across the country," Loretta said. She eyed Blair carefully, "But I don't think it is the physical demand of it all that is truly weighing on you."

Blair nearly spit her soup, "Excuse me?"

Loretta offered a calm smile, "The burdens we women carry. It is rarely the burdens of our time or toil that wear us down. It is the internal struggles, the ones of the heart that cause us to lose sleep."

Blair considered the innkeeper's words and shrugged, "It has been wonderful and tough taking over my grandparents' store. Putting a life that I had worked so hard to build for myself in New York on hold with people back there still counting on me."

"The highway of life. You're driving along towards the big city and you see a wonderful advertisement for this idyllic small town if you take the next exit. You need to figure out if you're going to take that exit," Loretta said, her hand on Blair's wrist.

"Something like that," Blair breathed.

"It must be a scary proposition, especially with the publishing house closing," Loretta said.

Blair nodded, "I'm worried about the other families more than myself. I keep wishing there was something I could do."

"You've already done a great deal. You've given hope. The gingerbread contest, the games, foster night, carrying on The Toy Chest during the most important season. I'd say your impact on the people of Evergreen has been profound," Loretta suggested.

Blair appreciated the sentiment, but her heart still hung heavy. Finishing her soup, she said, "I like my time with you and not just because you say nice things."

Loretta laughed, "I like my time with you, too. Know I can tell the hard truth when necessary as well."

"I believe it," Blair smiled. "Thank you again for dinner."

"My pleasure. Why don't you join me in the living room with Sam the rest of the guests for a while?" Loretta said grabbing Blair's soup bowl.

Despite exhaustion setting in, sitting in the living room by the fire for a while sounded nice. With a nod, she carried her wine glass into the living room, saying hello to everyone as she did. Curling into the wingback chair, right next to the fire that was offered for her, she settled in, almost feeling absorbed into the fabric.

The soft glow of the lights from the Christmas tree and the sundry of candles around the room, the light conversation and the warmth emanating from the fireplace were ethereally comforting. Partaking in light banter with the guests in the room, Blair faded into a blissful state where everything melted in the background. Her eyelids fell heavy and her head met the support of the wingback chair to steady her.

Loretta pulled her half empty wine glass from her hands and instructed Sam to cover her with a blanket. With a smile, she inspected her husbands' handiwork as she studied Blair looking content as she slumbered.

Twenty Four

Blair was happy to be in The Toy Chest. The sights, sounds and even smells were a mix of comforting familiar and nostalgia. She knew it was a bit of a false sanctuary as owning the store didn't come with guarantees. As Todd had told her many times, owning a retail store is challenging even in good economic times. Paychecks and even keeping the store open would be a lifelong battle with little room for upside growth.

She comforted herself in the fact that maybe that is why this was so fun to her. She wasn't dependent on its success, she could enjoy owning a toy store, even if for one brief Christmas season.

Whatever the rationale was, she took in a deep breath and enjoyed the moment as she opened the store. A light snowfall and forecast for more throughout the day only provided Blair an additional boost. She felt like she was receiving a hug.

Her phone sat in her desk drawer. She knew she would be getting calls and messages from Roberta, Ann Marie and Candace on the updates for Lorent. She worked on them over coffee and planned to tackle more improvements later that day. She didn't want their interruptions to take away from her fleeting experience.

The front door jingle bells rang as a smiling Nella burst through, "Good morning, Blair!"

"Good morning, Nella," Blair chimed.

"The kids were still talking about the gingerbread contest when I got home last night. They had a blast," Nella said. "When I walked in, Scott had all sorts of cardboard pieces and art supplies out and they made a little faux gingerbread village in the middle of the living room."

"He's a good man," Blair acknowledged.

Nella nodded, "He is. I am proud of him for focusing on the kids and Christmas when I know he is eaten up inside about the future."

"He's great with kids, too!" Blair said. "It's too bad I couldn't hire him on here at the store."

"That would be kind of fun. Kind of hectic, too. I think he'd just play with kids all day," Nella laughed.

"I think that was my grandpa's role here. Lift heavy things and play with children while my grandmother actually ran the store," Blair nodded.

As they welcomed Kris in with the day's hot beverages, a stream of shoppers funneled in. Each took a cup as Kris set up and waved to them before returning to the coffee shop.

Only days away from Christmas, Evergreen and the toy store were busier than ever. By the afternoon, shoppers turned into browsers, the store having recorded its best day yet since Blair arrived.

As Blair and Nella enjoyed a bit of calm, Luke Marsten entered the store, walking with purpose. "Ladies," he greeted, flashing a charming smile. Walking directly up to them, he fished into the breast pocket of his coat and produced a pair of envelopes. "I hope you will be my guests at the holiday food and wine pairing tomorrow evening."

Nella looked hesitant, shaking her head, "Luke, we'd love to, but we can't even afford a babysitter right now."

"I know. That is why my mother has invited them over to their annual s'mores in the snow party with their guests' children. I believe they are roughly the same age," Luke said.

"Wow, thank you. I'll check with Scott...," Nella started. A sparkle formed in her eye as she reconsidered. "Never mind. We will be glad to come. Thank you, Luke."

"Genuinely, my pleasure," Luke bowed gallantly. Turning to Blair, he proposed, "Ms. Cooper, would you accompany and join me at the chef's table tomorrow evening?"

Like Nella, Blair hesitated, but for her own slate of very different reasons.

"Unless... you have other plans?" Luke asked.

Blair shook her head, "No, I..."

"Great!" Luke snapped, handing her the envelope. Spinning to leave, he paused midway and cocked his head towards Blair, "Say, I have to do some final Christmas shopping. I was wondering if you would walk with me. I could sure use a world class marketer's opinion."

Blair looked reticent until Nella all but shoved her out the door, "Go. Things have settled down and you didn't even take a lunch break."

"I'll have her back in no time," Luke promised.

"Take your time," Nella sang.

Luke held the door as Blair gathered her coat and followed him out. "Thanks, I really appreciate you helping me out," he said as their gaits fell in line with one another's. The sidewalks were busy, forcing them to walk closely together. The day's snow had picked up, lighting on their shoulders as they walked.

"It's nice to stroll the streets of Evergreen at Christmas," Blair admitted. "I really haven't had time to check out the rest of the shops."

"Well, here's your chance," Luke said, enjoying their leisurely pace. "Nella said you haven't had lunch. Do you need to stop and eat?"

Blair shook her head, "No, I'll find some nibbles along the way. Your mom feeds everybody at the Holly Bough like royalty.'"

Luke chuckled, "That she does. She is one of the people I was hoping your keen eye might help me with."

"I'd love to help you find a gift for your mom," Blair perked up.

"How about you? Got all of your gifts bought this year? How about that boyfriend of yours?" Luke asked, his voice casual.

Blair frowned, "Oh, we don't really exchange gifts."

Luke stopped, "You don't exchange Christmas presents?"

"We go out to dinner," Blair said.

"No presents?" Luke was amazed.

"Nope."

"Do you have a tree?" Luke asked.

"A little one."

"Stockings?" Luke pressed.

Blair nodded.

Luke turned to face her, "But nothing goes in the stockings or under the tree?"

"I put the presents my parents send me under the tree and cards in the stocking. My friends and I do a gift exchange, so I have a few presents under the tree," Blair defended. "Todd is very... practical."

"I see," Luke said. "Just seems odd for someone who loves Christmas as much as you do…"

"Todd says it will be an evolutionary step in our relationship," Blair said, hearing the words out loud ring rather oddly to herself. "It's a big city relationship thing."

"Hmm," Luke mumbled. "Let's duck in here!"

Holding the door open for Blair, they entered the warmly lit store. Immediately hit with fragrance, they circulated amongst the wares. Blair nodded, "Good choice. This store has lots of things your mom would like. It is very…country chic. Everything is elegant with a touch of Americana. Very much like the Holly Bough."

Luke watched Blair as she described the store and placed herself in Loretta's shoes. "You have a way of looking at the world and describing it so enticingly. You must be very good at your job."

"I was. I think I might be losing a step," Blair grumbled.

"Why do you say that?" Luke frowned.

"It's the new client I started working on. Mixed in with events around town and running the toy store, I haven't really given it much of my attention," Blair shrugged.

"I'm sure they can appreciate your circumstances," Luke said.

Blair scoffed, "In that world, it is what have you done for me today because there are five more just as good as you clamoring to take your spot."

"Sounds fun," Luke chided.

"It's fun when you give your full attention and are on top of your game. I kind of feel like a racehorse. One little misstep and I'm off to the glue factory," Blair said. Happy to change the topic, she asked, "What are you looking to get your mother? Something sweet, simple, Christmassy…"

"Yes," Luke grinned, nodding. "All of that!"

"Alright, let's see what we can find," Blair said, taking an earnest look at the store's offerings.

Item by item, she began leading Luke around the store, eyeing décor that seemed to fit Loretta's tastes.

"Is there anything that your mother…complains about? Anything that she wishes for or struggles with?" Blair asked.

Luke looked thoughtful for a moment, "She wants bookcases that would sit on either side of the fireplace. She wanted to fill it with seasonal books for visitors to read and maybe even host writer's retreats." He was excited with his revelation, but then, his face fell. Scrunchy his nose, he said, "There aren't any furniture stores in Evergreen. Maybe the antiques shops, but it would be hard to find matching cases."

Blair looked at Luke, "The answer isn't in a store. I think it is in your workshop."

Luke frowned.

"Could you build your mother bookcases from your wine barrels or similar wood?" Blair asked. "Your mother would appreciate no gift greater than one that came from your own hands."

"You think?" Luke asked.

Blair smiled and nodded, "Oh, yeah."

"Hmm. I could do that," Luke mused. "I guess this isn't going to be all that long of a trip after all."

"If you've got the time, I wouldn't mind continuing to stroll through the shops," Blair suggested.

Luke nodded, "Happy to."

With an even more relaxed pace, the pair ventured through the shops enjoying the experience engulfing every sense of Christmas as they peered through windows, tasted samples of peppermint fudge and luxuriated in scents of pine, pomegranate, cinnamon and cardamom as they traveled.

The chill in the air cut more fiercely as the afternoon wore on, but it did not deter the visitors as they wound their way through the streets and shops of Evergreen. The busy sidewalks and blustery day pushed Luke and Blair close together as they navigated the Christmas village.

"Time for a cocoa?" Luke asked.

"I have a store to close. How about a fully caffeinated peppermint mocha?" Blair suggested.

"Sounds good," Luke said. "We can grab one for Nella, too. I appreciate her letting me steal you away yet again."

"She's a good one, that Nella," Blair said.

Luke nodded, "She is. Her whole family is."

Heading into the coffee shop, they placed their orders and sat by the window. Blair couldn't help but to be distracted observing the couples and families on the sidewalk. "There are no bad days in Evergreen around the holidays, are there?" she mused.

"It is a matter of perspective, I suppose, but yes, it would take a serious blow to knock one's spirit awry here. Kind of like being on a beach in Hawaii. When life is joyous and peaceful, it's hard to fight happy," Luke acknowledged.

"I like watching the people together and happy. My favorite time in New York is at Christmas time. Even in the chaos and bustle of the big city, Christmas is a bit more special. People are kinder, more generous, more considerate," Blair said.

Luke watched Blair ogle the families as they passed. "Two different worlds, both with their appeal, just very different," Luke said.

Blair nodded as Jessica flagged them down for their coffees.

"This has been nice. Thank you for letting me tag along," Blair said.

"Thank you for the brilliant, gold star Christmas present idea for my mom," Luke said. "I guess I should get back and get to work!"

They gathered their drinks and headed back outside. Stepping next door, they stood outside the toy store entrance. "I'll see you tomorrow night at the holiday pairing?" Luke asked, his voice hopeful.

"I'll try," Blair said.

"There'll be an empty seat at the chef's table if you don't," Luke warned, looking woeful.

Blair shook her head and chuckled, "Fine. I'll be there."

"Great!" Luke brightened. "I'll see you tomorrow night."

With that, he was gone in a flash. Blair watched him disappear down the sidewalk as she backed into the store with coffees in hand.

Entering the toy store, she handed Nella her cup and took over helping a guest. As the purchase was rung up, Blair went to the back to remove her coat. As she did, she patted her pockets realizing the luxuriously quiet phone day was a result of it being stashed in the desk drawer.

Reluctantly sliding it open, a glance at her phone warned of a litany of messages waiting for her. Squeezing her eyes shut for a preparatory moment, she snatched the phone and began scrolling through the missed calls, text and emails.

Her expectation of being assaulted by Candace and Roberta were unfounded, though each had reached out at least once while the phone was stowed. The majority of the pings were courtesy of the realtor who listed The Toy Chest.

Dispensing with the messages from Roberta and Candace first, each requesting a daily update that Blair resigned to do from her room at the Holly Bough, while each of her counterparts were slumbering. A call from Todd without a message and a pair of calls from Bradley Marcom, the real estate buyer, Blair cast off to deal with later.

Focusing on the messages from Meredith Kohl, she sifted through the texts and emails first. Moving backwards through the chronology, most of the hits were pings referencing the earlier communication.

Finding the meat of the notes, the realtor intoned that she was needing signatures and final decisions, that she needed a call from Blair as soon as possible.

Glancing out on the sales floor, seeing Nella straightening items by the front window, Blair dialed Meredith Kohl's number.

"Blair, my goodness. I've been trying to get a hold of you. Mr. Marcom is anxious to complete the deal. He is going to make a surprise offer to another location to launch the project if you don't sign," the realtor said.

Blair stared out at the store. She knew the sale was imminent. She wasn't thrilled to be the catalyst to fundamentally change Evergreen forever.

As she pondered how to respond to Meredith, Scott entered with the kids.

"How'd the interview go?" she heard Nella ask her husband. A simple shake of his head told Blair all that she needed to know.

Nella's head drooped. "The bank called too. They won't extend us. You're going to have to take that job in Seattle," Nella resigned. As she glanced back towards the office, Blair averted her gaze.

"Meredith, will you find out from Mr. Marcom how quickly he can begin hiring people from the publishing house? If they can find a path to employment in January…he has a deal," Blair said.

"Alright. I will. I have to warn you, this is likely his last attempt to close before he moves on," Meredith cautioned.

"I understand," Nella said, watching the Swanson family at the other end of the store.

"You had me draw up the papers for a reason, you must know it is the right thing. Let's get this sealed and you can enjoy your holiday, with much, much more money in your bank account," Meredith said. "You can get back to that life of yours in New York."

Blair hung up the phone. She glanced around the store. She would be sad to see it go, but it was no longer about her and her grandparents' legacy but about a hail Mary to help the people of Evergreen.

Twenty Five

Loretta slid in next to Blair at the dinner table. She watched Blair take a bite of her huckleberry and chicken salad. Receiving an approving nod, the hotelier smiled.

"My son ran out of here this evening. Said he had things to do based on advice you had given him," Loretta mused over her tea.

Blair looked up from her plate, "I offered some elfish ideas."

"He seems to enjoy spending time with you," Loretta observed.

Blair paused her forkful of greens, "You have a talented and gallant son. We've developed...a nice friendship."

Loretta studied Blair in her response. Shifting in her seat, she asked, "Is your boyfriend coming for Christmas? We can try and find a room for him."

Blair bristled, "I, uh…I'm heading to New York for the holiday, right after the foster kids Christmas party."

"I see. I suppose you would have already had plans," Loretta nodded. "Are you getting together with his family, then?"

Blair frowned, "No. We have dinner reservations. Todd has to work the day after Christmas. I have some projects I need to work on as well."

"When do you head back? I can reserve your room for you," Loretta offered.

Blair put down her fork and nearly choked, "Yeah, I, uh…I'm not sure. January is typically a slow retail month. I figured it would be a good time to get my affairs in order."

"I see," Loretta nodded. "How does…Todd…feel about you and the store?"

"He sees it as a nice gesture from my grandparents and a bit of a windfall, in some respects," Blair said.

"Sam was so wonderful when I suggested we start the bed and breakfast. He was still a few years from retirement, but we saw it as an investment for our future. So many people work so hard right up to retirement and just keel over before they had a chance to really live outside of their employer's shadow," Loretta reflected.

Blair nodded, not entirely sure where Loretta was going with her story.

"We have enough to pay the bills and enjoy our time together. I couldn't ask for a better husband with that one. And then to have Luke so close, it has been the biggest blessing to live in Evergreen," Loretta continued. "What kind of work does Todd do? Will he be able to find work here?"

"What?" Blair squeaked, a piece of frisee falling off of her fork. "Oh, I, uhm, I'm sure he could. We haven't really discussed him moving out here."

"Right, Luke said it was an 'evolutionary' relationship," Loretta smiled. "You two don't exchange gifts at Christmas?"

"Presents denote a certain amount of intimacy in a relationship...," Blair absently quoted Todd.

Loretta raised an eyebrow.

Blair looked sheepish, "The idea is to live in the moment. Enjoy the shared moment of the holiday without material things."

Loretta stuck out her lip and nodded, though she was far from understanding. "There is something to that, I suppose," Loretta offered. "But there are treasures that, yes, have little material value, but they can serve as permanent reminders of those shared experiences. Take the tree topper in the living room. That ratty thing has been on every tree since our first Christmas together, older than Luke. I wouldn't trade it for anything, because each year, I get to take it out of its box and every Christmas over the past forty plus years gets to flood my memory banks. I love that. I cherish that. The angel itself was probably three dollars back then and worth nothing now. To me, it's priceless."

Blair finished her plate. She looked at Loretta, "This conversation isn't really about 'things' and presents, is it?"

Loretta smiled, "No, dear. It isn't."

Blair chuckled and reached across the table to put her hand on Loretta's arm, "I like you."

"The feeling is most mutual," Loretta said. Motioning towards the living room, she asked, "You have time to visit?

Blair grimaced, "I am supposed to work on this project for back east."

"They're playing games…," Loretta teased.

"Games? What games?" Blair craned her neck to see into the living room.

"I'll make you some tea," Loretta said, nudging Blair forward.

Blair followed the sounds of animated conversation. Peering over shoulders, she found everyone on their knees, huddled over the coffee table. Joelle Hubbard rolled dice while her parents cheered her on. When the numbers came to light, cheers erupted.

"Joelle's the winner!" everyone but her brother Niles chimed. Niles studied the board before relenting that his sister was indeed the winner and clapped her on the back.

"Who's up for another round?" Sam called, resetting the meeples to the start of the board. "Hi, Blair! Are you in?"

Blair knew she should have retreated to her room to work, but grinned and nodded, "I'm in!"

Sam shifted over so that Blair could shift in and kneel between he and Joelle. Joelle, still excited for her first win, happily accepted a high-five from Blair.

As she settled into play games with the guests, she marveled at Sam. He was a master wrangler at getting people involved and weaving everyone into the same conversation.

"Blair, here, was a marketer in Manhattan before taking over her grandparents' toy store," Sam said as they kicked off the next round. "Gil runs a distribution company selling products into stores all around the world. Some of the toys in the store probably get there through his network."

Gil offered a modest nod as he took his turn, "It's true. Department stores, online retailers, book stores and yep, toy stores. I have a soft spot for small retailers. I set up a special network for independent shops."

"It must be exciting to see your work spread to stores around the country," Blair said.

"The world," Gil corrected. "I don't see it as my work. I'm just the connector helping the designers and manufacturers get their items out there. There's a series of toys in your shop that came from a husband and wife team.

They wanted to design play that would create hours of exercise without ever seeming like exercise."

"I love those, they've been selling well. I just wished they had an adult version," Blair quipped as the play came around to her turn.

"Me too," Gil laughed.

Loretta leaned in the doorway watching her guests.

"Come on in, Mama. We'll get you for the next round," Sam offered.

"You can take my spot, it looks like Niles is going to win this one in a moment," Blair said as she observed the board.

"I am?" the young boy looked up.

Blair drew a route to victory with her eyes. It took a moment and then Niles' eyes lit up and excitedly executed his winning move.

Getting up from her spot, Blair said, "Thank you for letting me play. I do have a bit of work to do. Good night, everyone!"

Blair exchanged smiles with Loretta and excused herself. Heading up the stairs to her room, she could hear the group in the living room laughing as they prepared for the next game. She heard Joelle and Niles squeal, "We want to play Blair's game!"

Blair chuckled and pushed into her room.

Settling in, she sat at her desk. She sifted through her notes and storyboards trying to engage. A large part of her preferred to stay in the living room with the families playing games. Relenting to the fact that Lorent was going to either be a career maker or career ender, she forced herself to focus.

With her content solid, it was a matter of cleaning up the details from the artwork, the flow and the complete storyline. Those were the rough edges she needed to transform. Those were the creative areas of marketing where Blair typically flourished.

Since she landed in Evergreen, her mind had been fractured. Nostalgia, new friends, the plight of the community all fighting for attention versus Blair's life in New York, her friends there and of course, her work.

Her resolve to the sell the toy store in the interest of retaining jobs in Evergreen helped her regain some of her focus and create a much more complete presentation for Lorent. She surfed through the pages nodding to herself as she put the sparkle in the marketing package she was known for.

Blair's spirits were high as she felt things as they should be were falling into place. Evergreen and a romanticized life in Evergreen running her grandparents' toy store had a strong emotional appeal, but her life in New York and career that was about to take a gigantic leap forward felt right for the first time in days.

Satisfied, she slid back from her desk just as her phone rang.

"Hello!" she sang.

"Well, you seem to be in a good mood," Todd answered.

"I think I finally got my act together on the Lorent portfolio. It just needed a little artistic flair, that's all," Blair replied.

"Good. You seemed pretty distracted recently," Todd said.

Blair studied the phone before responding, "I had to come to terms with letting my grandparents' store go. It wasn't easy. It still isn't."

"Your grandparents wanted you to have a legacy, I'm sure they would have wanted it to be *your* legacy," Todd counseled. "So, you've worked out the details with the buyer?"

"Close. I am waiting on one piece of information, how soon they can turn around and hire the people that lost their jobs when the publishing house closed," Blair reported.

Todd paused, "With all due respect, how does that affect the sale of the store? I mean, didn't the workers know in advance it was coming?"

"They did. They were loyal to the owner and there just aren't a lot of similar jobs in this market," Blair said. "These people were my grandparents' neighbors and friends. *My* friends. If I can make their transition easier with the sale, everyone wins."

"I suppose," Todd said. "Either way, it will get you back to New York where you belong."

Blair didn't expect those words to sting, but they did. She didn't have time to ponder as Todd asked her about Paris.

"I need to make the rest of the arrangements. I rolled the diced and booked flights," Todd said.

"I don't know. Roberta and Candace might need me in New York instead of Paris," Blair said.

"Try to find out tomorrow. The window is tight, and I don't want to block out my calendar if I'm not traveling," Todd said.

Blair nodded to herself, "Okay, I'll have an answer tomorrow."

She hung up the phone. She was bewildered why she was so hesitant to agree to the trip. Since she began working on the Lorent proposal, she dreamed of going to Paris to visit and to work. Something deep in her mind was causing her to apply the brakes.

Shrugging, she reviewed her updates to the Lorent package and sent them forward without hesitation. Glancing at the clock, she flopped on her bed. She would get a goodnight's sleep for the first in several nights.

Twenty Six

Blair awoke the next morning to heavy snowfall outside her window. She loved snowy days. They were an amalgamation of exciting and peaceful, of chilly and warm. She smiled as she pulled the covers up to her chin and watch the flakes dance past her window.

She breathed deep. She felt content. The conflict of to sell or not sell the toy store, her senseless resistance to her life in New York were gone and she knew her work on Lorent was some of her best. She could relax and enjoy her time in Evergreen for what it was, a nice respite and homage to her grandparents and the wonderful memories her family shared there.

With a bounce in her step, she dressed and danced her way down the steps. "My, you're hitting the day with vigor," Loretta said as she handed off the cup of coffee and breakfast bag.

"It is a good day, Loretta," Blair sang.

Loretta tried to decipher the blossoming of her guest, "I certainly hope so, dear. It's a blustery one though, keep your coat zipped."

Blair smiled and entered the snowy landscape. She was glad she had donned ankle boots as the fresh snow was to be her path to work that day.

The Christmas village of Evergreen was only more idyllic under the blanket of white. Sprigs of Evergreen and burning Christmas lights made for beautiful contrast off the wintry canvas.

By the time she hit downtown, she followed footsteps, most leading to Kris' coffee shop. Offering a wave to the ladies inside, Blair opened up the Toy Store.

Classic Christmas tunes filled the store as the rest of the lights came on to join those left burning overnight in the display window. Dancing through the store, she straightened, filled gaps on the shelves and admired the store.

Nella pushed through. Blair giggled, her friend's outfits became more and more decked for Christmas as each day passed. Candy cane earrings dangled from her ears as a short string of red and white swirled garland draped over her neck.

"You are looking wonderfully festive," Blair said.

"The garland was Sophie's idea, but when I looked in the mirror, I kind of liked it," Nella admitted.

"I like it too," Blair smiled. Her phone buzzed, with a glance, she excused herself, "I need to get this."

Moving towards the back of the store, she answered, "Hello!"

"Blair, it's Roberta."

"Hi, Roberta," Blair said.

"I just got a call from Candace at Lorent, and I have to say, I was expecting it," Roberta said. "It looks like you were working late last night."

Blair stammered, "I was. I sent an updated portfolio."

"Probably a huge risk with tired eyes. I have to say, it was some of the best work I have seen. Not just from you, from anyone this agency. Candace thought so, too. She is presenting to Lorent today," Roberta said. "Great work, Blair."

"Thank you," Blair gushed at the praise.

"I knew I could count on you. You are going to have a magnificent career here. I hope you don't mind; I am sharing your work with the partners. I think they might want to visit with you when you return to New York," Roberta shared.

"Wow. I don't even know what to say," Blair said.

"Your work speaks for itself. You don't have to say anything. I just wanted to let you know, after the last iteration with Lorent being met with…mixed reviews, you hit a home run with this one," Roberta said. "Let's have lunch when you're back."

"Sounds good," Blair said, staring at the phone as it went dead.

Nella slid into the office and hung her coat up, "Good news?"

Blair looked at Nella and nodded, "One of my last New York projects was really well received."

"Good for you," Nella winked. "Nice to leave things on a high note, right?"

Blair was hesitant in her response, "Right."

Nella's eyes grew wide, "I can't wait for the tasting tonight. It is going to be epic. Scott and I don't get out much. It is going to be fun to dress fancy for once."

"It will be good," Blair agreed.

"That's right, you got a little preview," Nella grinned.

"Bring your appetite. You won't be disappointed," Blair promised.

A pair of shoppers entered, the jingle bells announcing them. With nods, Blair and Nella separated to greet them and help find the perfect gift items.

Blair enjoyed the afternoon helping guests browse the store. Each serious shopper was a grand hunt for the just the right present to put under the tree. Guests just enjoying wandering through were a delight themselves in relaxed, holiday banter.

By the time afternoon rolled around and the typical lag set in, Blair's phone rang from the office. Rushing to get it, she snatched it just before it was set to go to voicemail.

"Good, I caught you," Meredith Kohl's voice came through the phone.

Blair greeted the realtor, "Hi Meredith!"

"I have news for you. Straight from Mr. Marcom. He will have some positions ready by the end of January or beginning of February at the latest. If you sign before Christmas, he will post jobs the week after Christmas and begin interviewing in January for Evergreen residents only to start," Meredith explained.

"Meredith, that is wonderful news. That will at least give people some hope to look forward to," Blair said.

"So…," the realtor pressed.

"It's a deal! Thank you, Meredith!" Blair called.

Bursting into the toy store floor, she located Nella and said excitedly, "Have Scott polish his resume!"

Nella shot Blair a questioning glance.

"I'm working on something. Something big. I'm not ready to divulge just yet, but I hope to offer good news…soon!" Blair said, her eyes wide.

"Ms. Cooper, what mysterious deed have you cooked up?" Nella scowled.

"A compromise of sorts. That's all I can say, for now," Blair said.

Nella studied Blair for a moment and then shrugged, "Alright. I trust you."

Blair's affect changed, softening, "I have genuinely enjoyed becoming friends."

"Me too," Nella nodded.

Twenty Seven

Blair descended the steps of the Holly Bough to gushes from Nella and Loretta.

"My stars, young lady. You are positively stunning," Loretta called.

"I'm not so sure I want to enter with you, golly," Nella teased.

Blair's face turned a shade of red competing with her dress, "I'm just glad they had my size. Isn't it a little...too glitzy?"

Loretta and Nella studied Blair. Her hair up in ringlets, shining earrings allowed to dangle free along her neck. The dress she found minutes before departing downtown flowed from her shoulders. Subtle metallic sparkles in a matching monochromatic deep red shimmered softly in the light giving way to layers of sheer fabric.

Sam and Scott appeared in the doorway; their jaws hung open. Loretta lifted her husband's chin to close his mouth while Nella's quick elbow to Scott's ribs jarred him from his folly.

Clearing his throat, Sam held his arm out at the foot of the stairs, "Ms. Cooper, you look divine this evening."

Loretta rolled her eyes as her husband helped Blair from the last step to the foyer.

"The kids are already running around together. One mentioned something about a "Blair" game," Scott informed the group.

Sam helped Blair into her coat. Scott put his arm around his wife and opened the door, "Shall we?"

Blair nodded and stepped onto the porch as the door was held open for them.

Nella craned over her shoulder, "Thank you again for letting the kids come play!"

"It is our pleasure. Have fun and if my son tempts you with too much wine, don't hesitate to have Sam come fetch you," Loretta said.

"We'll behave," Scott insisted.

Nella's head shot to her husband and teased, "Speak for yourself. I don't get out much!"

The winery was in full holiday gala. Massive wreaths adorned the outside of the tasting room, red bows hung from every light fixture and elegant white Christmas lights bordered the building.

The parking lot was filling up, surprising Blair with the number of people attending. "Wow, this is kind of a big deal," she remarked as she followed Scott and Nella into the tasting room.

A hostess met them at the door and received their invitations. She showed Scott and Nella to their table, instructing them to feel free to leave their things at their seats and welcome themselves to the tasting bar.

Seeing Blair's invitation and sizing up her elegant dress, the hostess flashed a bright smile. "The Chef's table. Follow me," with her arm out, the hostess guided Blair to a table set up on a small stage.

The room was abuzz with guests mingling about, sampling small glasses of wine and tasting appetizers. The kitchen door would swing and servers would spring out with trays of hors d'oeuvres.

By the cellar door, Luke Marsten was moving from guest to guest while occasionally interacting with a frantic server. His typically casual demeanor was supplanted with a gallant, if nervously rigid posture. Blair watched and smiled. Luke was in his element. He was happy to talk wine and mingle with guests. The amount of attention he was receiving seemed to overwhelm him, but not so much that his charm didn't conquer the situation anyway.

As he conversed with a guest, his gaze swung in Blair's direction as his eyes flittered about, taking in the room, ensuring he had greeted everyone. His head snapped back as he did a double-take upon seeing Blair. He held a finger up and excused himself. Carving his way through the crowd, singularly focused, he presented himself to Blair.

"You made it!" he smiled. Stepping back, he took her vision in, "My, I, I mean…wow. You look amazing!"

Blair blushed slightly, "You look very well put together yourself." Blair admired his tie-less shirt and vest. His jacket slung across the back of the chair next to the one Blair was presented by the hostess.

"I uh, thank you for coming," Luke said.

"Thank you for inviting me. Wow, this is quite the crowd," Blair's head bobbed around the room.

Luke's head bounced back and forth, "Yeah, it's become pretty popular. Christmas, vintage release and our annual grape stomp are the big events outside of the usual Labor Day and Thanksgiving weekends like most wineries."

"Grape stomp?" Blair scowled.

"Yeah," Luke nodded. "You probably wouldn't wear that dress, which is lovely, by the way. We put out barrels of grapes and people mush them with their feet to get the juice out. The most produced in three minutes gets a case of wine. It's a lot of fun. Very messy."

"I see. Sounds fun…if you like squishy stuff between your toes, I guess," Blair said.

Luke chuckled, "It's not for everyone but the event is phenomenal. And some of the proceeds from each event go to charity. Tonight's event goes to the foster kid program, which it sounds like you are hosting tomorrow."

"I am," Blair admitted.

"It sounds like we get to spend more time…together," Luke's voice trailed as he recognized how awkward that sounded. "Let's get you a glass. I recommend starting with Pinot Gris which is our first pairing anyway."

Luke escorted Blair to the wine server and held up two fingers motioning for the light white wine. Blair brought it to her lips, the slightest effervescence tickling her nose. "It's good."

"It has bit of natural CO_2 from the yeast. I kind of like that way," Luke said. Before Luke could continue, he was pulled away for an introduction. "Excuse me," he said as he was reluctantly led away.

Blair watched him get pulled through the crowd and then bounced from guest to guest.

"He's a good man," the wine server said.

"What?" Blair's head snapped to the server.

"Luke Marsten. He's a good man. You're a lucky woman," the server said.

"Oh, we're…we, uh, we're just friends," Blair stammered.

"Hmm," the server pursed her lips and studied the elegant Blair.

Blair raised her glass and scanned the tasting room for Nella and Scott, "Thank you!"

Darting through the crowd, Blair slid to her friend's side.

Nella's eyes were wide with glee, "This is so wonderful!"

"Have you tried the mushroom caps? They're delicious!" Scott said. "So's the rumaki."

Blair chuckled, "The way to a man's heart."

"You aren't kidding!" Nella beamed. "The way to mine – a reason to put on a dress and a nice glass of wine!"

As they sat at the tasting bar, several familiar faces streamed in stopped to say hello. Blair reached out and gave Mr. Martin a hug. Stepping back, he introduced Blair to his wife.

"Your husband is a remarkable man," Blair said.

Mrs. Martin smiled, "You must be the one pulling him out of retirement for brief ventures at the publishing house."

"I am," Blair admitted.

"It's sounds like you share his altruism. It is a pleasure to meet you," Mrs. Martin said.

"Merry Christmas!" Blair called.

Mayor Stowe was the next to stop by. "This was better attended than my best city council meeting," she lamented.

"Have you considered wine and hors d'oeuvres at you council meetings?" Blair quipped.

The mayor snapped her fingers, "No, but I think you might be on to something."

They laughed as the mayor's husband pushed through and greeted the group. When the room seemed as full as it could get, the hostess stood on the small stage and turned on a microphone. "If you would all begin to take your seats…yes, the ones I presented to you, we will get the main event underway. With that, I present to you Chef Raul Bautista and your host for the evening, Luke Marsten."

The crowd cheered as Chef Raul and Luke took the stage. The chef pointed towards Luke to lead off the event.

Luke stepped up to the microphone. "I'd like to thank you all for coming. This is one of my favorite events all year. I am honored to spend part of the holidays with you all. I am also honored to say that with your generosity, we will be able to write a sizable check for the foster children's program. Thank you."

He stepped away from the microphone for a moment as he scanned the crowd, "If you'll permit, I'd like to say a blessing over the food and we'll begin."

Luke bowed his head and said grace. Lifting his head when he said 'amen', he bounced back to the microphone. "For those of you who do not know him, I'd like to introduce Chef Raul. Yes, I borrowed him from the Seattle area, but Chef Raul is one of the best chefs I have ever met and was blown away when he accepted my invitation to join me in creating tonight's pairings."

"Tonight's first course is a frisee, pomegranate and walnut salad alongside a light curried butternut squash soup served alongside Pinot Gris. Enjoy," Chef Raul said as servers placed the first course at the diner's settings. With a slight bow, he retreated for the kitchen to oversee the preparations for the next course.

Luke left the microphone and sat next to Blair.

"What do you think?" he asked.

"I think this is amazing! A little awkward eating on a stage with everyone looking at me, but this is a nice evening. Thank you," Blair said.

"My pleasure," Luke said.

Blair ate a few bites of her opening course, "This with the wine is divine!"

"That's the idea. Give me a taste of possibilities, hoping they get some ideas to play around with flavors themselves. But mainly, it is just a great reason to pull people together for the holidays," Luke said, looking out over the crowd.

"It's quite the audience," Blair observed.

Luke nodded, "We get the usual who's who from Evergreen. We get a lot of folks who stay in Evergreen over the holidays and a few who come up just for the event, driving almost three hours to be here."

"You're good with the crowd," Blair said.

"I like the people part, if I could do away with the spotlight, I would," Luke admitted.

Blair studied him for a moment.

"What?" Luke raised an eyebrow.

"You don't like the spotlight?" Blair asked.

Luke offered a wry smile, "It sometimes finds me. I don't seek it out."

"You're good in it, just the same," Blair said.

"Thanks," Luke said, scanning the crowd. "I don't know everyone who attends, but I do know most of them. I purposely mix up the crowd. If you come with someone, I'll keep you together, but I take those I give tickets away to with those who can easily afford it. Of all times of the year, Christmas is the most magical time of the year to bring people from different worlds and have them enjoy each other."

"How many tickets do you give away?" Blair asked.

"Quite a few. I gave some for Chef Raul to hand out as well," Luke said.

"That's nice of you," Blair said.

Luke shrugged, not willing to accept high praise for his actions. "Take Scott and Nella. Great couple. Hard working. Kids at home. They wouldn't be able to afford this, but I want them to the have the opportunity to enjoy themselves here."

Blair nodded, glancing at her friends enjoying themselves and then at the man who put all of this together. "Cheers, Mr. Marsten," Blair raised her glass.

"Salut!" Luke smiled. Luke looked restless for a moment as Raul appeared in the doorway of the kitchen. "Excuse me."

Luke waved Raul up to the stage, "How was the first course? Amazing, right? Chef Raul is going to entice us to keep going. What do you say?"

Chef Raul stepped up to the microphone and explained the three mini-dishes he was serving for the entrée. Luke's wine servers poured thee subsequent modest samples to match each of the three dishes. Both encouraged the guests to eat and drink from left to right to allow their palates to make the most of the flavors.

"Three dishes?" Blair asked as Luke sat back down.

"We couldn't decide, so we cheated. Get the best of both worlds or all three, in this case," Luke grinned.

"It is all wonderful," Blair said. "How is your mother's gift going?"

Luke looked up from his plate, "I have gathered everything and come up with the design. With the pairing and a few other projects I haven't been able to work on it fully yet. I'll be up late with Santa on Christmas Eve, I'm afraid."

"I'd offer to help, but the design phase is about all that I'd be good for," Blair said.

"Nice of you to offer, just the same," Luke said.

Blair frowned, "Speaking of your parents, I thought they would be here."

Luke nodded, "They come some years. Some of their guests are here. I think the Hubbard's got here late. Mom and Pops hang at the Holly Bough to watch the kids. They've turned it into this big annual event with games, cookies and s'mores by the fire. It's more their thing, anyways."

Blair scanned the crowd. As her eyes landed on the Hubbards, she gave a little wave across the sea of tables.

"They sure are proud of you," Blair said. "With good reason. You've done well."

"I wasn't so sure, at first. When I ditched the career, I got my degree for to open a winery I was worried what they would think. Opening it so close to Evergreen was my way of softening the blow. That and I love it here," Luke said.

"Change is tough. It is a big risk to open a bed and breakfast or a winery. You are a very enterprising family," Blair said.

Luke looked at Blair, his eyes shining from the Christmas lights. "You have it in your blood, too. Your grandparents and The Toy Chest. They were the anchor for Evergreen to become the Christmas village that it is. Of the originals, that store is the last one standing. Fortunately, other complementary shops have moved in over the years that only helped to keep Evergreen the town that it is. And now you're here."

Blair swallowed hard as she drunk in the words that Luke shared.

"Oh, I'm up again. Dessert time!" Luke excused himself and pushed his chair away.

As Luke and Raul explained their next course, Blair stared out at the audience. Luke's words rattled through her head as she scanned the crowd. Visitors who drove for miles to visit Evergreen, some who have made it an annual trek. Locals who staked their lives on the town. People like herself who have a lifetime of memories in the little piece of idyllic main street holiday.

The people who worked at the publishing house and have little prospect for jobs other than moving away from the town they love, where they dreamed of raising their children. Blair rationalized to herself, they'd rather provide for their families at the risk of a few changes, wouldn't they?

She knew her grandparents had been in Evergreen a long time. She didn't know they were the catalyst for what Evergreen had become.

A voice broke her thoughts, "Are you okay?"

Luke slid back into his seat.

"Yeah," Blair nodded. "Just thinking about my grandparents."

"They'd be proud of you," Luke assured.

Blake's head snapped and she scrunched her eyes, "But what if they wouldn't make the same decisions I might need to make?"

"They entrusted you with the store because they had faith you would do the right thing, whatever that thing might be," Luke countered.

Blair nodded absently.

As the dessert was finished and the attendees began mingling once more, Luke nudged Blair, "You want to go for a quick walk, get some air?"

"I could use air," Blair agreed.

Putting their napkins by their plates, they slid out from the table.

Blair followed Luke out of the tasting room and into the cool night air behind the building. A series of outdoor wine barrels stacked side by side under a metal roof lined the exterior of the tasting and wine making facility.

"What are all these?" Blair asked.

"These are some wines that are nearly finished. I wanted to slow their final process down, so I moved them out here for cold fermentation. Not all winemakers like the process and these are a bit of an experiment for me. Want to try some?" Luke said.

"Sure," Blair shrugged.

Luke found a couple of glasses on a shelf and grabbed the siphon.

"You just have glasses...everywhere?" Blair asked.

"Sometimes. I figured folks might migrate out here. Somewhere out there," Luke pointed towards the hills, "Is a special little cave where I am trying my hand at ice wine."

"Like for dessert?" Blair asked.

Luke nodded, "Exactly. Syrupy and sweet. When done well, they are really good."

Luke pulled some of the wine from the barrel. "These have nice clarity if I hit the right chord," he held the glass to the light and handed it to Blair. Siphoning some for himself, he leaned on the rail as they watched the snow fall beyond the metal roof.

"My mom says her guests really liked the game you made," Luke said.

Blair laughed, "The kids were asking to play it again last night."

"It's nice to have creative outlets," Luke said.

"For me, it's like putting a puzzle together. I have these random fragments of ideas and try to figure out how to make it all mesh into a complete picture, an enticing picture," Blair shared.

"I get it. Sometimes for me it's experimenting with wine," Luke held his glass up, eyeing the soft garnet liquid in the light from the Christmas lights. "Sometimes it is fiddling with a chunk of wood and seeing what I can make of it."

Blair stared off at the falling flakes drifting down to the ground. "I used to feel that about marketing. Telling a story, creating eye-catching and memorable images," she said.

"But you don't anymore?" Luke frowned.

"More often than not it is trying to capture someone else's vision and too often it is a variation of a tried and true theme. Not entirely inspiring," Blair said.

"I get that," Luke nodded.

That sat in silence for a few minutes, listening to nothing but the crystalizing snow pitter-patter off the tin roof.

"You're amazing at making games, why not do something with that?" Luke suggested.

"Like, as into make a living?" Blair was astonished.

"Sure. Why not? You light up when you talk about your games," Luke said. "You clearly have a passion for it. It would be a nice sideline as owner of The Toy Chest. With your marketing prowess, I am sure you could grow both businesses."

"I have a job," Blair protested.

Luke looked directly at Blair, "Are you as passionate about your job in New York as making games?"

"I like it. I'm good at it," Blair admitted.

"That's now what I asked," Luke pressed.

Blair bristled and scanned the winery, "Not everyone can say I want to own a winery and poof, be successful."

"I worked in high tech for years. I found creating things with my hands, from the dirt, a hunk of wood, a barrel of grapes exhilarating. Wholly more fun than punching a time clock. I probably work more, but it doesn't feel like it. It feels like I'm doing what I'm supposed to be, because I am," Luke professed.

"My situation is different," Blair shrugged.

"Is it?" Luke asked. "Your grandparents gave you an amazing gift. You can start something amazing. Right here in Evergreen."

"Starting a game company from scratch...," Blair shook her head as though the idea were absurd as it sounded.

"Not from scratch, with an iconic, functional toy store," Luke said.

Blair remained dubious, "In a town that is struggling and about to struggle more?"

"It'll bounce back," Luke remained undeterred.

"Is that realistic? The store is already struggling. If I stay and somehow manage to keep the store going, never mind kick off some long shot game enterprise, that won't help the families like Nella's. They need help now. The town needs a big employer," Blair said.

Luke was suddenly struck with why Blair was considering selling the store. Nodding slowly, he said, "I see what you're up against. Not only the struggle between a possible life here and your life in New York, but you feel the opportunity to save the town is in your hands."

Blair blinked, "Yes."

Luke stood close to Blair and looked down into her eyes, "With a little faith, a better solution will present itself. I know it will."

"A job in hand for the people of Evergreen is better than a maybe a job will come along wish. They have mortgage payments that will be due in thirty days. Even if they can survive that, can they survive the next thirty?" Blair said.

"They want to stay, not because of some patch of dirt, because it is Evergreen. If Evergreen is bought up and bulldozed, they lose anyway without any hope of getting it back," Luke said.

The energy between them grew charged. It was good and bad. Their lips hovered close enough that their wine soaked breaths intertwined with the other.

Blair's heart raced. Squeezing her eyes tight, she took a step back. "We should go inside," Blair turned and walked toward the tasting room door.

Luke cursed himself as he slapped his hands against the rail. As he did, he caught a slight vibration to his left. Cocking his head, he saw Blair's phone, the screen suddenly illuminated. The words, "Couldn't wait, tickets to Paris bought. Love ya, Todd" scrolled on the screen.

Luke's throat tightened. His cursing himself only grew more vivid. Snatching the phone, he ran after Blair. Weaving his way through the thinning crowd, ignoring the attempts of the servers to stop him for a question, he scanned the room. At the front door, he saw Blair slip out with Scott and Nella.

Heading towards the door to chase after them, Luke was halted as Chef Raul stepped in front of him, "The Food Channel wants a quick word and photo op with us." Snatching Luke's arm, he spun him towards his assistant who was waiting with a camera.

Luke looked over his shoulder, but the light on the camera was lit, forcing his attention on the interviewer.

Twenty Eight

When the kitchen was cleaned and packed up. The last table was rolled away and the linens bagged for laundry, Luke congratulated Chef Raul on an amazing event and shut down the lights inside the tasting room.

Patting the phone in his pocket, he headed for his truck. Sweeping off the fresh layer of snow, he let the vehicle's powerful heater warm up the cab and defrost the windows.

Luke enjoyed driving in the snow. It was peaceful, at least when he and his fellow drivers had good grip. The fresh snow actually helped coat the roads on top of what might well have been ice that night. His four-wheel drive got him faithfully to the Holly Bough Bed and Breakfast.

It was late enough in the evening and he knew all the guests that were registered for the week had already arrived so that he could park in front of the stately home.

Unsure if most or all guests would be retired for the night, he made his way stealthily up to the porch of the inn.

Slipping his key in the lock, he turned it slowly and used both hands to carefully open the door. Kicking his soles together to knock of the snow, he crept inside.

Seeing a shadow played in the firelight of the living room, Luke poked his head in. A recognizable figure was half awake in one of the wingback chairs.

"Hey, Pops!" Luke hissed.

Sam shook himself, "Luke? I didn't expect you this evening."

"I didn't expect I'd be coming by," Luke admitted.

"It sounds like the holiday pairing was a success," Sam said.

Luke nodded, "It was a good evening."

"Night cap?" Sam offered.

Luke chuckled, "Oh, no. Not after the tasting. I'm good, but no sense in testing my limit. I might take a coffee though."

Sam pushed up from his chair, "We can probably whip something up."

Moving to the kitchen, Luke followed his father. Using a cannister of pre-ground beans Loretta kept on hand for such a late night instance and not wake guests with the grinder, they began lording over a brewing pot.

"What brings you out here?" Sam asked.

Luke fished a cellphone out of his pocket and set it on the counter, "Blair left this behind. I thought she might need it."

Sam frowned, "I'm sure it could have waited until the morning, especially with most of contacts on the east coast."

Luke bit his lip and looked sheepish, "I didn't mean to, but I saw a message and thought she might need it sooner."

"Message? What kind of message?" Sam asked.

"A pair of tickets booked by her boyfriend to Paris kind of message," Luke said, a sour note of dejection detectable only by a keen parent's ear.

Sam studied his son, a concerned, yet wry look in his eye, "Seems like the message was a kick to your midsection, son. Why would that be that case?"

Luke looked flabbergasted, his expression like he had just bitten a lemon, "What? It doesn't bother me, just sounded important, that's all."

Sam was unshaken by Luke's feigned retort.

"I just think, I have seen some things this week. I, uh, think she's on a path she's not sure she wants to be on but doesn't know how to change," Luke stammered.

Sam's look of concern strengthened, "The boyfriend part or the Paris part? And where do you fit into it?"

"Fit into it?" Luke gasped. Pouring his coffee with gusto. "I've just been a friendly ear. A sounding board."

Sam chuckled, "I see."

He stared at his son who tried his best to nonchalantly sip coffee that was a bit too hot to be drinkable at that moment. Tapping the phone, Sam said, "Well, it's here. What would you like to do now?"

Luke scrunched his face, "Nothing. I just delivered it."

A new voice caused Luke spin in horror, not knowing who might have heard any part of their conversation.

"What are you boys up to? Luke, what are you doing here?"

Luke smiled and moved to give his mother a kiss on the cheek, "Hi, Mom."

"Luke found Blair's phone. He was being a good Samaritan," Sam said.

"She was wondering what she did with it. She and Scott tore their car apart looking for it while Nella got the kids ready to go," Loretta said. She suddenly eyed her husband and son, darting from one to the other as a suspicious mother might. "Anything else?"

Sam and Luke exchanged glances and each shrugged, "Nope, nothing."

"Well, I'll see she gets it. I'm sure she'll be happy to know the mystery is solved," Loretta said.

"What mystery?" Blair's voice suddenly called softly as she entered the kitchen. Her hair was tussled as she transformed from gala wear to pajamas.

Luke's eyes went wide as Sam couldn't fight a knowing grin. Loretta raised a brow as she studied the boys before turning to Blair, "Luke found your phone, it seems, and was kind enough to bring it by."

"I thought you might need it," Luke blurted.

Blair looked at Luke in the same manner Loretta had.

"I just made some coffee. Would you like some?" Luke said, his voice accelerated.

"I was coming down for tea," Blair said.

"Luke, why don't you put some tea water on for Blair? I need to get ready for bed myself," Loretta suggested.

Luke nodded and grabbed the kettle for water.

Sam, leaning against the kitchen counter received a sharp look from his wife. "Right, I should too. A solid tooth cleaning regimen, you know, two minutes at least," he nodded and scurried after Loretta.

"Kind of gives you the feeling they were giving us the room," Blair suggested.

"Well intended, I'm sure," Luke offered meekly.

"Thank you for bringing my phone. You didn't have to come all the way out here tonight, but it is appreciated," Blair said, sliding her phone towards her as she waited for the water in the kettle to heat.

"It was no problem. I thought you might need it," Luke suggested. Feeling awkward, he turned towards the cupboard and found a mug for Blair's tea.

Blair studied him as he nervously held out a selection of teas for her to choose. Selecting an herbal, he set the tray down.

"Is everything alright?" Blair asked.

Luke frowned, "I hope I wasn't too forward or pushy at the winery. I just know what it is like to have dreams that don't fit the career path you find yourself on."

"You're fine. I know you were just trying to be helpful," Blair said. "I'm sorry I left abruptly."

Luke poured hot water into a mug and handed it to her. For a moment, both of their hands shared space on the mug, their fingers overlapping, their eyes locked on one another.

Blair breathed, "If anything, you were too close to pulling a string I might have been tempted to follow."

Luke fought to infer what part of their conversation resonated in such a way, his fingers frozen in place on the mug.

"Being here has brought up some questions for me. Questions of what I really want…in many aspects of my life," Blair said, looking deep into Luke's eyes.

Their breathing collectively stopped. Their eyes were the only things that remained in motion, each seeking meaning in the moment, neither realizing it. Blair pulled gently on the mug, releasing its grip from Luke's hand, their fingers sliding apart from one another.

"What we talked about," Blair continued. "There's so much more than me to consider."

"Like Todd?" Luke blurted in spite of himself.

"Todd?" Blair cocked her head questioningly.

Luke's shoulders slumped, "I, uh…when I found your phone, a message flashed about him taking you to Paris."

Blair let out a big sigh, "I'm not going to Paris, not with Todd, at least."

Luke didn't know how to react.

"My relationship with Todd is one of those things this trip has caused me to think about it," Blair admitted. "I don't know where it's going or more importantly where I want it to go. And don't go thinking it is about you, because it's not."

Blair cast her hair defiantly.

"I didn't…I wasn't…," Luke shrugged.

Blair took a dangerous step forward, closing the gap between them, "You are a different matter entirely. I could allow you to sway me, but I won't. It isn't about you or Todd. It's about the store, Evergreen, Nella and her family. It's about the career that I have built and a dream client in Lorent who loves my work. It's the past and the future. It's toys and games and worldwide marketing campaigns."

Luke was stunned as he listened to Blair equivocate.

Blair slapped her hand against Luke's chest and gave him a stern glare directly into his eyes, "Not that you aren't sway worthy. You...you are an amazing man, Luke Marsten. One that deserves a girl who knows what she wants and where she wants to be."

"Whatever, wherever, I have enjoyed getting to know you. To see how you treat the world around you. You are special yourself. I am happy to call you my friend if that is all I ever get to call you," Luke said. The words tumbled out of him as though he were having an out of body experience. He was shocked, excited and appalled all at the same time.

The words brought a smile to Blair's face.

"I should be going. Enjoy your tea, Blair," Luke said. On his way out of the kitchen, he turned back to Blair who didn't move from her spot at the counter, both hands cupping her tea. "Sleep on your next steps. Pray on them."

Blair offered a slight nod as Luke disappeared down the hall and out the front door.

Twenty Nine

Blair awoke the next day with a big stretch in her astoundingly comfortable Holly Bough bed. Sitting up, while her mind was churning full of conundrums and competing ideas, she wasn't rushed and she wasn't late. That for her, was a win she would take.

Getting ready, she descended the stairs to find Loretta scrambling to meet her at the door. Blair smiled, "I was thinking I might have breakfast here today?"

"My dear, I think that is a wonderful way to get your day started. Come on, you can sit at the counter if you don't mind ramblings of an old woman first thing," Loretta said, spinning to carry Blair's to go coffee cup and bagged breakfast to the kitchen island.

Setting Blair up on one side of the island, Loretta worked on the business side of the kitchen, preparing the day for the rest of the guests.

"How was the holiday pairing? Always quite elegant affairs," Loretta said, the corner of an eye on Blair while tending to her tasks.

"It was wonderful. The who's who of Evergreen, minus you and Sam, of course. Great food, wonderful wine, Christmas music from a string quartet. It was lovely," Blair said. "How about you? It is awful nice of you and Sam to forego your son's event to allow your guests to go."

"It alternates from year to year. We like seeing our son in action and the people's reaction to his handiwork for sure. The winery is a strong connection for the Holly Bough, so we do our part," Loretta said while whipping up a batter. "Besides, it is a lot of fun here with the kids, too. In fact, your game was part of the festivities. The kids really seem to like it."

"How did you and Sam choose to move to Evergreen?" Blair watched Loretta over the edge of her coffee cup.

"We realized home didn't feel as much like home after visiting here. Evergreen felt more like home to us, so we made it so," Loretta said.

Blair nodded thoughtfully as her phone rang. Todd's name popped up on the screen. Blair's finger hovered over the buttons before settling on the red 'decline' button. His text from the previous evening as the last communication. She stared at the words, "Tickets to Paris bought". She quickly cleared the screen.

As she returned her attention to Loretta and her breakfast her phone kept beckoning, rattling off another call from Todd and a message stating he needed to talk to her. Two messages from her boss Roberta, one from Candace at Lorent and her friend Ann Marie texting when would she be back to New York and was wondering what was going on.

Loretta glanced at the active phone, "You can take that, if you like."

Blair sighed. Loretta was busy but busy in her element, commanded by her own schedule. She admired that.

"I suppose I should before a missing persons is called out on me," Blair nodded. "Thank you for breakfast and the visit."

"Anytime, dear. Anytime," Loretta cooed, removing Blair's dishes from the counter. "I'm still on to help at the foster party!"

Blair smiled, "Good. I'll see you there. I think it is setting up to be the highlight of my day."

As Blair strolled to open The Toy Chest, she simultaneously enjoyed the wintry white scenery while checking her messages. She was pleasantly surprised to see the messages from Roberta and Candace were complimentary and a slew of appointments were being scheduled for after the Christmas holiday.

She studied Todd's messages but what wasn't quite ready to tackle that conversation. She had a few things to sort out first.

Her thumb moved to the next message. Realizing she hadn't communicated with Ann Marie aside from a few project related requests, she owed her friend a call. Pressing the phone symbol by her name, Ann Marie picked up on the first ring.

"Where have you been? What is going on out there?" Ann Marie's voice sprang through the phone.

"Sorry," Blair conceded. "The trip out here has been more complicated than I could have ever expected."

"Sheesh! To watch Roberta fume the halls cursing your name to spinning around and lauding praise was a wild thing to watch," Ann Marie said.

"Yeah, I had some complications with the first round of the storyboard package," Blair admitted.

There was a brief pause in the conversation. "So, when are you coming home?" Ann Marie asked.

"The plan is to come home tomorrow on Christmas Eve," Blair said, surprised by the hesitation in her own voice.

"The plan? What is going on, Blair?" Ann Marie asked. Suddenly her voice rose several octaves, "You met someone!"

Blair paused, "That's not what it's about…"

"Blair Cooper, I can hear in your voice it is at least a factor. A sizable factor. What about Todd?" Ann Marie noted.

"Todd. Todd is something I need to deal with when I am back in New York. I have realized, with some distance, I don't want to be one of his associates which is how our relationship seems to work," Blair said. "It's all head and no heart."

"He's rich, charming in a cocktail dinner kind of way, handsome…he checks a lot of boxes," Ann Marie countered.

"Not the important one," Blair muttered.

Ann Marie fumbled with the phone, "See! I knew it! You did meet someone!"

"I met lots of people here in Evergreen. People who knew my family. New friends. It has been a surprisingly good, busy, confounding trip," Blair said.

"Confounding?" Ann Marie queried.

Blair sighed, "Take the store, for example. It was supposed to be an easy decision, sell it, take the money, close a chapter. But being here. Being in my grandparents' store felt like I was cutting off a limb on the family tree."

"Keep it and let someone local run it," Ann Marie suggested.

"I thought about that. The margins are pretty tight and tough to make ends meet without some serious changes," Blair said. "I did find a buyer."

"That's great!" Ann Marie exclaimed.

"They want to knock it down. Buy up most of the shops along Main Street and put in a big highway center," Blair said.

"Eww. I mean, you can't control what other people do with the things they buy from you," Ann Marie countered.

Blair breathed, "I hold the key to this town's future with my grandparents' store."

"It sounds like another head and heart debate," Ann Marie suggested.

"I wish I could put the two together," Blair said.

"It sounds like you have a day and half to figure it out," Ann Marie said. "Listen, if you aren't going to spend Christmas with Todd, let me know. The ladies in my building get together for a Christmas pajama party. You'll just need to scrounge a white elephant gift on your way home."

"I might take you up on that," Blair said as she stood in front of The Toy Chest. "Thanks, Ann Marie."

"Good luck."

Blair went through the motions of opening up the toy store, including letting Kris in to set up the treat table and double check arrangements for the foster kids' party. Mostly she was on autopilot as her conversation the previous evening careened and merged with Ann Marie's. She wished there were some magical way to make everything work out.

She entertained Luke's idea. Was there a way to embellish the role of The Toy Chest affecting more jobs for publishing house employees? Hiring another employee in place of her position was the best she could do. That wouldn't even put a dent in the town's needs.

When Nella arrived for the day, she wore the troubled look again.

"News?" Blair looked concerned.

"Sorry I'm late. I think my car finally died and so Scott had to take me in. We've been sitting on an expensive repair for a while. There's no way we can get to it now," Nella said.

"Could I give you an advance?" Blair asked.

Nella's expression softened to one of gratitude, "It would take three months' worth of advances to solve this problem. We had a bit of a tense car ride as Scott suggested we move in with his parents in Tacoma."

"Nella, I'm sorry," Blair said. Seeing the personal plight gave Blair the resolve to do what she needed to with the store. It was the closest she could get the head and heart equation to play out. She just couldn't get the Pottersville vision from *It's a Wonderful Life* out of her head every time she pictured selling to the developer.

Meredith Kohl and Bradley Marcom were coming up that afternoon with final papers. The stores and the town's destinies were sealed.

Blair and Nella were each helping last minute gift shoppers. The jingle bells at the door had been a steady chorus throughout the day. She didn't flinch when they sounded again. As she led her guests up to the counter, Nella looked over her shoulder, "I'll ring them up."

Blair turned to see Luke Marsten standing with a wooden box in his hands. Thanking her guests, she walked up to Luke. Her brow wrinkled, "What's up?"

Luke grinned wide, "I have something for you." Stepping forward, he opened the lid of the hinged box to reveal the contents inside.

Rows of hand carved figures were held in separate felt sections. Blair studied them and then her eyes widened with recognition. "Are those...?"

"What did you call them, meeples?" Luke asked. "Mr. Martin said if you had a form mold, you could make 3D prints instead of the flat cardboard printed ones."

Blair studied the pieces, her fingers gliding along the figures. Pulling one of the meeples from its soft perch she held it in front of her. "Luke," she gasped. "These are...perfect!"

Feeling overwhelmed, she led Luke to the back room. Diligently, he carried the box and set it on the desk, the lid flopped open.

Blair looked at Luke with incredulous eyes. "I don't know what to say."

"Say you'll take a chance on your own dream. Take a chance that you can take your grandparents' legacy and make it your own," Luke urged.

"When I put the game together, I dreamed of having it produced and stacked on shelves in The Toy

Chest and stores all over. I pictured families gathering in their homes, snow falling outside their windows and a fire in the fireplace playing the game. Pulling families and friends together. Ridiculous, huh?" Blair said, her cheeks red and her eyes distant as she dreamt aloud.

Luke shook his head, "Not at all. No more ridiculous than clearing some brush and planting vines hoping that in seven years, they'd bear fruit."

"I do have other game ideas. I hadn't thought of games for years, but ever since I found that dusty old box on that shelf, I have been churning them in my head," Blair said excitedly.

"Run with it!" Luke said excitedly. "Follow your dream with The Toy Chest being the epicenter. It can be the vehicle to grow and carry your ideas forward. Who knows, in time, this might be just what Evergreen needs, not some big developer that wants to change Evergreen forever."

Blair's face fell as she began to mull the reality of the fantasy they cobbled together. "It all sounds magical, but it's just not realistic. I barely have the funds to keep this store running and that is through the busy season. I've dipped into my savings to prop up some of the events. There is no way I could invest in a game company, as nice as that sounds," she relented.

"By the time I pay capital gains, I won't have a dime left, especially if I don't sell. Never mind invest in a game factory. And I've got my life in Manhattan. The Lorent account…," Blair rationalized.

"And Todd," Luke muttered.

"What about the people here, in Evergreen? It would take years, if ever, for me to grow to the point where I could afford to hire anyone. They need help *now*," Blair argued.

Luke studied Blair, "If they survive to live on in a town that is no longer Evergreen, they might as well move on. Another small town with classic charm and history wiped off the map, forever," Luke said. He chewed his lip. "Come with me."

"What?" Blair looked astounded. She started to place the carved meeple back in the box.

"Take that with you. I want to show you something," Luke said. Snatching Blair's coat from the rack, he held it for her to slip her arms into. "Nella, do you mind…"

Nella cut Luke off with a wave as he paraded Blair out of the store and to the passenger door of his truck. Without a word, he circled to the driver's door and climbed in.

Putting the truck into gear, Luke pulled away from the curb, swinging the truck out of town. Just past the city limits sign, he swung the truck through a thick patch of snow and engaged the four-wheel drive. With steady pressure on the accelerator, he wound through the trees until a curve brought them to the edge of the snow-covered hill.

In this spot, the road skirted the side of the hill leaving a spot bare of trees. Directly below them was Main Street, the Christmas village of Evergreen in all its holiday splendor. The wreath strung lamp posts, lit trees along the sidewalk and the giant town tree looming at the end of the drive were majestically presented before them.

"This is amazing. I've seen this view before," Blair said.

"It's on the town webpage and almost every postcard stand," Luke laughed. "This is Evergreen. There's The Toy Chest. There's the coffee shop…"

Blair nodded, "I get it."

She fumbled with the meeple in her hand. Luke reached over and softly guided her hand to the dash of the truck, depositing the meeple overlooking the town.

"I don't know," Blair breathed.

"I didn't know until I planted the first vine. My parents didn't know until they registered the first guest at the Holly Bough. Your grandparents didn't know until they turned the sign on The Toy Chest door to read 'open'," Luke pressed.

"You really think I can do this?" Blair asked.

Luke shrugged, "In truth, I don't know. I do absolutely know that if you don't try, you most certainly won't."

Blair stared out at the town, seemingly through the blank stare of the meeple on the dash.

Quietly, she turned to Luke, "Would you take me back? I think I have a lot of work to do and very little time to do it."

Luke nodded and fired up the truck.

Blair raced through the store and tossed her coat on the rack. Diving to her desk, she snatched open her laptop and pulled out a notepad. In a fury like she had never worked before, she began storyboarding for what might be the most important pitch of her life.

Nella manned the store while Blair worked through the morning in the office. Fueled by a kindly delivered latte, Blair scanned through her presentation. The concept was solid and the marketing plans worthy of Madison Avenue. What she wasn't sure of was the numbers. She did her best research to create realistic scenarios, but it was the realm of accountants and investors.

Hesitating, she stared at her phone. Biting her lip, she picked it up and dialed.

"Blair! Thank goodness, I was starting to worry," Todd spat into the phone.

"Sorry, it has been hectic as I'm down to the wire here in Washington," Blair said.

"I thought I scared you off with the trip to Paris...," Todd started.

Blair sighed, "Todd, I can't go to Paris with you. But I have something important to run by you."

"What? I...," he started before Blair cut him off.

"I have an opportunity that I need your financial expertise on. I am thinking about starting a game company," Blair said.

Her statement was met with silence. When Todd finally did speak, he repeated, "You want to start a game company. With what expertise? What resources? You'll need manufacturing, likely foreign and domestic options. Distribution. A *lot* of start up capital in an extremely high risk, fairly low return venture...Blair, that is not a good idea. Sell the store, come back to New York and rocket your career with Lorent. And I'm not saying that just because it is you. I would be obligated to say that to anyone who asked my advice."

"Is it doable?" Blair asked.

"With prayers, hard work and a bit of magic...maybe. Look, I have to go. Send me what you've got. I'll take a look at it, but, I'm not convinced my advice will be any different," Todd admitted.

"Thank you. That is all I ask," Blair said.

Thirty

Blair didn't realize how much of her day was slipping by as she scrambled in the toy shop office. Scouring her contact lists for clients she had run marketing campaigns for from manufacturers to distributors, she began filling gaps in her business plan.

The toy store office was wall papered with sketches and spreadsheets and call logs. Much like the Lorent presentation, she took a solid concept and wrapped it in elegance and completeness.

Through her industry contacts, she was able to come up with staffing models and estimated financials for starting the business. Her own keen marketing prowess created company and game campaigns that would rival any larger game company.

Arms crossed, she stared at her walls. She amassed everything that Todd had requested and more. She had manufacturers and distributors as well as the costs to use them. Blair was able to calculate the cost per game to print, produce and ship.

Her staffing map wasn't as robust as she'd like, but she would be able to create several jobs from the publishing house to take orders, assist with marketing and oversee production and sales.

Excitedly, she sent Todd her final package.

As she worked through the process of developing the game company she was inspired and put ideas for two new games down on paper. Soon, her office walls were plastered with game sketches and mock-ups, replacing the pages she had pasted of the business model.

Simple games with colorful balloons and migrating jelly fish to adventure games that could take a family hours to play to Blair's favorite, a Main Street Christmas game that leads to the crescendo of a town tree lighting, the ideas spilled out of her and onto the pages.

Lost in her work, she was startled when she caught a figure in the corner of her eye.

"I didn't mean to disturb you, I was worried. You had hadn't been out of there all day," Nella said. Stepping inside the back room, she spied the sketches taped on every available surface. "What is all of this?"

Blair looked at Nella, not wanting to get her hopes up until she had the financial details solved, "I am working on something big. Think of it like a giant Christmas present. I just have a few things to work out to make it real."

"More games?" Nella asked. "We love your games."

"It is a little more than that, but it gave me a few ideas that I had to get out of my head and down on paper," Blair said.

Nella inspected one in particular, "Wow. This looks great! You just...created it?"

Blair shrugged, "I mean, it's not done. It's just the original concept, but yeah."

"Your grandparents would be so joyful to see your games in the store that they created," Nella said.

"You think so?" Blair frowned.

"Are you kidding me?" Nella beamed. "They talked about you all the time. And your brother Derek, of course. But there was a special affinity with you."

"Derek liked the toys, but never took interest in the store. Playing toy store was my favorite thing," Blair reminisced.

"Well, whatever you are cooking up, I hope it is a success," Nella said. "I'm going to keep an eye out for guests. Let me know if you need anything."

"Thanks. I'll be out in a bit," Blair said.

The jingle bells at the front door chimed as though on cue. Blair dropped back down to the final sketch she was working on.

A soft knock on the doorjamb broke Blair's attention. "Luke!"

Luke stood in the doorway. As he strode forward, he held out the game piece Blair had placed on the dash of this truck while they looked over the town of Evergreen. "You forgot this."

Blair's eyes grew wide, "Oh, my gosh! I got so excited to work on plans, that I must have forgot it on the dash!"

"I'm not sure how long this little guy hung in up there, it was rattling around the floor board as I was heading into the hills to the winery," Luke laughed.

Blair snatched it like it was a prize jewel. She looked at Luke with grateful eyes, "Thank you." Excitedly, she pulled out her stack of papers on the game company specs, "You've got to see this."

Running through the full presentation she had sent to Todd, Luke looked impressed.

"Blair, that's amazing. That is just what this town needs. The injection of hope that can keep it together for things to sort out," Luke said.

Blair looked less convinced, "It doesn't bring in that many jobs. I wish I could do more there."

"For those you can give a job to, imagine the blessing it will be on their lives," Luke said. "And you give Evergreen a fighting chance to stay Evergreen."

Blair smiled. Placing an arm on Luke's shoulder, she breathed, "You have a lot of faith in me."

"You have a spark that lights up the room, energizes everyone around you. I think Evergreen lost that spark when your grandparents…left us," Luke said.

The words resonated with Blair.

"Great work," Luke said. "I've got to run and get things tied down at the winery so that I can be at the foster party with bells on."

Blair nodded. Holding up the wooden game piece, she admired, "Thanks, Luke!"

She placed the game piece in her pocket as she cleaned up her mad scientist explosion of papers and ideas she had scattered around the office. As she did, she uncovered the mail. Inspecting the envelopes, she carefully opened them, lining them out. Doing quick math in her head, she swallowed hard. The receipts she had taken in since she opened the store would be barely enough to cover the overhead and outstanding invoices, never mind Nella's salary.

Blair sighed and rubbed her head. She still had to come up with the capital gains tax for inheriting the store. It would have exhausted her savings had she not paid out of pocket for the coffee and cocoa, helped pay for the gingerbread contest and supplied the food and presents for the foster party. The check from the holiday pairing would have paid for the party, but Blair insisted it go into the foster program's coffers.

Chewing her lip, she was hopeful Todd came back with good news. For her, The Toy Chest and for Evergreen.

Pushing her bills and papers aside, she marched out onto the sales floor for an invigorating boost she received when greeting guests into the store. It didn't take long before the bounce in her step was back. Her Christmas spirit refilled and she looked forward to the foster children's party that evening.

After an afternoon of helping visitors finding the perfect Christmas gift, Blair's phone rang. She felt a pang of guilt as she hadn't been as a excited to receive a call from Todd since she arrived in Evergreen.

"Excuse me," she called across the toy store as she scurried to the office to take Todd's call.

Clicking on the phone, she asked excitedly, "So?"

There was a brief hesitation before Todd spoke, "Blair, this was a really solid presentation. My firm should hire you to put together our investment portfolios, we'd be a whole lot more successful."

"So, you liked it!" Blair squealed.

"I shared it with a few others, they liked it too," Todd said. "The concept is great. The products you are creating are amazing. I had no idea that was something you did or even wanted to do. Linking it the store in your little Christmas village is cute and tells a nice story."

"That's what I was hoping," Blair admitted.

"You did everything I needed you to do from marketing to production to distribution," Todd said. "Once you factor in those outsourced costs, your profit gets eaten up. With the cost of manufacturing and the time to profit from spin up and buoyancy…the numbers just don't pencil out. I tried everything, even with my most aggressive investors and analysts."

Blair sunk against the wall as the words crashed down on her, her heart plummeting to the pit of her stomach.

"I'm not just saying this, it was excellent work. Your plan was solid. The numbers don't lie. I can't make this work. Not with the costs to do business. I just can't. No one could. I'm sorry, Blair," Todd said.

Blair fought for breath and choked, "Thank you. I know you put a lot into running through all this for me.

"Of course, Blair. I wish there was more that I could do. Even if it was close, I'd invest myself," Todd said.

"Thank you," Blair said. "I need to go. I have an appointment to keep I was hoping I could cancel."

Blair hung up the phone. Her mood was heavy. She was riding so high, lifted on the promise that she could do some real good in the community. The news from Todd brought her crashing down. She knew Todd, if there was a way, he would have done it.

With a sigh, she returned to the solace of the Christmas infused toy store sales floor.

Thirty One

Blair's respite serving guests in the store was short lived, as her phone announced the arrival of Meredith Kohl and Bradley Marcom. Blair desperate to not be the thief that stole the town's Christmas, sought a place away from Main Street to meet with the realtor and the developer.

Excusing herself, yet again, she grabbed her coat and climbed into the Mercedes that parked out in front of the store. With a forced smile, she nodded and the luxury vehicle pulled away from the curb.

"Thank you for picking me up, I didn't want to do this at the store," Blair said. As they drove past the coffee shop, "Or in town."

"Change is difficult, but there is a light at the end of the tunnel if my company can begin hiring people. Re-instill some hope for the New Year and the future," Bradley Marcom smiled.

Blair nodded.

The driver pulled into a little roadside café that was most often used as a quick stop for folks either heading into or out of the mountains.

Pushing into the rustic general store that sold everything from gas to pies to fishing bait and firewood. A few tables covered with vinyl table clothes served as their meeting table and the three reluctantly ordered cups of coffee to rent their space.

Meredith placed a large file of papers on the table, landing with a thump. "We would have done this digitally, but Mr. Marcom wanted to do this in person," the realtor said.

"I can be a little old fashioned," Marcom grinned. "Antithetical for a progressive developer, I know."

Again, Blair nodded silently.

Meredith began flipping pages that required signatures or initials or both. Blair hardly heard the words as Meredith's voice faded to a murmur. Blair's mind was flooded with images of Evergreen. Two competing lenses pulled and yanked at her mind and her heart.

One lens was the iconic Christmas village. Locals and visitors delighting in the quaint and undeniably beautiful town set at the foot of the Cascade mountain range. A respite for families and travelers to enjoy a piece of Americana throughout the year, most particularly at Christmas. One of the last refuges to experience a Norman Rockwell Christmas. Evergreen was a place to live a Courier and Ives Christmas postcard.

The second lens brought her to the table with pen in hand. The people of Evergreen desperate to find a way to make a living as the publishing house doors closed. Blair wondered if she had done all that she could. If she had thought of everything.

With a sigh, she signed the last page. Her hand hovering the final 'r' in her name. Looking up, she placed the pen on the table.

Mr. Marcom reached his hand across the table. "You have set the future of Evergreen into motion, Ms. Cooper," he smiled.

Blair knew it was meant as a positive, but the words instead stung her. She simply offered a lifeless hand and a numb nod in return.

"We should find a place with champagne to celebrate!" Meredith offered.

"I need to get back. I am hosting the town foster event tonight," Blair said softly.

"You have a heart of gold, Blair," Meredith beamed.

Blair shook off the compliment, feeling anything but kind-hearted at the moment. She felt like the town had nothing to fill their stockings, so she graciously just signed them up to receive a lump of coal. In this case, she was curious if something under the tree was truly better than nothing.

She fought for a last second moment of inspiration, but her mind was blank.

"Oh, and as promised. You have signed before Christmas, as such, you get this," Mr. Marcom reached in his jacket and produced a sizable check, handing it to Blair.

Blair studied it. It was the largest check she had ever received. She should have felt excited holding that windfall in her hand, but it surged the pangs of guilt to new levels.

"Let's get you back to the store so that you can prepare for your party. We'll get back to Seattle. Good luck to you, Blair," Meredith said, shaking her client's hand.

"If I can ever do anything for you, here is my card," Mr. Marcom handed Blair a business card.

Blair nodded and slipped the card in her pocket along with the check she folded in half.

Luke Marsten whistled along to the Christmas song as he drove towards town. He had a quick stop at the bed and breakfast before he would meet up with Blair for the foster children's Christmas event. As he descended the hill, he checked his fuel gauge. It was going to be a cold night, he liked to keep the tank full.

Pulling into the gas station, he hopped out and slid the nozzle into the tank and clipped the trigger into place to let the pump run. Hands in his pockets, he stomped his feet to shake of the cold as he waited for the pump to fill his tank.

Glancing towards the store of the gas station, he saw three people gathered around a table at the window. Seeing Blair, he instantly brightened. He was surprised to see her out this far out of town, but instinctively strode to pop in and say hello.

As he walked, he studied the exchange. He watched as the man across from Blair handed her a check and the woman next to Blair slid a large folder into an attaché. He froze as recognized the woman, a realtor from Seattle who had approached his parents on more than one occasion to sell the bed and breakfast.

The man turned so Luke could see his face as they rose from the table. Luke's brow twitched as he too, was recognized. The developer that wanted to purchase his winery as part of some grand development where the mountain roads met the interstate.

Watching Blair pocket the check, Luke shook his head and cursed.

Spinning on his heels, he retreated for his truck. The pump had shut off and was ready for him. Hastily replacing the nozzle with the pump and closing his fuel door, Luke climbed in the cab of his truck and rocketed out of the gas station parking lot towards town.

Blair walked into The Toy Chest with the movement akin to a zombie. The lights, the Christmas displays, the crooning Christmas carols played over the store's speakers failed to penetrate her veil of sadness. Her brain told her she did the right thing. She provided a path for livelihoods for the people of Evergreen, but her heart was broken.

Her grandparents' store, the face of Evergreen, the very icon of Christmas celebration was signed away. Forever changed.

Nella called from across the store, "Is everything okay?"

Blair couldn't bring herself to look at Nella, she just nodded, "I'm fine."

Sulking all the way to the backroom to hang up her coat, Blair hardly looked up from the floor.

Nella quietly followed. Softly, she said, "You don't seem fine."

Blair looked up, her eyes welling, "That big project I was trying to do. It's not going to work."

Nella cocked her head, "I'm sure it's okay, whatever it was. It sounds like you tried."

"You don't understand," Blair gasped.

"Do you want to talk about it? I'd like to help, if I can," Nella said.

Blair shook her head and wiped her cheek, "No. I don't want to talk about it. At least not now. I want to focus on the kids coming in this evening."

Nella bit her lip and nodded. Putting her arms around Blair's shoulders, she squeezed, "Okay."

"I think...I think I need to clear my head before the kids arrive," Blair stammered.

"Sure," Nella said. "I've got everything here."

Blair thanked her. Grabbing her coat, she hastily left The Toy Chest and wandered aimlessly along Main Street. As she walked past the wreath adorned shops, the fabulous window displays of the small shops, most of them family businesses. She knew they all struggled this season as well. You couldn't tell from how they greeted everyone who walked into their stores.

Blair's gut wrenched with having signed those papers. She helped out a part of the town only to doom the other. It would take a little time, but the slope had been slipped on. The Christmas village would one day in the not distant future be the scene of a giant travel mall.

The sun set quickly behind the hills, allowing the Christmas lights to make an early appearance, leading all the way to the Christmas tree. It made the scene that much more magnificent and Blair's lament that much stronger.

As was the town tradition, many locals and visitors alike gathered around the town Christmas tree at five o'clock. Gathering in a circle around the tree, they began to sing. When they hit the second chorus, the tree shimmered to light.

Blair was frozen, watching the event take place. Her eyes lit upon families that she had grown to know over the past week. Many of which she knew were directly and profoundly impacted by the shuttering of the publishing house. She watched astonished as they gleefully held hands and sung alongside the Christmas tree. They rejoiced and celebrated as though nothing was wrong. Many were perched to lose their livelihoods, their homes and yet here they were, spirits undaunted.

Part of Blair was furious as her own anguish boiled. Why weren't they more worried? Why did they not fret?

As she continued gazing, hands reached from family to family. Smiles were shared through cheeks plump with song. Families, neighbors, visitors sharing a moment. A moment of hope. A moment of peace. A moment of togetherness and love.

Blair was suddenly moved by inspiration. She glanced at her watch. She had very little time before the foster party. She grinned a hopeful grin, it was enough time to at least get the wheels in motion.

As she marched back to The Toy Chest, she placed two very important calls.

Thirty Two

Blair burst into The Toy Chest a new woman. She knew it was another long shot, but it was reason for hope. That hope would get her through the foster Christmas event and through the night where she would see if her plan would work the next morning.

The abrupt change in affect wasn't lost on Nella. Her gaze pivoted, "That was a good walk."

Blair grinned sheepishly, "Nothing a little song around a Christmas tree couldn't fix."

Nella nodded, "Yeah, that is a good experience. When I first heard about Scott's early dismissal, it helped me gather myself."

"Ready for this? We have some kids that deserve some holiday cheer themselves. Let's give them a great party!" Blair exclaimed. She headed to the store room to start retrieving the presents she had prepared for the kids in addition to the money they got to spend on siblings and friends in the store that night.

Kris and Jessica began carrying in treats for the party while Nella closed out the sales for the day.

Mayor Stowe, Mary Kay and June Kennedy arrived. All three women looking casually elegant for the event. Mayor Stowe thanked Blair and Nella for facilitating the party. As the room began to fill with supporters, volunteers and streams of children, Blair craned her neck of the crowd to find Luke.

She approached Nella, "Have you seen Luke?"

Nella shook her head.

"I thought he would have been here by now," Blair said, eyeing the door.

Her attention was quickly swayed by a little hand tugging on her skirt. Looking down she saw a pair of large brown eyes staring up at her, "'Scuse me. Can you help me?"

Blair stooped closer to the girl, "Of course, I can. What are you looking for?"

"I want something for my sister. But, I don't know what," the little girl said.

"How old is your sister?" Blair asked.

"She's ten," the girl replied.

"How old are you?" Blair asked.

"Seven."

"That's a good age. What's your name?" Blair asked.

"Lucy. My sister's name is Brianna."

"It's nice to meet you, Lucy," Blair said. Do you have an idea what you are looking to get for Brianna?"

Lucy looked sheepish, her eyes glancing at the floor before the large brown saucers once more met Blair's. "I want something that she will keep with her. Something that will reminder her of me if we ever get separated again."

The words instantly melted Blair's heart. Her problems and the problems of Evergreen suddenly became so minute in scale compared the kids that were visiting her store that night.

With a gentle hand, she guided Lucy to some items in the store that she thought would fit the bill.

At one point in the evening, Nella came over to Blair and whispered, "A lot of the kids coming up don't have enough, what do I do?"

Blair chewed her lip, "I know part of the event is a bit of lesson in economics and empowerment. I tell you what, discount everything to thirty-percent below our margin. If they still don't have enough, send them back out to find something cheaper. Team them up with a volunteer to help them."

"Can we afford that?" Nella hissed; her nose wrinkled.

Blair shrugged with a bit of a giggle, "I'll figure it out later."

"You're the boss! And a darn good one," Nella said and jogged back over to the register.

Blair didn't hear the door chimes. Mayor Stowe's voice rang above the crowd, "Luke Marsten! I was wondering where you were!"

Blair's head spun to face them. Luke nodded in conversation with the mayor and produced the check from the funds he collected from the Holiday Pairing.

Mayor Stowe waved the check towards the foster program director. Weaving her way through the crowd, the director met with the mayor and Luke. Mayor Stowe found Blair and waved her over to join them.

"Blair, this is Stacy Richards. She runs the county's foster program," the mayor introduced. "Stacy, this is Blair Cooper. Granddaughter of the Noelles."

Stacy looked at Blair, "Your grandparents were the most generous, kindest people I have ever met. It seems like that runs in the family."

"Thank you, Stacy. It is a pleasure to meet the kids and help them," Blair said. She noticed Luke wouldn't make eye contact with her. He gazed his way out of the conversation and across the store.

"I've watched you. You get to know them first. That's just what they need. To see that people care enough to get to know who they are," Stacy lauded.

"Luke and Blair make a powerful partnership," Mayor Stowe added, catching Luke's attention. His eyes flitted on Blair's briefly, his lips tight before turning his gaze to the mayor and smiling.

"I'm glad to have been able to help. If you don't mind, I'd like to visit with the kids," Luke said and wandered off to a section of toy cars several boys were inspecting.

Mayor Stowe pulled something from her pocket and held it out for the ladies to see, "Luke made one of these ornaments for each of the children."

Blair studied the wooden ornament dangling from a piece of gold string. The wooden ball depicted the town tree with a ring of silhouettes of various sizes circling the tree, hand in hand.

"That is amazing, I just experienced the power of that scene this evening before the party," Blair said.

Stacy nodded, "I try to get the kids and the foster families to attend during the season. I love the sense of community at that very moment."

"As mayor, I strive to keep that feeling throughout the year. I don't think I've achieved it yet, but it is my dream."

"It's a good dream," Blair nodded.

Mayor Stowe looked at Blair, "I have had to learn to never give up. The people of this town haven't ever failed me in that faith. Even in bleak times. As one of our newest residents, you'll come to see that."

"I think I'm on the accelerated course of that sentiment," Blair laughed.

When the children completed their purchases and each had a sufficient pile of cookies on their plates, Santa Claus burst through the door to an uproar of cheers from the children.

"Ho, Ho, Ho!" Santa bellowed as she entered, a sack slung over his back.

"This looks like a room full of exceptionally good boys and girls," Santa eyed the children in the room. "I know you all have been busy with the important part of presents, the giving part. As, uh, sort of an expert in this field, I can tell you that is where the greatest joy comes from. But every so often, it is okay to find joy in receiving. Especially when it is something special. I worked on these in my workshop myself, just for you."

Blair stared at Santa's eyes. They flitted on hers but refused to land. She knew those eyes. She knew that voice.

Santa reached into his pack and began handing out presents. When each child had one, he nudged, "Well, go on. Open them up!"

The kids unwrapped their present at their own varied pace. Some tore into the package with paper and bows flying. Others carefully slipped the bows off and gently placed them in as new condition in front of them while finding the edges of the tape to release the paper which they folded in neat sheets in front of them.

They all admired their gift. It wasn't a car, a doll, a train or a toy of any sort. It was a Christmas ornament that spoke love and togetherness. One girl hugged it. A little boy scanned the room and quickly slid the prize in his pocket.

"Ho, ho, ho!" Santa laughed. "I'll see you all again on Christmas Eve! Be sure to follow the rules of your households and get to sleep early that night so I can do my work! Merry Christmas, kids!"

"My staff has the gifts you put together already loaded. That was very generous of you," Stacy whispered to Blair.

Blair nodded, "Happy to."

"He's a good Santa, isn't he?" Stacy chuckled.

"Yeah," Blair agreed. "He is."

They watched as Santa hugged and high-fived his way across the room, heading out the door.

"Excuse me," Blair said. "I need a word with Santa."

Slipping towards the entrance, she streaked after Santa.

Parked around the corner so the children didn't seem climb into his truck, Santa slipped into the dark.

"Santa!" Blair hissed. "Luke!"

Santa spun, seeing Blair chase after him, his shoulders slumped.

"I need to talk with you!" Blair called.

Luke opened his door, "I need to go Blair. Nice event for the kids."

Without waiting for a response, he climbed in the cab and started the truck. Still clad in Santa garb, he pulled away from the curb and drove off into the night. Blair stood on the sidewalk, crossing her arms to fend off the chill as she watched his taillights disappear.

Thirty Three

Blair kicked out of bed the next morning with the excitement of a child on Christmas morning. She burst out of the covers and quickly got ready for the day. It was only Christmas Eve, but she was hoping for a gift or two that day.

Stopping to have coffee with Loretta on her way out the door, the intuitive hotelier studied Blair. "Your have some vim and vigor today," Loretta said. "I know that look. It is the same one Luke had right before he opened a winery in the middle of nowhere."

"And look at him now," Blair grinned over her mug. "Have you seen him? I needed to talk to him after the foster Christmas party."

"He stopped quickly, flashed one of his fake smiles and dashed out," Loretta admitted. "Anything wrong?"

Blair shook her head, "I don't know."

"He's got something in his head. The Marsten boys are resilient and resourceful but stubborn as they come," Loretta warned.

"Yeah, I know the type," Blair grinned. Glancing around the inn, she asked, "Do you have a meeting room? I have someone stopping by that I need to have an important conversation with in private."

"We do. It's down that hall. Our offices are on the other end. It is full of paper snowflakes and clay gingerbread men ready for painting. We used it for arts and crafts the night of the winery event," Loretta. "It's your when you need it."

Blair glanced at her watch, "I gotta go. Thanks for coffee!"

Jumping out of her counter stool, she paused as she passed Loretta. Leaning in, she wrapped her arms around the bed and breakfast proprietor, "You're wonderful!"

Scampering out, she dashed through the front door and bound down the steps while still pulling her winter coat on. High-stepping over the new snow that fell overnight, she danced her way into town. Passing the coffee shop, Blair gave a little wave. Dialing Nella, she asked if she would mind opening The Toy Chest. Receiving a rousing "of course", Blair arrived at her destination.

"If I wasn't so painfully obvious in my adoration for my wife and about half a century your senior, people might begin to talk with our clandestine meetings, Ms. Cooper," Mr. Martin teased, a playful twinkle in his eye.

"You're as honorable as you are charming. Your sterling reputation should remain intact," Blair said. "Mine, however, is in a bit of jeopardy."

Mr. Martin frowned, "How so?"

"Have you ever tried to do the right thing only to unleash a line of dominoes with unintended consequences?" Blair sighed.

"Like keeping the publishing house open past its due date? I tried to encourage my employees to seek other jobs. I even brought in experts to help them. They wouldn't take me up on it. Loyal to the last day," Mr. Martin nodded.

"That's exactly what this is about," Blair said. Her face falling serious. "I was approached to sell The Toy Chest."

She swallowed hard as her eyes welled and she bit her lip, "That was my intention when I flew out here. Sell The Toy Chest. When I got here, I saw the town for the first time in years. Stepped in my grandparents' store, I began to have a change of heart. And then I started to see the struggles of the families that worked at the publishing house. The investor suggested a path to reclaim jobs. I even got him to agree to hire Evergreen applicants first and to bring them on early."

"Sounds noble so far," Mr. Martin said. Leaning against the reception desk of the publishing house.

"I signed the papers yesterday," Blair breathed so deep her chest swelled and then fell. "He wants buying my store to be a catalyst for the rest of Main Street. They want some sort of travel mall for interstate traffic as we're about halfway from the Canadian border to Seattle."

"I see," Mr. Martin winced. The vision of Evergreen turned interstate center was a gut wrenching one. "That is a strong business case. And you say they'd hire my former employees?"

"They'd have priority," Blair nodded. Her face fell, "I'm afraid Evergreen won't be Evergreen anymore."

Mr. Martin nodded, "You didn't bring me out here to tell me all that."

"No, sir. I didn't," Blair admitted. She looked at the newly retired Mr. Martin and then at the offices behind him. "The publishing house bought your company. Did they by the building?"

"I own the real estate. It was offered as part of the package, but they had no use for it once our deal was done. It goes on sale next month once they send a crew out to see if they want any of our equipment. I'm letting them have it at cost," Mr. Martin said.

"What if another buyer had use for those machines? You said they could do more than print books?" Blair asked. She pulled the wooden game piece that Luke carved from her pocket and handed it to Mr. Martin.

He grinned and nodded, "It can. This would make a fine mold for the 3-D printer."

Mr. Martin leaned back, staring at the game piece in his hand and scratched his chin with the other. "I'd be willing to sell the equipment at cost, but this building and the property…it's not Manhattan prices out here, but it's not cheap. I'd give you a sweetheart deal, but…"

He scratched out a figure on a piece of paper that was in line with what Blair expected. It was a hurdle that made her swallow hard just the same.

"It's difficult to tell," Mr. Martin waved a finger in the air. "This property goes all the way to the frontage road that runs along the interstate."

Blair's eyes widened and a grin flashed across her face.

Mr. Martin put an arm around her, "You know, convincing your buyer to change their plans is a long shot."

"I'll have to give the marketing presentation of my life!" Blair gleamed.

"Alright. If you can get the investor to agree, you have my support," Mr. Martin said.

"Thank you, thank you, thank you!" Blair squeezed. In a flash, her arms were held wide and she gave the old publisher a mighty hug. Backing off, she shrugged meekly, "Sorry. Hugging is just a thing with me today."

"Quite alright, so long as the paparazzi doesn't take it out of context," Mr. Martin laughed. "If you need anything, don't hesitate to call. Merry Christmas, Blair."

"Mr. Christmas, Mr. Martin."

Blair dashed out of the publishing house foyer and raced through the streets of Evergreen.

Thirty Four

Blair slipped through the front door of the bed and breakfast intent on grabbing her laptop and documents she created to make revisions for her big, final pitch. Focused on her task, she nearly ran headlong into a figure, stopping inches from his chest. Looking up, her eyes went wide with surprise.

"Todd!" Blair was astonished. "What are you doing here?"

Todd smiled, his hands alongside Blair's arms, "Two Paris tickets buy you a lot of domestic travel clout. I got here as soon as I could."

"Why?" Blair frowned.

"To help you, Blair."

Blair's shoulders slumped, "Todd…"

Todd waved his hands in front of him, "Just to help you. That's all. If you can use a *friend* and a little expertise."

Blair looked wounded, "I signed the papers."

"I see," Todd nodded. "That complicates things. Were they executed?"

Blair wrinkled her brow.

"Did you receive a copy with the buyer's signature? Did you cash any checks? If not, you may, just may have a window," Todd said. "Let's see what we can do."

Blair pushed into him and gave him a hug, "Thank you."

A cold blast of air hit her as she released from Todd. Turning, she saw Luke standing in the doorway. His face fell into a knowing nod. Spinning on his heels, he walked back out, closing the door behind him.

Blair looked up at Todd, "Excuse me for a moment."

Dashing out the door herself, she chased after Luke who was just about to climb into his truck.

"Luke! Stop, please," Blair pleaded.

Luke stood with the door open, "I don't think there is much left to say."

"Luke, you don't understand," Blair breathed.

"I saw you with the real estate investor and the realtor. They're both predators I am well familiar with. I guess I shouldn't be surprised. They fit your plan perfectly. Now you can go back to New York with your…boyfriend,"

Luke snapped. "I liked you, Blair. I really liked you. Now I see you've been lying the whole time. Making me and the town the fools."

"Luke…" Blair started.

"It's Christmas Eve. I've got to go," Luke said, slamming the door shut and bringing the truck roaring to life.

For the second time in as many days, Blair watched Luke's truck disappear out of sight.

When Blair returned to the Holly Bough foyer, Loretta and Sam were getting acquainted with Todd. Blair flashed a sheepish smile.

"I see you met our son," Sam said to Todd.

Todd shot a confused look.

"He owns a winery just outside of town and is a big advocate on keeping Evergreen as it is," Blair said. Glancing to Loretta, "Can we use the meeting room?"

"Of course," Loretta said. "Can I get you two anything?"

"Coffee would be great. I've got to grab a few things, could you show him the way?" Blair asked, a foot already on the first step of the stairwell.

Rushing through the house, she gathered what she needed in both arms, using her heel to close the door to her room behind her. Scampering down the stairs, she slipped midway down, recovered and continued her decent.

Pushing through the glass French doors of the meeting room, Blair felt like she was back on Madison Avenue in Manhattan. Arms full of storyboards and documents, she set her laptop down and glanced at Todd, "We have a lot of work to do and not a lot of time to do it!"

"Let's see what you've got. I have a few ideas too, but I have to warn you, this is going to take a Christmas miracle!" Todd said.

"I know," Blair nodded. Laying her items out and pulling the sheets she updated since she sent the presentation to Todd, she handed them to him.

Chewing on her lip, she watched intently as Todd reviewed the numbers. Mumbling and pulling out a calculator, he began penciling notes. "Get your computer fired up. We're going to have to do a little magic before your investor sees this," Todd said.

"But there's hope?" Blair asked tentatively.

"With pulling in the cost of doing the design, marketing, production and distribution in house, it is a different ballgame. Mathematically, at least," Todd said, looking up from the spreadsheets. Frowning, he asked, "This might change things for my investors, but this doesn't change your buyer's plans."

Blair breathed deep, "I know. You work on your investors. I'll work on Mr. Marcom."

Todd nodded and dropped his head, on his own work. Pulling out his laptop, he began casting the net with his contacts.

Blair calculated the travel time from Seattle, she had an hour to make the presentation of her life.

Blair and Todd were two coffees in and heads still buried in their work when a light rap at the meeting room door stole their attention. Shuffling her papers quickly into order and resetting her digital presentation to the opening screen, she looked up and nodded.

Loretta held the door open for Mr. Marcom to enter.

"Thank you, Loretta!" Blair waved.

Mr. Marcom turned and smiled, "Yes, thank you."

Loretta nodded and closed the door, giving the people in the room a once over before reluctantly scampering off.

"Lovely woman," Mr. Marcom remarked as Loretta walked away.

Todd rose from his seat as Blair introduced them. "Mr. Marcom this is Todd Allen, my..."

"Financial Advisor, from New York," Todd said, extending his hand. "You must be Bradley Marcom. I'm familiar with some of your projects, in fact, my investors have stakes in several of them."

"Pleasure to meet you," Mr. Marcom said, his voice full of trepidation. Turning to Blair, he scowled, "Ms. Cooper, what is this all about?"

Blair steadied herself, "Thank you for coming up here. Especially on Christmas Eve."

"You intrigued me enough to get me up here. I certainly hope this isn't a fanciful goose chase," Mr. Marcom warned.

"I had the same thought when I boarded my flight from New York," Todd quipped, hoping his remark would be encouraging.

Mr. Marcom took off his coat, "Alright. Let's see what you've got!"

Settling into one of the meeting room chairs, Mr. Marcom folded his hands together.

Todd gave Blair a reassuring nod. With a deep breath, Blair turned on the monitor and beamed her presentation to it.

"With your current plan, travelers on Interstate 5 would need to get off the highway here heading south bound and here heading north bound only to have traverse either direction on Main Street to return to the highway," Blair said.

"With most of the small shops removed and a few improvements, the travel would be improved and not inhibitory," Mr. Marcom nodded.

"What if your travelers didn't come all the way to Main Street to reach your travel center, but could access the frontage road instead?" Blair suggested. She showed a clip of the proposed highway access points.

Mr. Marcom studied the design, "I'll admit, being as close to the interstate is ideal. The challenge is purchasing the property, getting zoning sign offs, town approval…"

"What if I have that all arranged for you?" Blair asked.

Marcom leaned forward, "I'm listening."

"The owner of the land that stretched from here to here on the frontage road includes all this space," Blair said.

"The publishing house land," Mr. Marcom nodded. "We looked at it. The cost was prohibitive with the commercial building."

Todd frowned, "It is cheaper to buy up a bunch of small shops like…Blair's?"

Mr. Marcom cleared his throat, "Under the right economic pressures…yes."

The room was quiet just for a moment.

"I get it, it's business. Your job is to get your investors the best deal. It's not your fault if a town is struggling. Progress is progress," Todd jumped in. "Reviewing Blair's numbers that she already has the seller's stamp of approval on, this plot of land gives you nearly the same footprint at a drastically reduced cost."

Mr. Marcom studied the document Todd slid over to him, "Splitting the property. Smart. What happens to the commercial space?"

Blair squirmed in her seat. Todd nodded, encouraging her to proceed.

"I…we are gathering investors to convert the book publishing house to a game publishing house. Using much of the same assets," Blair said.

Mr. Marcom frowned.

"I know," Todd laughed. "I thought the same. But look at these numbers and with Ms. Cooper's Masdison Avenue experience, distribution channels…I already have seventy-five percent of the needed backing."

"I see," Mr. Marcom said. "Can I see your proposal for that?"

Blair hesitated and showed him the updated presentation packet she had made for Todd.

After a few quiet minutes, Mr. Marcom nodded, "Interesting. Not my area of expertise, but fascinating."

Blair licked her lips and straightened, "There's more."

Mr. Marcom chuckled at the enthusiasm, "Sure. Why not?"

"I made some mock-ups of your travel center," Blair said. On the screen behind her, a sprawling array of buildings with lodge style facades flashed on the screen. "Using some of the same motifs as you see in and around Evergreen will beckon people to stop. Not just fill up on gas because their tank is low, but pull into experience your center a destination."

Mr. Marcom looked dubious, "This looks great, our centers have a known look and feel to them. The build out isn't custom. We use wide open landscape, red and white buildings as a beacon. And the cost…"

"Running the numbers as a *premium* travel center, makes up the difference in two years. It becomes additional profit starting year three including the additional maintenance," Todd interjected. "Your travel center on the way to Vail. It is your most profitable by square footage of all your centers."

"What's more, there is a serious lack of lodging available. This bed and breakfast turns away ninety-percent of its requests and is booked out for the next two Christmases already. They would refer overflow to your…," Blair moved to the next image. "Your hotel on property."

Mr. Marcom's head swiveled from Todd to Blair and back to Todd again. "I know, our property in Vail has a hotel nearby that is enormously profitable," he said before Todd could reply.

"Mr. Marcom, your travel center integrates with a town that is a loved destination by so many people. You see how busy the town is this time of year," Blair said.

Mr. Marcom sighed, sorting through all of the papers. "You have both done some exceptional work. This, in every aspect, is a better proposal and monumentally more profitable than our original plan," Mr. Marcom said. "I can get our investors on board."

Blair shot Todd a thankful look.

"There's just one thing," Mr. Marcom snapped, seizing Blair's heart mid-gallop. "I want in on that game company. I'll cover the remaining twenty-five percent."

Blair clutched her chest, "Thank you, Mr. Marcom."

"Thank you, Ms. Cooper. I sensed your hesitation with selling the toy store. It had nothing to do with numbers, did it?" Mr. Marcom asked.

"I love this town, sir. The store is a piece of my family history I wasn't ready to let go of," Blair pulled the bonus check she had received the day prior and handed it back to the real estate investor.

"What are you going to do with it?" Marcom asked.

"It will be the flagship store for our games," Blair said.

Mr. Marcom smiled, "We aren't used to decorating for Christmas with the same zeal that the town of Evergreen does. Suppose we could get a hand with that next year?"

"I think you will have a town full of helpers next year, Mr. Marcom," Blair assured.

"Well, it is Christmas Eve and believe it or not, even a land developer has a family waiting on him," Mr. Marcom rose from his chair. "Have the papers drawn. We'll get this done by the new year."

Mr. Marcom shook Todd's hand. Spinning to shake Blair's, she surprised him with a hug. "Merry Christmas!"

"Merry Christmas, Ms. Cooper."

Marcom pulled on his coat and nodded, leaving Blair and Todd to decompress in the meeting room.

Blair collapsed in her seat, exhausted and overwhelmed.

Glancing over at Todd who was quietly putting his papers in order, Blair said, "I don't know how I can ever thank you."

Todd put the papers down. He looked across the table and said, "Make my investors profitable and find your happiness. Here, in Evergreen. Where you belong."

"Todd...," Blair rolled her head on her shoulders.

"I know. Merry Christmas, Blair."

Thirty Five

Blair and Todd emerged from the meeting room feeling elated. Bursting into the kitchen, Blair couldn't hide her excitement.

"I take it went well?" Loretta asked.

"It went great!" Blair squealed. Looking at Todd, she added, "I couldn't have done it without your help."

"You did all the hard work," Todd assured.

"You two have time to celebrate over lunch? I was just about to get it ready for the guests," Loretta asked.

Todd shrugged, "I have a couple hours before I need to head back for the airport."

"You're heading back to New York?" Loretta asked.

"I am. It was a quick, very purposeful trip," Todd said.

With a glance at Blair, he asked, "Weren't you flying back as well? I could give you a ride."

"I, uh, I think I need to stay. There are a few things I need to tend to that really can't wait," Blair said. Blair looked at Loretta who shrugged, knowing what she was inquiring.

"Listen, you stay here and enjoy lunch. Loretta's cooking is the best. You'll end up kicking yourself for not staying for Christmas," Blair said. "But I need to run and share the news. Could I borrow your car?"

Todd looked hesitant for just a moment but relented, fishing the keys for his rental car out of his pocket.

"Thanks!" Blair jingled the keys in her hand.

Darting out of the Holly Bough, she scanned the cars on the street for the one that flashed. Finding the lights on a European luxury vehicle flashing, she nodded, "Of course!"

Slipping behind the wheel, she started the posh SUV up and pulled away from the curb. Winding her way out of town and up into the hills as snowflakes speckled the windshield.

Finding her way to the long tree-lined drive of the winery, she pulled in front of the tasting room, parking next to Luke's pick-up truck. Trying the handle, she found it locked. Peering in through the frosty windows, the tasting room was dark.

Jogging through the snow to the nearby house, she tried it. Knocking on the door and ringing the bell to no avail, she traversed along the porch, peering through the windows with her hands shaded over her eyes.

The house was silent.

Confounded, she circumnavigated the winery, trying each door and peering in each window. With a bit of inspiration, she circled to the back where the outdoor barrels were. It too was empty.

Hands on her hips, she scanned the grounds. Looking over the rows of snow dusted grapevines, to the back of the house, her eyes finally gazed on something that made her pause.

A barn, much smaller than the winery building, was tucked behind the house. Its small, rustic windows glowed with light. Marching through the snow, she was guided by a separate set of prints.

The sound of rustling and clanking of tools emanated from the small barn. Closing her eyes for a moment, Blair reached out for the handle and tugged. The door opened to a tidy barn bathed in soft light. Shelves of wooden carvings lined the walls next to racks of tools. In the center of the barn, several unfinished toy boxes sat on a long, sturdy table. Against a wall covered with tools, a figure hunched over a workbench.

Alerted by the wisp of cool air and the splash of natural light, the figure turned and glanced at Blair. Without flinching, the man went back to his work.

Blair walked up and placed a hand on his shoulder, "Luke…"

Reluctantly, Luke sighed and put down the tools he was using. Turning, he looked directly at Blair, unmoved, "What do you want, Blair?"

"There's some things that you need to know," Blair declared.

"I know. You're selling the store. Your bags are packed, you're heading back to New York with Mr. Striped Suit," Luke scowled. "It's your life. I get it. I just don't like being played for a fool. Worse, I don't like my town being played for a fool."

Luke spun to face Blair directly, "It's not just your store. It is every business in Evergreen. I looked up Marcom's work. He's going to turn Evergreen into a giant truck stop."

"Look. It's unfair to put all that on you. It's not. The Toy Chest has just become a symbol of what's to come. What really gets me, is you had me believing you cared about all of this, all of us. You only opened the store to ensure you got max payout when you sold," Luke said, his eyes turning away.

"It's true," Blair admitted. "I did open the store to help the sale. But being here in Evergreen. Spending time with your Mom, with Nella and her family…*you*. I realized there was way too much at stake. I fell in love with this town all over again."

"And you signed the papers anyway," Luke blurted. "I saw you yesterday at the general store at the bottom of the hill."

"You saw us," Blair breathed. "That's why you were so upset at the foster Christmas party."

"Am I wrong?" Luke asked.

Blair shook her head slowly, her eyes damp, "You're not wrong. I did sign the papers. The moment I did, I regretted it."

"You didn't mind the check that Marcom wrote, did you?" Luke said.

Blair bit her lip, "I gave him the check back."

Luke's head snapped, "You what?"

"Today, when I asked him to come back up. I handed him the check back and rescinded the deal on The Toy Chest," Blair said. "I agreed to sell when I thought Marcom would provide jobs to the families like Nella's. I thought of what you said, and I listened to myself every time I walked down Main Street. Every time I turned the lock at The Toy Chest. I didn't sell. Evergreen is Evergreen. I couldn't be a part of changing that."

Luke was astounded. Shaking his head, he frowned, "Marcom went with that?"

Blair nodded, "I pitched him a better deal. A stake in a game company and property closer to the highway."

Luke blinked trying to take in all that Blair had laid out on him.

"I needed a little help. Help from Mr. Martin and help from Todd," Blair said softly. "That is why Todd came. As an investment strategist, not as anything else. I'm not flying back to New York with Todd tonight. He will be getting on the plane on his own."

Luke sat stunned.

"You're not wrong for feeling the way you do. I felt the same towards myself. That is why I knew I had to fix it," Blair said. Her voice trembled as she looked into Luke's eyes, "I didn't just fall in love with Evergreen again. I fell in love with you, too."

Luke stared back, his icy disposition melted, "Blair, I don't know what to say."

"You don't have to say anything," Blair said. The soft wind from her lips brushing against Luke's. "I didn't come expecting to be swept off my feet. I came to share the news with you."

Turning away, she took a step towards the entrance of the barn. A hand gently landed on her shoulder with just enough pressure to suggest that she turn back. Luke grasped her hand and pulled her close, "Falling in love with you and thinking you would just fly away and leave all of us here that you've come to mean so much to, *that* is what hurt the most."

"I know. It hurt me too," Blair breathed, inching towards him on her toes. "I'm not going anywhere. Evergreen is home."

Luke wrapped his arm around her waist as she laced her fingers around his neck pulling him close, their lips meeting.

Thirty Six

Blair stood in front of the town Christmas tree, staring at it. Even during the day, if aided by the snow burdened clouds, the lights dazzled. She felt a contentment she couldn't recall, certainly not in her adult life.

"I thought I'd find you here," Todd's voice called. "You always did love Christmas trees."

Blair turned and nodded, "Yes, everything in this town just makes Christmas seem more magical."

"It's a nice town," Todd admits.

"Look, Todd. This is isn't easy, but I don't think…," Blair started.

"I know. I have seen a different side of you here. I haven't seen you so completely in your element, ever. The way you are in this town and the way the town reacts to you. You have something special here, it is everything the stories you shared about your grandparents. This is your Manhattan. This is where you belong," Todd said.

"Todd…," Blair began.

"It's okay," Todd reached his arm around her. "I have to get back to New York. You have a new company to run. And I'd hate for you to disappoint my investors."

"I won't," Blair looked up at Todd and promised.

Todd grinned, "I know you won't. Hey, I'd love to be your financial advisor, if you'd have me."

"There's no one I would want more to help me," Blair said.

Todd stepped away from her and held out his hand.

"Really?" Blair scoffed, reluctantly shaking Todd's hand.

"I'll call you after the New Year and we'll work out the details," Todd said. With a glance at his watch, he wrinkled his nose, "I better get going or I'll be spending Christmas at the Sea-Tac Airport."

He paused and waited expectantly, "Blair, you still have my car keys."

"Oh," Blair flushed, digging the keys out of her pocket. "Merry Christmas, Todd."

"Merry Christmas!" Todd nodded. Hands in his coat pockets, he strolled down Main Street.

Thirty Seven

Blair took a few more moments enjoying her moment at the town tree before making her way down Main Street herself.

With a new sense of ownership, she stopped in at The Toy Chest. She found Nella wrapping up with a very last-minute shopper.

"Well, hello, stranger," Nella called. "You missed one of my favorite The Toy Chest days of the year. I love Christmas Eve. Everyone is at their peek festiveness. Joy and peace abound in the air. I love it!"

"Thank you for manning the shop. It has been quite the day," Blair said. Her glow hid an undercurrent of exhaustion. She was sure that she was still upright with pure adrenal only. "I did come by to give you an early Christmas present. It's really for Scott, too. The whole family."

Nella cocked her head and came out from behind the register.

"Scott can forget about his resume," Blair said. "That is, if he'll accept a position at The Toy Chest games based right here in Evergreen, Washington!"

Nella's eyes grew wide, "What are you talking about?"

Blair wrapped her arm around Nella's shoulders, "It is a long story that I'll share at game night. Until then, just know I prayed for a Christmas miracle and it was delivered with the help of a few earth-bound angels, or people who helped in angelic ways at the very least."

Nella's eyes welled with tears, "We can stay?"

Blair nodded, "Oh, you're staying alright. You're the manager of our corporate store. And part owner through stock if you're in."

"Oh, I'm in!" Nella squealed.

Blair helped Nella close up the shop. As they were just locking up, a pair of figures appeared outside their door. Exchanging glances at one another, the ladies shrugged and stepped outside, turning the lock on The Toy Chest.

With furrowed brows, they looked past the grins on Luke's and Scott's faces at the horse carriage parked alongside the sidewalk. Each held their arms out as they linked arms with their unexpected dates.

Helping each into the carriage and settling into opposing seats, the gentlemen covered the ladies' legs with wool blankets. Luke pulled Blair close with their backs to the carriage driver, facing Scott and Nella.

From under the bench, Luke slid out a bucket with four glasses and a bottle of champagne. Popping the cork, he exhausted an explosion of sparkling wine and turned sheepishly to his carriage-mates, "Horse rides can be a little tough on champagne."

Pouring glasses, he handed them out and held his glass in the air as the jingle bell adorned carriage streamed them down the entirety of Main Street. "To the newest resident of Evergreen, Blair Cooper!" he toasted to chorus of cheers from Scott and Nella.

"This is nice," Blair said.

"It's the least I could do, especially after doubting you," Luke said.

Undaunted, Blair sipped her champagne and shrugged, "Who could blame you? I doubted me."

Blair's eyes brightened, "Can I make a toast? To Scott Swanson, the newest employee of The Toy Chest Games, if he'll accept?"

Scott choked on his champagne, "What? What's the role? The pay? Oh, who cares, I accept!"

They cheered an even more raucous cheer as they rolled past the town Christmas tree. Expecting the carriage driver to loop the tree and head back down Main Street, she was surprised when the driver rolled right past into the darker streets beyond Main Street.

Pulling into the publishing house parking lot, the driver halted in the center of the lot.

"A final toast," Luke stood, holding Blair's hand, encouraging her to stand with him.

Spinning her to face the building, bathed in darkness. As they turned, a Christmas tree at the very top of the building, topped with a brilliant star came to light.

Like a fuse, lights traveled from the base of the tree down the façade of the building until the parking lot was ablaze with Christmas lights. Illuminated from the shadows was most of the town of Evergreen. Residents, visitors and former publishing house employees.

Each person raised a glass of champagne or apple juice high in the air.

Blair looked at Luke in amazement.

Luke grinned, "I added a little note to your game boxes before Mayor Stowe had them delivered. The rest is all them, here for you."

In a loud voice, Luke called out, "To Blair Cooper and to all the people of Evergreen. Residents, guests, inheritance collectors, you are all family in Evergreen. Merry Christmas!"

"Merry Christmas!" the crowd roared.

Tears filled Blair's eyes. She looked out at the crowd. Loretta and Sam, all of their guests. Mr. Martin and his family. Kris and here entire crew from the coffee shop. Mayor Stowe and the ladies' auxiliary.

Blair wiped a tear from her cheek and raised her glass, "To Evergreen and all her loved ones. Merry Christmas!"

"Blair," Luke began.

Blair looked up at him, "No more toasts. You talk too much." Launching up on her toes, she pushed her lips against his. "Merry Christmas!"

"Merry Christmas, Blair."

Thirty Eight

Blair awoke on Christmas morning. Kicking off her blankets, she dressed and hurried downstairs with the zeal she hadn't felt since she was a child. Meeting Loretta in the kitchen, she was surprised when the children staying at the Holly Bough were already up, seated at the kitchen counter drinking cocoa with candy canes hanging on the rims of their mugs.

"Go figure, the children are up early today," Loretta called over her shoulder.

"Merry Christmas, Loretta."

"Merry Christmas, Blair."

Blair put her arms around the children's shoulders. "Merry Christmas, guys!"

"Merry Christmas, Blair."

The front door opened and Luke, laden with presents stopped to set them by the tree before joining everyone in the kitchen.

Smiling at Blair and the children, he made a beeline to his mother, giving her a kiss and wishing her a Merry Christmas.

"Are you guys excited to see what Santa brought?" Luke egged the children, conjuring a robust bellow of anxious cheers.

"Stop, Luke. Their parents are still sleeping," Loretta said.

Luke grinned, "I get to be kind of like the uncle. Get everyone all riled up and turn them back over to their parents."

"That's why you work at a winery and not here at the Holly Bough," Loretta quipped. "Now put your immense work experience to use and pour Blair and me a mimosa."

"Yes, ma'am," Luke saluted. As a sleepy figure appeared in the doorway, Luke called, "Good morning, Pops!"

"Merry Christmas, son!" Sam returned.

"Mimosa?" Luke asked.

"Coffee and a healthy amount. Then I'll consider such concoctions," Sam said.

Luke nodded and handed his mother and Blair each a mimosa. Pouring himself a glass of champagne, he held his glass high towards Blair and winked. Her smile grew.

Handing Sam a cup of coffee, Luke led Blair by the hand.

Stopping in front of the Christmas tree, Luke spun Blair to face him.

"I have a couple of things," Luke said. Sliding a piece of paper from his pocket, he handed it to Blair, "Not from me. Well, not entirely, at least."

Blair took it and unrolled it, her eyes swelled. "This, this is a deed."

Luke nodded, "To the publishing house, or I should say, the game company. My new friend Todd had funds wired to Mr. Martin while he was waiting at the airport. Technically, the publishing house and its property belongs to The Toy Chest."

Blair gasped as she clutched the document.

"I am part owner, you know. I invested. Most of the town did," Luke said. "There's more. This is more from me and Mr. Martin."

Luke fished in his pocket and pulled out a small figurine, handing to Blair.

"Our first meeple!" she bounced up and down as she clutched the game piece.

Blair suddenly looked aghast. "In all the excitement, I, I don't have anything to give you."

Luke wrapped his arms around Blair, "You have given me, and the town of Evergreen, way more than anyone could have deserved to ask for. I love you, Blair Cooper."

Blair's eyes sparkled in the Christmas tree light, "I love you, Luke Marsten!"